A VISION OF THE WORLD

ALSO BY JOHN CHEEVER

Novels

The Wapshot Chronicle
The Wapshot Scandal
Bullet Park
Falconer
Oh What a Paradise It Seems

Short Stories

The Way Some People Live
The Enormous Radio
The Housebreaker of Shady Hill
Some People, Places, and Things
That Will Not Appear in My Next Novel
The Brigadier and the Golf Widow
The World of Apples
The Stories of John Cheever

Journals

The Journals of John Cheever

Letters

The Letters of John Cheever
(edited by Benjamin Cheever)

JOHN CHEEVER

A Vision of
the World

Selected Stories

SELECTED AND WITH AN INTRODUCTION BY
Julian Barnes

VINTAGE

2 4 6 8 10 9 7 5 3 1

Vintage
20 Vauxhall Bridge Road,
London SW1V 2SA

Vintage Classics is part of the Penguin Random House group of companies
whose addresses can be found at global.penguinrandomhouse.com

Penguin
Random House
UK

The stories in this volume previously appeared in the
New Yorker and *Esquire*

First published in Great Britain by Vintage Classics in 2021

penguin.co.uk/vintage

A CIP catalogue record for this book is available from the British Library

ISBN 9781784875824

Typeset in 12 pt/15 pt Bembo
by Integra Software Services Pvt. Ltd, Pondicherry

Printed and bound in Great Britain by Clays Ltd, Elcograf S.p.A

The authorised representative in the EEA is Penguin Random House
Ireland, Morrison Chambers, 32 Nassau Street, Dublin DO2 YH68

Penguin Random House is committed to a sustainable future for
our business, our readers and our planet. This book is made from
Forest Stewardship Council® certified paper.

Contents

Introduction

ONE VERSION: JOHN Cheever was born in Quincy, Massachusetts, in 1912. He published his first short story in the *New Yorker* in 1935, at the age of twenty-two, the start of a lifelong association with the magazine. His literary reputation grew slowly, until in 1958 he won the National Book Award for his first novel, *The Wapshot Chronicle*. In 1964 *Time* magazine put him on its cover – an accolade that brought coast-to-coast fame back then; zealously alliterative, it dubbed him 'Ovid in Ossining', after the town in New York State where he lived for many decades. The inside story describes the writer's idyllic life with his wife Mary and three children in a beautiful house. The photograph of his wife is captioned, in reference to his highbrow uxoriousness and her cooking: 'Sometimes a tribute in Latin to the quality of the roast.' In a section subheaded 'The Monogamist' we are told that 'Cheever, almost alone in the field of modern fiction, is one who celebrates the glories and delights of monogamy'; further, that 'He delights in dancing, and enjoys his liquor with zest.' Four years later, in 1968, his best-known story, 'The Swimmer', was made into a movie starring Burt Lancaster. His novels are good, but his art was made for the shorter form. *The Stories of John Cheever* (1978), which won him the National Book Critics

Circle Award and the Pulitzer Prize, are one of the high points of twentieth-century American literature. He used to say, ironically, to his children, 'I'm a brand name, like corn flakes, or shredded wheat.' But this was true, and when he died in 1982, he was full of honour.

Or: John Cheever was the son of a dominant mother and alcoholic father; he and his brother both grew up to be alcoholics. When the Army tested him, they found he had a low IQ; though when re-examined, he did adequately. Despite his early success, he feared that he wasn't in 'the big league' like Norman Mailer, and was equally daunted by the worldly baubles of Irwin Shaw and the brilliance of John Updike. Though he wrote around two hundred stories, there was no relaxed facility about his creative process: in 1947 he told a friend, 'I want to write short stories like I want to fuck a chicken.' Within that reportedly idyllic marriage he was often intensely lonely and sexually tormented; outside it, frequently unfaithful with both men and women. He and Mary had week-long stand-offs, and nearly split up countless times. 'I am so sensitive,' he wrote in his Journal in 1955, 'that I seem to be insane ... I have wept too many tears, gin tears, whiskey tears, tears of plain salt, but too many.' He suffered 'scrotum-tightening vertigo' on station platforms and bridges. His self-pity was accentuated by feeling that he was always the lover, never the beloved; nor could he ever admit his homosexuality, except to his private diary. He had sex with the photographer Walker Evans and an affair with the actress Hope Lange, who described him as 'one of the horniest men I've ever met'. Such revelations, which emerged after his death in his *Letters* (1988) and *Journals* (1991), foolishly blurred his literary reputation for some years.

The writer with whom Cheever is most often lumped together in the general literary mind is Updike: both wrote novels and short stories about the East-Coast suburban middle-class, and both were star *New Yorker* names. Yet Updike, born in 1932, was a whole generation younger. In terms of simple years, Cheever was closer to Scott Fitzgerald (b.1896) or Hemingway (b.1899); or to the similarly underrated John O'Hara (b.1905). One writer born between Cheever and Updike, and who shared some of their world and their very male literary tradition, is the now rediscovered and revalued Richard Yates (b.1926). In his most famous novel, the exactly titled *Revolutionary Road*, Yates described how the American Dream had finally petered out in the backways of consumerist suburbia. Updike's Rabbit initially tries to flee just such a milieu, but soon returns to enjoy its offerings, and then – bought up as the rest of America has been bought up – becomes a Toyota dealer: his defeat is as much economic as spiritual. Cheever's world is pitched a little earlier, mainly in the Truman and Eisenhower years, before the Sixties took hold, when American expansionism and power seemed uncomplicated, and consumerism not just exciting, but in a way almost pure. As one husband puts it of his Westchester wife: 'You might say that she is prideful, but I think only that she is a woman enjoying herself in a country that is prosperous and young.' In 1956, in his Journals, Cheever refers to himself as being a member of 'this cheerful generation'. The Sixties made the Fifties look drab, but give any decade enough time and it can become glamorous again. It's no coincidence that in *Mad Men* Don Draper's creator decided that his ad man should live in Ossining.

Cheever's suburbia has its full share of joyful Updikean adulteries: as another of his suburban husbands says of his wife, 'She knows that I fool around, but if I wasn't unfaithful ... I wouldn't be true to myself.' Yet its spiritual roots, and therefore spiritual malaise, lie much further back – way beyond the American Revolution – in the essential nature of man and woman. Ezekiel Cheever, the first Cheever in America, was a Puritan schoolmaster of the stern belief that 'man is full of misery and all earthly beauty is lustful and corrupt'. His descendant's view was more nuanced: beauty – which Cheever's characters, like Cheever himself, encounter mainly in nature, in woods and weather and sunsets and panoramas, but also in human beings – was not in itself sinful, though human beings, given their fallen natures, were always likely to contaminate it. So life was 'a perilous moral adventure', and spiritual peace is found less often in church (where a well-dressed woman is always likely to catch a male protagonist's eye) than in physical activity, especially when water, in its liquid or frozen forms, is concerned. In 1963 Cheever goes tobogganing 'to purify my feelings'; while shovelling snow moves him 'from despair into hopefulness'. Cheever characters, like the writer himself, find temporary redemption in seas and rivers and even in suburban pools. But it is frozen water that calms him, and them, even more; and his work contains many passages of joy, and even spiritual resolution, when a solitary figure skates on a frozen lake. Knowing, of course, that however deep the freeze, ice is always metaphorically thin. In 1979 he notes in his Journal: 'The motion of skating, and the lightness and coldness of the air involve quite clearly for me a beauty – a moral beauty. By this I mean that it corrects the measure and the nature of my thinking.'

Many novelists who write directly about the erotic life persuade themselves that they are doing so truthfully for the first time in literary history; also, that they have somehow taken the matter the full distance. Cheever was prepared to bow to the *New Yorker*'s editorial prudishness when tactically necessary; but proud (in 1957, with *The Wapshot Chronicle*) of becoming the first writer to get the word 'fuck' into the Book-of-the-Month Club. Yet every literary pioneer finds successors who go farther: in Cheever's case, two in particular: Updike and Philip Roth. So a mere twelve years later, all of a sudden, what is he but a writer born way back in 1912:

> John [Updike]'s new novel (*Couples*) has made him a millionaire ... It is obsessively venereal but the descriptions of undressed women are splendid. Great advances have been made here recently in writing about venereal sport. The pure, correct and ancient vocabulary is used freely, the techniques of masturbation are discussed and the sense is of freedom, discovery and newness. Phil Roth leads the group. While all my friends are describing orgasms I still dwell on the beauty of the evening star.

Cheever is being deliberately comic, and deliberately disingenuous (he carried on writing about sex, and Updike was similarly interested in the beauty of the evening star). But as he knew, 'The rivalry among novelists is quite as intense as that among sopranos.' His relationship with

Updike was bound to be edgy, given that to the casual eye, the younger man seemed to be taking over Cheever's turf. He often denounces the younger man in his letters, yet always in a self-aware fashion. 'I think his magnanimity specious and his work seems motivated by covetousness, exhibitionism and a stony heart. I put all this down to show how truly innocent and generous I am.' Similarly: 'Updike and I spend most of our time back-biting one another. I find him very arrogant but my daughter tells me that I'm arrogant.' However, Cheever learned to separate the man from the work: he tells Updike that *Rabbit Redux* is 'great' – and 'Thinking that I might have deceived myself I read it again and came to the same conclusion'; while *Rabbit is Rich* is 'the most important American novel I have read in many years'. In 1981 the two men appeared on *The Dick Cavett Show* and were asked to describe their differences. Cheever said that Updike was the only writer he knew who gave a sense of American lives being performed in an environment of a grandeur that escaped them. In reply and counter-praise, Updike emphasised that Cheever was a transcendentalist, feeling and conveying a radiance which he, Updike, was unable to feel and convey.

Updike is suaver and more celebratory; Cheever is edgier, odder and more pessimistic. There are other significant differences. Updike's *Rabbit* quartet is built upon the armature of American public events; whereas Cheever – despite the times he lived through – was, according to his son Benjamin, 'as uninvolved in politics as it is possible for a literate man to be'. The daily news forms little part of his stories. Nuclear war may be alluded to, but it is felt more as a bad dream or a lingering migraine than a thermonuclear reality.

'The Brigadier and the Golf Widow' turns on a kerfuffle over access to a domestic nuclear shelter; Cuba and Russia are mentioned, but are mere words put into the comic mouth of a golf-club bore. Meanwhile, in the non-fiction world of Cheever's Letters, a rare geopolitical prediction, in March 1943, turned out to be deliriously wrong: 'I think Churchill's exaggerating when he says it's going to take another two years to win the war.'

In life, Cheever was an excellent dreamer: pithy, witty and to the point. Among the dreams noted in his Journals are the following:

- 'I dream about the White House. It is after supper in a bedroom that I have seen on postcards. Ike and Mamie are alone. Mamie is reading the *Washington Star*. Ike is reading *The Wapshot Chronicle*.'
- 'I dream that my face appears on a postage stamp.'
- 'I dream that I am walking with Updike. The landscape seems out of my childhood. A familiar dog barks at us. I see friends and neighbours in their lighted windows. Updike juggles a tennis ball that is both my living and my dying. When he drops the ball I cannot move until it is recovered, and yet I feel, painfully, that he is going to murder me with the ball. He seems murderous and self-possessed. Here is a museum with a turnstile, a marble staircase, and statuary. In the end I do escape.'
- 'I dream that a lady, looking at my face, says, "I see you've been in the competition, but I can't tell by your face whether or not you've won".'

- 'Last night I had a dream that a brilliant reviewer pointed out that there was an excess of lamentation in my work.'
- 'I go to bed at half past eight and have a horrendous dream in which Mary is made president of the college. There is a hint of ruthlessness here. I remember watching her father seize a position of power. I retaliate by having a homosexual escapade, unconsummated, with Ronald Reagan.'

Shortly after that last nocturnal invention (of 1966), Cheever notes: 'I have dreams of a density I would like to bring to fiction.' When we say 'dreamlike' we often mean ethereal, woozily enjoyable. 'Dreamlike' for Cheever means something else: density, as he says, but also an internal logic that seems completely unarguable at the time, but only half-cogent when we wake; further, an ability to change register suddenly without announcing the change, and without our being troubled by it. 'The Death of Justina', one of his most famous stories, moves, in the space of fewer than twenty pages, through grave reverie on the hazard of life, puckish reflections on the state and origin of America, satirical business about office life and zoning regulations, pathetic details of the death of an elderly aunt, comic details about the same, wry thoughts on giving up smoking, a phantasmagorical dream, and angry expostulation on the nature of death and the unwillingness of others to spot it. The story switches from one tone to another with the untroubled transitions of dreaming, though we never doubt that this is a string of real events.

Or take 'The Swimmer'. Neddy Merrill, a man in early middle age, at a Sunday afternoon neighbourhood party, decides to swim the eight miles home via all the private (and one public) pools he knows. It sounds like a harmless suburban whim and perhaps a picaresque short story. This first pool he dives into, that of his hosts, is fed by an artesian well: 'To be embraced and sustained by the light green water was less a pleasure, it seemed, than the resumption of a natural condition.' To begin with, the day is sunny and the neighbours welcoming; but gradually pool-owners become more indifferent, the summer seems to turn to autumn, Neddy's memory of his friends and acquaintances becomes less reliable, he encounters unexpected hostility and enigmatic remarks about his own life; his muscles seem to grow weaker, his stroke feebler, and when finally he arrives home, he discovers that his house is dilapidated, locked and abandoned. Is he swimming from a 'natural condition' to a social one; is he swimming from the present into his future life, or into a gradual realisation of the truth about his existing life? Is he swimming from metaphor into truth, or from truth into metaphor? Something transcendent is going on, though if transcendence means spiritual enhancement, perhaps is it a reverse transcendence that he is swimming into. Here, certainly, is the density that Cheever sought.

In 1975 Cheever examined a short-story anthology 'from which I have been conspicuously excluded', and agreed with the editors: what they had chosen was 'more substantial and correct than my flighty, eccentric, and sometimes bitter work, with its social disenchantments, somersaults, and sudden rains'. Sometimes Cheever appears to be writing satire, and sometimes he is. But he reserves the right to shift register and tone at will, if only for a sentence. And, often, something weirder is going on. Stories may end with a shimmer of the fantastical or the otherworldly. 'The Country Husband', for example, is a seemingly realistic story of disharmony, rage and sin among a typical suburban family. After a catalogue of disruptive and potentially lethal events, the family arrives back to (almost) the moral place where it was at the beginning; and everybody retires to bed. Whereupon the final sentence erupts: 'Then it is dark; it is a night where kings in golden suits ride elephants over the mountains.' And is that just another dream? It is certainly much more than an authorial whim: Cheever had the line in his head before he even had the story.

In 1972 Cheever, then teaching at the Writers' Workshop at the University of Iowa, flew home via Chicago with a Pan Am stewardess either seated beside him or in close attendance: 'At the end of the flight she embraced me ardently and said: "You are one of the most charming and interesting men I have ever met and by far the craziest." She wore a red cape.' A lesser writer might have started off with 'a Pan Am stewardess in a red cape'; Cheever delays this sartorial detail until after the anecdote's supposed kicker, which turns it into a poignant and amusing detail. As his children testified, he was always – in life as in fiction – a comic and subversive presence. He once described himself as 'the sort of iconoclast ... who will ridicule the establishment endlessly and expect to be seated at the head of the table'. In 1977 the *New York Times* asked him to comment on the 100th anniversary of Peter Rabbit. Cheever replied, 'My money has always been on Mr McGregor.'

Cheever's restless, divided spirit, which caused him much grief, sought the usual sources of temporary escape and temporary coherence: sex and drink. But for the longer term? In 1955 he wrote of his life: 'It seems to me that I try to repair a web that is always broken; that with every reparation I find that a new part has been broken or kicked loose.' If you have violent thesis and antithesis in your life, where do you find synthesis? In one of two ways: you hope for it in God, or you create it for yourself in art. Cheever was a diligent social churchgoer rather than a writer with an active theology. So for him, the saviour and the synthesis could only be literature:

> I know almost no pleasure greater than having a piece of fiction draw together disparate incidents so that they relate to one another and confirm the feeling that life itself is a creative process, that one thing is purposefully put upon another, that what is lost in one encounter is replenished in the next, and that we possess some power to make sense of what takes place.

Cheever hoped, in the final words of the final story in his collection *Some People, Places, and Things That Will Not Appear in My Next Novel*, 'to celebrate a world that lies about us like a bewildering and stupendous dream'. The same story features 'my laconic old friend Royden Blake', a writer who in mid-life finds, and is spoiled by, success and money. As a result, 'In his pages one found alcoholics, scarifying descriptions of the American landscape, and fat parts for Marlon Brando. You might say that he had lost the gift of evoking the perfumes of life: sea water, the smoke of burning hemlock, and the breasts of women. He had damaged, you might say, the ear's innermost chamber, where we hear the heavy noise of the dragon's tail moving over the dead leaves.'

Writers often invent other writers who exemplify their own secret fears; and Cheever was no exception. He certainly had more than a quorum of alcoholics in his fiction, and though he wrote no fat parts for Marlon Brando, he found that he had, without knowing it, written a fat part for Burt Lancaster. But for all his chaotic life and self-destructive drinking, his working brain retained a sober clarity: he never harmed the ear's innermost chamber, and he always heard the swish of the dragon's tail.

Julian Barnes

The Enormous Radio

J IM AND IRENE Westcott were the kind of people who seem to strike that satisfactory average of income, endeavor, and respectability that is reached by the statistical reports in college alumni bulletins. They were the parents of two young children, they had been married nine years, they lived on the twelfth floor of an apartment house near Sutton Place, they went to the theatre on an average of 10.3 times a year, and they hoped someday to live in Westchester. Irene Westcott was a pleasant, rather plain girl with soft brown hair and a wide, fine forehead upon which nothing at all had been written, and in the cold weather she wore a coat of fitch skins dyed to resemble mink. You could not say that Jim Westcott looked younger than he was, but you could at least say of him that he seemed to feel younger. He wore his graying hair cut very short, he dressed in the kind of clothes his class had worn at Andover, and his manner was earnest, vehement, and intentionally naïve. The Westcotts differed from their friends, their classmates, and their neighbors only in an interest they shared in serious music. They went to a great many concerts – although they seldom mentioned this to anyone – and they spent a great deal of time listening to music on the radio.

1

Their radio was an old instrument, sensitive, unpredict-able, and beyond repair. Neither of them understood the mechanics of radio – or of any of the other appliances that surrounded them – and when the instrument faltered, Jim would strike the side of the cabinet with his hand. This sometimes helped. One Sunday afternoon, in the middle of a Schubert quartet, the music faded away altogether. Jim struck the cabinet repeatedly, but there was no response; the Schubert was lost to them forever. He prom-ised to buy Irene a new radio, and on Monday when he came home from work he told her that he had got one. He refused to describe it, and said it would be a surprise for her when it came.

The radio was delivered at the kitchen door the follow-ing afternoon, and with the assistance of her maid and the handyman Irene uncrated it and brought it into the living room. She was struck at once with the physical ugliness of the large gumwood cabinet. Irene was proud of her living room, she had chosen its furnishings and colors as carefully as she chose her clothes, and now it seemed to her that the new radio stood among her intimate possessions like an aggressive intruder. She was confounded by the number of dials and switches on the instrument panel, and she studied them thoroughly before she put the plug into a wall socket and turned the radio on. The dials flooded with a malevo-lent green light, and in the distance she heard the music of a piano quintet. The quintet was in the distance for only an instant; it bore down upon her with a speed greater than light and filled the apartment with the noise of music amplified so mightily that it knocked a china ornament from a table to the floor. She rushed to the instrument and

2

reduced the volume. The violent forces that were snared in the ugly gumwood cabinet made her uneasy. Her children came home from school then, and she took them to the Park. It was not until later in the afternoon that she was able to return to the radio.

The maid had given the children their suppers and was supervising their baths when Irene turned on the radio, reduced the volume, and sat down to listen to a Mozart quintet that she knew and enjoyed. The music came through clearly. The new instrument had a much purer tone, she thought, than the old one. She decided that tone was most important and that she could conceal the cabinet behind a sofa. But as soon as she had made her peace with the radio, the interference began. A crackling sound like the noise of a burning powder fuse began to accompany the singing of the strings. Beyond the music, there was a rustling that reminded Irene unpleasantly of the sea, and as the quintet progressed, these noises were joined by many others. She tried all the dials and switches but nothing dimmed the interference, and she sat down, disappointed and bewildered, and tried to trace the flight of the melody. The elevator shaft in her building ran beside the living-room wall, and it was the noise of the elevator that gave her a clue to the character of the static. The rattling of the elevator cables and the opening and closing of the elevator doors were reproduced in her loudspeaker, and, realizing that the radio was sensitive to electrical currents of all sorts, she began to discern through the Mozart the ringing of telephone bells, the dialing of phones, and the lamentation of a vacuum cleaner. By listening more carefully, she was able to distinguish doorbells, elevator bells, electric razors, and

Waring mixers, whose sounds had been picked up from the apartments that surrounded hers and transmitted through her loudspeaker. The powerful and ugly instrument, with its mistaken sensitivity to discord, was more than she could hope to master, so she turned the thing off and went into the nursery to see her children.

When Jim Westcott came home that night, he went to the radio confidently and worked the controls. He had the same sort of experience Irene had had. A man was speaking on the station Jim had chosen, and his voice swung instantly from the distance into a force so powerful that it shook the apartment. Jim turned the volume control and reduced the voice. Then, a minute or two later, the interference began. The ringing of telephones and doorbells set in, joined by the rasp of the elevator doors and the whir of cooking appliances. The character of the noise had changed since Irene had tried the radio earlier; the last of the electric razors was being unplugged, the vacuum cleaners had all been returned to their closets, and the static reflected that change in pace that overtakes the city after the sun goes down. He fiddled with the knobs but couldn't get rid of the noises, so he turned the radio off and told Irene that in the morning he'd call the people who had sold it to him and give them hell.

The following afternoon, when Irene returned to the apartment from a luncheon date, the maid told her that a man had come and fixed the radio. Irene went into the living room before she took off her hat or her furs and tried the instrument. From the loudspeaker came a recording of the 'Missouri Waltz.' It reminded her of the thin, scratchy music from an old-fashioned phonograph that she sometimes heard across the lake where she spent her summers. She waited until the waltz had finished, expecting an explanation of the recording, but there was none. The music was followed by silence, and then the plaintive and scratchy record was repeated. She turned the dial and got a satisfactory burst of Caucasian music – the thump of bare feet in the dust and the rattle of coin jewelry – but in the background she could hear the ringing of bells and a confusion of voices. Her children came home from school then, and she turned off the radio and went to the nursery.

When Jim came home that night, he was tired, and he took a bath and changed his clothes. Then he joined Irene in the living room. He had just turned on the radio when the maid announced dinner, so he left it on, and he and Irene went to the table.

Jim was too tired to make even a pretense of sociability, and there was nothing about the dinner to hold Irene's interest, so her attention wandered from the food to the deposits of silver polish on the candlesticks and from there to the music in the other room. She listened for a few minutes to a Chopin prelude and then was surprised to hear a man's voice break in. 'For Christ's sake, Kathy,' he said, 'do you always have to play the piano when I get home?' The music stopped abruptly. 'It's the only chance I have,' a woman said, 'I'm at the office all day.' 'So am I,' the man said. He added something obscene about an upright piano, and slammed a door. The passionate and melancholy music began again.

'Did you hear that?' Irene asked.

'What?' Jim was eating his dessert.

5

'The radio. A man said something while the music was still going on – something dirty.'

'It's probably a play.'

'I don't think it *is* a play,' Irene said.

They left the table and took their coffee into the living room. Irene asked Jim to try another station. He turned the knob. 'Have you seen my garters?' a man asked. 'Button me up,' a woman said. 'Have you seen my garters?' the man said again. 'Just button me up and I'll find your garters,' the woman said. Jim shifted to another station. 'I wish you wouldn't leave apple cores in the ashtrays,' a man said. 'I hate the smell.'

'This is strange,' Jim said.

'Isn't it?' Irene said.

Jim turned the knob again. '"On the coast of Coromandel where the early pumpkins blow,"' a woman with a pronounced English accent said, '"in the middle of the woods lived the Yonghy-Bonghy-Bò. Two old chairs, and half a candle, one old jug without a handle ..."'

'My God!' Irene cried. 'That's the Sweeneys' nurse.'

'"These were all his worldly goods,"' the British voice continued.

'Turn that thing off,' Irene said. 'Maybe they can hear *us*.' Jim switched the radio off. 'That was Miss Armstrong, the Sweeneys' nurse,' Irene said. 'She must be reading to the little girl. They live in 17-B. I've talked with Miss Armstrong in the Park. I know her voice very well. We must be getting other people's apartments.'

'That's impossible,' Jim said.

'Well, that was the Sweeneys' nurse,' Irene said hotly. 'I know her voice. I know it very well. I'm wondering if they can hear us.'

Jim turned the switch. First from a distance and then nearer, nearer, as if borne on the wind, came the pure accents of the Sweeneys' nurse again: "'*Lady Jingly! Lady Jingly!*'" she said, "'*sitting where the pumpkins blow, will you come and be my wife? said the* Yonghy-Bonghy-Bò ...'"

Jim went over to the radio and said 'Hello' loudly into the speaker.

"'*I am tired of living singly,*'" the nurse went on, "'*on this coast so wild and shingly, I'm a-weary of my life; if you'll come and be my wife, quite serene would be my life ...*'"

'I guess she can't hear us,' Irene said. 'Try something else.'

Jim turned to another station, and the living room was filled with the uproar of a cocktail party that had overshot its mark. Someone was playing the piano and singing the 'Whiffenpoof Song,' and the voices that surrounded the piano were vehement and happy. 'Eat some more sandwiches,' a woman shrieked. There were screams of laughter and a dish of some sort crashed to the floor.

'Those must be the Fullers, in 11-E,' Irene said. 'I knew they were giving a party this afternoon. I saw her in the liquor store. Isn't this too divine? Try something else. See if you can get those people in 18-C.'

The Westcotts overheard that evening a monologue on salmon fishing in Canada, a bridge game, running comments on home movies of what had apparently been a fortnight at Sea Island, and a bitter family quarrel about an overdraft at the bank. They turned off their radio at midnight and went to bed, weak with laughter. Sometime in the night, their son began to call for a glass of water and Irene got one and took it to his room. It was very early. All the lights in the neighborhood were extinguished, and from

7

the boy's window she could see the empty street. She went into the living room and tried the radio. There was some faint coughing, a moan, and then a man spoke. 'Are you all right, darling?' he asked. 'Yes,' a woman said wearily. 'Yes, I'm all right, I guess,' and then she added with great feeling, 'But, you know, Charlie, I don't feel like myself any more. Sometimes there are about fifteen or twenty minutes in the week when I feel like myself. I don't like to go to another doctor, because the doctor's bills are so awful already, but I just don't feel like myself, Charlie. I just never feel like myself.' They were not young, Irene thought. She guessed from the timbre of their voices that they were middle-aged. The restrained melancholy of the dialogue and the draft from the bedroom window made her shiver, and she went back to bed.

The following morning, Irene cooked breakfast for the family – the maid didn't come up from her room in the basement until ten – braided her daughter's hair, and waited at the door until her children and her husband had been carried away in the elevator. Then she went into the living room and tried the radio. 'I don't want to go to school,' a child screamed. 'I hate school. I won't go to school. I hate school.' 'You will go to school,' an enraged woman said. 'We paid eight hundred dollars to get you into that school and you'll go if it kills you.' The next number on the dial produced the worn record of the 'Missouri Waltz.' Irene shifted the control and invaded the privacy of several breakfast tables. She overheard demonstrations of indigestion, carnal love, abysmal vanity, faith, and despair. Irene's life was nearly as simple and sheltered as it appeared to be, and the forthright and sometimes brutal language that came from the loudspeaker that morning astonished and troubled her. She continued to listen until her maid came in. Then she turned off the radio quickly, since this insight, she realized, was a furtive one.

Irene had a luncheon date with a friend that day, and she left her apartment at a little after twelve. There were a number of women in the elevator when it stopped at her floor. She stared at their handsome and impassive faces, their furs, and the cloth flowers in their hats. Which one of them had been to Sea Island? she wondered. Which one had overdrawn her bank account? The elevator stopped at the tenth floor and a woman with a pair of Skye terriers joined them. Her hair was rigged high on her head and she wore a mink cape. She was humming the 'Missouri Waltz.'

Irene had two Martinis at lunch, and she looked searchingly at her friend and wondered what her secrets were. They had intended to go shopping after lunch, but Irene excused herself and went home. She told the maid that she was not to be disturbed; then she went into the living room, closed the doors, and switched on the radio. She heard, in the course of the afternoon, the halting conversation of a woman entertaining her aunt, the hysterical conclusion of a luncheon party, and a hostess briefing her maid about some cocktail guests. 'Don't give the best Scotch to anyone who hasn't white hair,' the hostess said. 'See if you can get rid of that liver paste before you pass those hot things, and could you lend me five dollars? I want to tip the elevator man.'

As the afternoon waned, the conversations increased in intensity. From where Irene sat, she could see the open sky above the East River. There were hundreds of clouds in the sky, as though the south wind had broken the winter into pieces and were blowing it north, and on her radio she could hear the arrival of cocktail guests and the return of children and businessmen from their schools and offices. 'I found a good-sized diamond on the bathroom floor this morning,' a woman said. 'It must have fallen out of that bracelet Mrs Dunston was wearing last night.' 'We'll sell it,' a man said. 'Take it down to the jeweler on Madison Avenue and sell it. Mrs Dunston won't know the difference, and we could use a couple of hundred bucks ...' '"Oranges and lemons, say the bells of St Clement's,"' the Sweeneys' nurse sang. '"Halfpence and farthings, say the bells of St Martin's. When will you pay me? say the bells at Old Bailey ..."' 'It's not a hat,' a woman cried, and at her back roared a cocktail party. 'It's not a hat, it's a love affair. That's what Walter Florell said. He said it's not a hat, it's a love affair,' and then, in a lower voice, the same woman added, 'Talk to somebody, for Christ's sake, honey, talk to somebody. If she catches you standing here not talking to anybody, she'll take us off her invitation list, and I love these parties.'

The Westcotts were going out for dinner that night, and when Jim came home, Irene was dressing. She seemed sad and vague, and he brought her a drink. They were dining with friends in the neighborhood, and they walked to where they were going. The sky was broad and filled with light. It was one of those splendid spring evenings that excite memory and desire, and the air that touched their hands and faces felt very soft. A Salvation Army band was on the corner playing 'Jesus Is Sweeter.' Irene drew on her husband's arm and held him there for a minute, to hear the music. 'They're really such nice people, aren't they?' she said. 'They have such nice faces. Actually, they're so much nicer than a lot of the people we know.' She took a bill from her purse and walked over and dropped it into the tambourine. There was in her face, when she returned to her husband, a look of radiant melancholy that he was not familiar with. And her conduct at the dinner party that night seemed strange to him, too. She interrupted her hostess rudely and stared at the people across the table from her with an intensity for which she would have punished her children.

It was still mild when they walked home from the party, and Irene looked up at the spring stars. '"How far that little candle throws its beams,"' she exclaimed. '"So shines a good deed in a naughty world."' She waited that night until Jim had fallen asleep, and then went into the living room and turned on the radio.

Jim came home at about six the next night. Emma, the maid, let him in, and he had taken off his hat and was taking off his coat when Irene ran into the hall. Her face was shining with tears and her hair was disordered. 'Go up to 16-C, Jim!' she screamed. 'Don't take off your coat. Go up to 16-C. Mr Osborn's beating his wife. They've been quarreling since four o'clock, and now he's hitting her. Go up there and stop him.'

From the radio in the living room, Jim heard screams, obscenities, and thuds. 'You know you don't have to listen to this sort of thing,' he said. He strode into the living room and turned the switch. 'It's indecent,' he said. 'It's like

11

looking in windows. You know you don't have to listen to this sort of thing. You can turn it off.'

'Oh, it's so horrible, it's so dreadful,' Irene was sobbing. 'I've been listening all day, and it's so depressing.'

'Well, if it's so depressing, why do you listen to it? I bought this damned radio to give you some pleasure,' he said. 'I paid a great deal of money for it. I thought it might make you happy. I wanted to make you happy.'

'Don't, don't, don't, don't quarrel with me,' she moaned, and laid her head on his shoulder. 'All the others have been quarreling all day. Everybody's been quarreling. They're all worried about money. Mrs Hutchinson's mother is dying of cancer in Florida and they don't have enough money to send her to the Mayo Clinic. At least, Mr Hutchinson says they don't have enough money. And some woman in this building is having an affair with the handyman – with that hideous handyman. It's too disgusting. And Mrs Melville has heart trouble and Mr Hendricks is going to lose his job in April and Mrs Hendricks is horrid about the whole thing and that girl who plays the "Missouri Waltz" is a whore, a common whore, and the elevator man has tuberculosis and Mr Osborn has been beating Mrs Osborn.' She wailed, she trembled with grief and checked the stream of tears down her face with the heel of her palm.

'Well, why do you have to listen?' Jim asked again. 'Why do you have to listen to this stuff if it makes you so miserable?'

'Oh, don't, don't, don't,' she cried. 'Life is too terrible, too sordid and awful. But we've never been like that, have we, darling? Have we? I mean, we've always been good and decent and loving to one another, haven't we? And we have two children, two beautiful children. Our lives aren't sordid, are they, darling? Are they?' She flung her arms around his neck and drew his face down to hers. 'We're happy, aren't we, darling? We are happy, aren't we?'

'Of course we're happy,' he said tiredly. He began to surrender his resentment. 'Of course we're happy. I'll have that damned radio fixed or taken away tomorrow.' He stroked her soft hair. 'My poor girl,' he said.

'You love me, don't you?' she asked. 'And we're not hypercritical or worried about money or dishonest, are we?'

'No, darling,' he said.

A man came in the morning and fixed the radio. Irene turned it on cautiously and was happy to hear a California-wine commercial and a recording of Beethoven's Ninth Symphony, including Schiller's 'Ode to Joy.' She kept the radio on all day and nothing untoward came from the speaker.

A Spanish suite was being played when Jim came home. 'Is everything all right?' he asked. His face was pale, she thought. They had some cocktails and went in to dinner to the 'Anvil Chorus' from *Il Trovatore*. This was followed by Debussy's 'La Mer.'

'I paid the bill for the radio today,' Jim said. 'It cost four hundred dollars. I hope you'll get some enjoyment out of it.'

'Oh, I'm sure I will,' Irene said.

'Four hundred dollars is a good deal more than I can afford,' he went on. 'I wanted to get something that you'd enjoy. It's the last extravagance we'll be able to indulge in this year. I see that you haven't paid your clothing bills yet. I saw them on your dressing table.' He looked directly at her. 'Why did you tell me you'd paid them? Why did you lie to me?'

'I just didn't want you to worry, Jim,' she said. She drank some water. 'I'll be able to pay my bills out of this month's allowance. There were the slipcovers last month, and that party.'

'You've got to learn to handle the money I give you a little more intelligently, Irene,' he said. 'You've got to understand that we won't have as much money this year as we had last. I had a very sobering talk with Mitchell today. No one is buying anything. We're spending all our time promoting new issues, and you know how long that takes. I'm not getting any younger, you know. I'm thirty-seven. My hair will be gray next year. I haven't done as well as I'd hoped to do. And I don't suppose things will get any better.'

'Yes, dear,' she said.

'We've got to start cutting down,' Jim said. 'We've got to think of the children. To be perfectly frank with you, I worry about money a great deal. I'm not at all sure of the future. No one is. If anything should happen to me, there's the insurance, but that wouldn't go very far today. I've worked awfully hard to give you and the children a comfortable life,' he said bitterly. 'I don't like to see all of my energies, all of my youth, wasted in fur coats and radios and slipcovers and –'

'Please, Jim,' she said. 'Please. They'll hear us.'

'*Who'll hear us?* Emma can't hear us.'

'The radio.'

'Oh, I'm sick!' he shouted. 'I'm sick to death of your apprehensiveness. The radio can't hear us. Nobody can hear us. And what if they can hear us? Who cares?'

Irene got up from the table and went into the living room. Jim went to the door and shouted at her from there. 'Why are you so Christly all of a sudden? What's turned you overnight into a convent girl? You stole your mother's jewelry before they probated her will. You never gave your sister a cent of that money that was intended for her – not even when she needed it. You made Grace Howland's life miserable, and where was all your piety and your virtue when you went to that abortionist? I'll never forget how cool you were. You packed your bag and went off to have that child murdered as if you were going to Nassau. If you'd had any reasons, if you'd had any good reasons –'

Irene stood for a minute before the hideous cabinet, disgraced and sickened, but she held her hand on the switch before she extinguished the music and the voices, hoping that the instrument might speak to her kindly, that she might hear the Sweeneys' nurse. Jim continued to shout at her from the door. The voice on the radio was suave and noncommittal. 'An early-morning railroad disaster in Tokyo,' the loudspeaker said, 'killed twenty-nine people. A fire in a Catholic hospital near Buffalo for the care of blind children was extinguished early this morning by nuns. The temperature is forty-seven. The humidity is eighty-nine.'

The Season of Divorce

MY WIFE HAS brown hair, dark eyes, and a gentle disposition. Because of her gentle disposition, I sometimes think that she spoils the children. She can't refuse them anything. They always get around her. Ethel and I have been married for ten years. We both come from Morristown, New Jersey, and I can't even remember when I first met her. Our marriage has always seemed happy and resourceful to me. We live in a walk-up in the East Fifties. Our son, Carl, who is six, goes to a good private school, and our daughter, who is four, won't go to school until next year. We often find fault with the way we were educated, but we seem to be struggling to raise our children along the same lines, and when the time comes, I suppose they'll go to the same school and colleges that we went to.

Ethel graduated from a women's college in the East, and then went for a year to the University of Grenoble. She worked for a year in New York after returning from France, and then we were married. She once hung her diploma above the kitchen sink, but it was a short-lived joke and I don't know where the diploma is now. Ethel is cheerful and adaptable, as well as gentle, and we both come from that enormous stratum of the middle class that is distinguished by its ability to recall better times. Lost money is so much a

part of our lives that I am sometimes reminded of expatri-
ates, of a group who have adapted themselves energetically
to some alien soil but who are reminded, now and then, of
the escarpments of their native coast. Because our lives are
confined by my modest salary, the surface of Ethel's life is
easy to describe.

She gets up at seven and turns the radio on. After she is
dressed, she rouses the children and cooks the breakfast.
Our son has to be walked to the school bus at eight o'clock.
When Ethel returns from this trip, Carol's hair has to be
braided. I leave the house at eight-thirty, but I know that
every move that Ethel makes for the rest of the day will be
determined by the housework, the cooking, the shopping,
and the demands of the children. I know that on Tuesdays
and Thursdays she will be at the A & P between eleven and
noon, that on every clear afternoon she will be on a certain
bench in a playground from three until five, that she cleans
the house on Mondays, Wednesdays, and Fridays, and pol-
ishes the silver when it rains. When I return at six, she is
usually cleaning the vegetables or making some other
preparation for dinner. Then when the children have been
fed and bathed, when the dinner is ready, when the table in
the living room is set with food and china, she stands in the
middle of the room as if she has lost or forgotten something, and this moment of reflection is so deep that she will
not hear me if I speak to her, or the children if they call.
Then it is over. She lights the four white candles in their
silver sticks, and we sit down to a supper of corned-beef
hash or some other modest fare.

We go out once or twice a week and entertain about
once a month. Because of practical considerations, most of

the people we see live in our neighborhood. We often go around the corner to the parties given by a generous couple named Newsome. The Newsomes' parties are large and confusing, and the arbitrary impulses of friendship are given a free play.

We became attached at the Newsomes' one evening, for reasons that I've never understood, to a couple named Dr and Mrs Trencher. I think that Mrs Trencher was the aggressor in this friendship, and after our first meeting she telephoned Ethel three or four times. We went to their house for dinner, and they came to our house, and sometimes in the evening when Dr Trencher was walking their old dachshund, he would come up for a short visit. He seemed like a pleasant man to have around. I've heard other doctors say that he's a good physician. The Trenchers are about thirty; at least he is. She is older.

I'd say that Mrs Trencher is a plain woman, but her plainness is difficult to specify. She is small, she has a good figure and regular features, and I suppose that the impression of plainness arises from some inner modesty, some needlessly narrow view of her chances. Dr Trencher doesn't smoke or drink, and I don't know whether there's any connection or not, but the coloring in his slender face is fresh – his cheeks are pink, and his blue eyes are clear and strong. He has the singular optimism of a well-adjusted physician – the feeling that death is a chance misfortune and that the physical world is merely a field for conquest. In the same way that his wife seems plain, he seems young.

The Trenchers live in a comfortable and unpretentious private house in our neighborhood. The house is old-fashioned; its living rooms are large, its halls are gloomy, and the Trenchers don't seem to generate enough human warmth to animate the place, so that you sometimes take away from them, at the end of an evening, an impression of many empty rooms. Mrs Trencher is noticeably attached to her possessions – her clothes, her jewels, and the ornaments she's bought for the house – and to Fraulein, the old dachshund. She feeds Fraulein scraps from the table, furtively, as if she has been forbidden to do this, and after dinner Fraulein lies beside her on the sofa. With the play of green light from a television set on her drawn features and her thin hands stroking Fraulein, Mrs Trencher looked to me one evening like a good-hearted and miserable soul.

Mrs Trencher began to call Ethel in the mornings for a talk or to ask her for lunch or a matinee. Ethel can't go out in the day and she claims to dislike long telephone conversations. She complained that Mrs Trencher was a tireless and aggressive gossip. Then late one afternoon Dr Trencher appeared at the playground where Ethel takes our two children. He was walking by, and he saw her and sat with her until it was time to take the children home. He came again a few days later, and then his visits with Ethel in the playground, she told me, became a regular thing. Ethel thought that perhaps he didn't have many patients and that with nothing to do he was happy to talk with anyone. Then, when we were washing dishes one night, Ethel said thoughtfully that Trencher's attitude toward her seemed strange. 'He stares at me,' she said. 'He sighs and stares at me.' I know what my wife looks like in the playground. She wears an old tweed coat, overshoes, and Army gloves, and a scarf is tied under her chin. The playground is a fenced and paved lot between a slum and the river. The picture of the well-dressed, pink-cheeked doctor losing his heart to Ethel in this environment was hard to take seriously. She didn't mention him then for several days, and I guessed that he had stopped his visits. Ethel's birthday came at the end of the month, and I forgot about it, but when I came home that evening, there were a lot of roses in the living room. They were a birthday present from Trencher, she told me. I was cross at myself for having forgotten her birthday, and Trencher's roses made me angry. I asked her if she'd seen him recently.

'Oh, yes,' she said, 'he still comes to the playground nearly every afternoon. I haven't told you, have I? He's made his declaration. He loves me. He can't live without me. He'd walk through fire to hear the notes of my voice.' She laughed. 'That's what he said.'

'When did he say this?'

'At the playground. And walking home. Yesterday.'

'How long has he known?'

'That's the funny part about it,' she said. 'He knew before he met me at the Newsomes' that night. He saw me waiting for a crosstown bus about three weeks before that. He just saw me and he said that he knew then, the minute he saw me. Of course, he's crazy.'

I was tired that night and worried about taxes and bills, and I could think of Trencher's declaration only as a comical mistake. I felt that he was a captive of financial and sentimental commitments, like every other man I know, and that he was no more free to fall in love with a strange woman he saw on a street corner than he was to take a walking trip through French Guiana or to recommence his life in Chicago under an assumed name. His declaration, the scene in the playground, seemed to me to be like those chance meetings that are a part of the life of any large city. A blind man asks you to help him across the street, and as you are about to leave him, he seizes your arm and regales you with a passionate account of his cruel and ungrateful children; or the elevator man who is taking you up to a party turns to you suddenly and says that his grandson has infantile paralysis. The city is full of accidental revelation, half-heard cries for help, and strangers who will tell you everything at the first suspicion of sympathy, and Trencher seemed to me like the blind man or the elevator operator. His declaration had no more bearing on the business of our lives than these interruptions.

Mrs Trencher's telephone conversations had stopped, and we had stopped visiting the Trenchers, but sometimes I would see him in the morning on the crosstown bus when I was late going to work. He seemed understandably embarrassed whenever he saw me, but the bus was always crowded at that time of day, and it was no effort to avoid one another. Also, at about that time I made a mistake in business and lost several thousand dollars for the firm I work for. There was not much chance of my losing my job, but the possibility was always at the back of my mind, and under this and under the continuous urgency of making more money the memory of the eccentric doctor was buried. Three weeks passed without Ethel's mentioning him, and then one evening, when I was reading, I noticed Ethel standing at the window looking down into the street.

'He's really there,' she said.

'Who?'

'Trencher. Come here and see.'

I went to the window. There were only three people on the sidewalk across the street. It was dark and it would have been difficult to recognize anyone, but because one of them, walking toward the corner, had a dachshund on a leash, it could have been Trencher.

'Well, what about it?' I said. 'He's just walking the dog.'

'But he wasn't walking the dog when I first looked out of the window. He was just standing there, staring up at this building. That's what he says he does. He says that he comes over here and stares up at our lighted windows.'

'When did he say this?'

'At the playground.'

'I thought you went to another playground.'

'Oh, I do, I do, but he followed me. He's crazy, darling. I know he's crazy, but I feel so sorry for him. He says that he spends night after night looking up at our windows. He says that he sees me everywhere – the back of my head, my eyebrows – that he hears my voice. He says that he's never compromised in his life and that he isn't going to compromise about this. I feel so sorry for him, darling. I can't help but feel sorry for him.'

For the first time then, the situation seemed serious to me, for in his helplessness I knew that he might have touched an inestimable and wayward passion that Ethel shares with some other women – an inability to refuse any cry for help, to refuse any voice that sounds pitiable. It is not a reasonable passion, and I would almost rather have had her desire him than pity him. When we were getting ready for bed that night, the telephone rang, and when I picked it up and said hello, no one answered. Fifteen minutes later, the telephone rang again, and when there was no answer this time, I began to shout and swear at Trencher, but he didn't reply – there wasn't even the click of a closed circuit – and I felt like a fool. Because I felt like a fool, I accused Ethel of having led him on, of having encouraged him, but these accusations didn't affect her, and when I finished them, I felt worse, because I knew that she was innocent, and that she had to go out on the street to buy groceries and air the children, and that there was no force of law that could keep Trencher from waiting for her there, or from staring up at our lights.

We went to the Newsomes' one night the next week, and while we were taking off our coats, I heard Trencher's voice. He left a few minutes after we arrived, but his manner – the sad glance he gave Ethel, the way he sidestepped me, the sorrowful way that he refused the Newsomes when they asked him to stay longer, and the gallant attentions he showed his miserable wife – made me angry. Then I happened to notice Ethel and saw that her color was high, that her eyes were bright, and that while she was praising Mrs Newsome's new shoes, her mind was not on what she was saying. When we came home that night, the baby-sitter told us crossly that neither of the children had slept. Ethel took their temperatures. Carol was all right, but the boy had a fever of a hundred and four. Neither of us got much sleep that night, and in the morning Ethel called me at the office to say that Carl had bronchitis. Three days later, his sister came down with it.

For the next two weeks, the sick children took up most of our time. They had to be given medicine at eleven in the evening and again at three in the morning, and we lost a lot of sleep. It was impossible to ventilate or clean the house, and when I came in, after walking through the cold from the bus stop, it stank of cough syrups and tobacco, fruit cores and sickbeds. There were blankets and pillows, ash-trays, and medicine glasses everywhere. We divided the work of sickness reasonably and took turns at getting up in the night, but I often fell asleep at my desk during the day, and after dinner Ethel would fall asleep in a chair in the living room. Fatigue seems to differ for adults and children only in that adults recognize it and so are not overwhelmed by something they can't name; but even with a name for it they are overwhelmed, and when we were tired, we were unreasonable, cross, and the victims of transcendent depressions. One evening after the worst of the sickness was over, I came home and found some roses in the living room. Ethel said that Trencher had brought them. She hadn't let him in. She had closed the door in his face. I took the roses and threw them out. We didn't quarrel. The children went to sleep at nine, and a few minutes after nine I went to bed. Sometime later, something woke me.

A light was burning in the hall. I got up. The children's room and the living room were dark. I found Ethel in the kitchen sitting at the table, drinking coffee.

'I've made some fresh coffee,' she said. 'Carol felt croupy again, so I steamed her. They're both asleep now.'

'How long have you been up?'

'Since half past twelve,' she said. 'What time is it?'

'Two.'

I poured myself a cup of coffee and sat down. She got up from the table and rinsed her cup and looked at herself in a mirror that hangs over the sink. It was a windy night. A dog was wailing somewhere in an apartment below ours, and a loose radio antenna was brushing against the kitchen window.

'It sounds like a branch,' she said.

In the bare kitchen light, meant for peeling potatoes and washing dishes, she looked very tired.

'Will the children be able to go out tomorrow?'

'Oh, I hope so,' she said. 'Do you realize that I haven't been out of this apartment in over two weeks?' She spoke bitterly and this startled me.

'It hasn't been quite two weeks.'

'It's been over two weeks,' she said.

'Well, let's figure it out,' I said. 'The children were taken sick on a Saturday night. That was the fourth. Today is the –'

'Stop it, stop it,' she said. 'I know how long it's been. I haven't had my shoes on in two weeks.'

'You make it sound pretty bad.'

'It is. I haven't had on a decent dress or fixed my hair.'

'It could be worse.'

'My mother's cooks had a better life.'

'I doubt that.'

'My mother's cooks had a better life,' she said loudly.

'You'll wake the children.'

'My mother's cooks had a better life. They had pleasant rooms. No one could come into the kitchen without their permission.' She knocked the coffee grounds into the garbage and began to wash the pot.

'How long was Trencher here this afternoon?'

'A minute. I've told you.'

'I don't believe it. He was in here.'

'He was not. I didn't let him in. I didn't let him in because I looked so badly. I didn't want to discourage him.'

'Why not?'

'I don't know. He may be a fool. He may be insane but the things he's told me have made me feel marvelously, he's made me feel marvelously.'

'Do you want to go?'

'Go? Where would I go?' She reached for the purse that is kept in the kitchen to pay for groceries and counted out of it two dollars and thirty-five cents. 'Ossining? Montclair?'

'I mean with Trencher.'

'I don't know, I don't know,' she said, 'but who can say that I shouldn't? What harm would it do? What good would it do? Who knows. I love the children but that isn't enough, that isn't nearly enough. I wouldn't hurt them, but would I hurt them so much if I left you? Is divorce so dreadful and of all the things that hold a marriage together how many of them are good?' She sat down at the table.

'In Grenoble,' she said, 'I wrote a long paper on Charles Stuart in French. A professor at the University of Chicago wrote me a letter. I couldn't read a French newspaper without a dictionary today, I don't have the time to follow any newspaper, and I am ashamed of my incompetence, ashamed of the way I look. Oh, I guess I love you, I do love the children, but I love myself, I love my life, it has some value and some promise for me and Trencher's roses make me feel that I'm losing this, that I'm losing my self-respect. Do you know what I mean, do you under-stand what I mean?'

26

'He's crazy,' I said.

'Do you know what I mean? Do you understand what I mean?'

'No,' I said. 'No.'

Carl woke up then and called for his mother. I told Ethel to go to bed. I turned out the kitchen light and went into the children's room.

The children felt better the next day, and since it was Sunday, I took them for a walk. The afternoon sun was clement and pure, and only the colored shadows made me remember that it was midwinter, that the cruise ships were returning, and that in another week jonquils would be twenty-five cents a bunch. Walking down Lexington Avenue, we heard the drone bass of a church organ sound from the sky, and we and the others on the sidewalk looked up in piety and bewilderment, like a devout and stupid congregation, and saw a formation of heavy bombers heading for the sea. As it got late, it got cold and clear and still, and on the stillness the waste from the smokestacks along the East River seemed to articulate, as legibly as the Pepsi-Cola plane, whole words and sentences. Halcyon. Disaster. They were hard to make out. It seemed the ebb of the year – an evil day for gastritis, sinus, and respiratory disease – and remembering other winters, the markings of the light convinced me that it was the season of divorce. It was a long afternoon, and I brought the children in before dark.

I think that the seriousness of the day affected the children, and when they returned to the house, they were quiet. The seriousness of it kept coming to me with the feeling that this change, like a phenomenon of speed, was affecting our watches as well as our hearts. I tried to remember the willingness with which Ethel had followed my regiment during the war, from West Virginia to the Carolinas and Oklahoma, and the day coaches and rooms she had lived in, and the street in San Francisco where I said goodbye to her before I left the country, but I could not put any of this into words, and neither of us found anything to say. Sometime after dark, the children were bathed and put to bed, and we sat down to our supper. At about nine o'clock, the doorbell rang, and when I answered it and recognized Trencher's voice on the speaking tube, I asked him to come up.

He seemed distraught and exhilarated when he appeared. He stumbled on the edge of the carpet. 'I know that I'm not welcome here,' he said in a hard voice, as if I were deaf. 'I know that you don't like me here. I respect your feelings. This is your home. I respect a man's feelings about his home. I don't usually go to a man's home unless he asks me. I respect your home. I respect your marriage. I respect your children. I think everything ought to be aboveboard. I've come here to tell you that I love your wife.'

'Get out,' I said.

'You've got to listen to me,' he said. 'I love your wife. I can't live without her. I've tried and I can't. I've even thought of going away – of moving to the West Coast – but I know that it wouldn't make any difference. I want to marry her. I'm not romantic. I'm matter-of-fact. I'm very matter-of-fact. I know that you have two children and that you don't have much money. I know that there are problems of custody and property and things like that to be settled. I'm not romantic. I'm hardheaded. I've talked this all over with Mrs Trencher, and she's agreed to give me a divorce. I'm not underhanded. Your wife can tell you that. I realize all the practical aspects that have to be considered – custody, property, and so forth. I have plenty of money. I can give Ethel everything she needs, but there are the children. You'll have to decide about them between yourselves. I have a check here. It's made out to Ethel. I want her to take it and go to Nevada. I'm a practical man and I realize that nothing can be decided until she gets her divorce.'

'Get out of here!' I said. 'Get the hell out of here!'

He started for the door. There was a potted geranium on the mantelpiece, and I threw this across the room at him. It got him in the small of the back and nearly knocked him down. The pot broke on the floor. Ethel screamed. Trencher was still on his way out. Following him, I picked up a candlestick and aimed it at his head, but it missed and bounced off the wall. 'Get the hell out of here!' I yelled, and he slammed the door. I went back into the living room. Ethel was pale but she wasn't crying. There was a loud rapping on the radiator, a signal from the people upstairs for decorum and silence – urgent and expressive, like the communications that prisoners send to one another through the plumbing in a penitentiary. Then everything was still.

We went to bed, and I woke sometime during the night. I couldn't see the clock on the dresser, so I don't know what time it was. There was no sound from the children's room. The neighborhood was perfectly still. There were no lighted windows anywhere. Then I knew that Ethel had wakened me. She was lying on her side of the bed. She was crying.

'Why are you crying?' I asked.

'Why am I crying?' she said. 'Why am I crying?' And to hear my voice and to speak set her off again, and she began to sob cruelly. She sat up and slipped her arms into the sleeves of a wrapper and felt along the table for a package of cigarettes. I saw her wet face when she lighted a cigarette. I heard her moving around in the dark.

'Why do you cry?'

'Why do I cry? Why do I cry?' she asked impatiently. 'I cry because I saw an old woman cuffing a little boy on Third Avenue. She was drunk. I can't get it out of my mind.' She pulled the quilt off the foot of our bed and wandered with it toward the door. 'I cry because my father died when I was twelve and because my mother married a man I detested or thought that I detested. I cry because I had to wear an ugly dress – a hand-me-down dress – to a party twenty years ago, and I didn't have a good time. I cry because of some unkindness that I can't remember. I cry because I'm tired – because I'm tired and I can't sleep.' I heard her arrange herself on the sofa and then everything was quiet.

I like to think that the Trenchers have gone away, but I still see Trencher now and then on a crosstown bus when I'm late going to work. I've also seen his wife, going into the neighborhood lending library with Fraulein. She looks old. I'm not good at judging ages, but I wouldn't be surprised to find that Mrs Trencher is fifteen years older than her husband. Now when I come home in the evenings, Ethel is still sitting on the stool by the sink cleaning vegetables. I go with her into the children's room. The light there is bright. The children have built something out of an orange crate, something preposterous and ascendant, and their sweetness, their compulsion to build, the brightness of the light are reflected perfectly and increased in Ethel's face. Then she feeds them, bathes them, and sets the table, and stands for a moment in the middle of the room, trying to make some connection between the evening and the day. Then it is over. She lights the four candles, and we sit down to our supper.

Goodbye, My Brother

WE ARE A family that has always been very close in spirit. Our father was drowned in a sailing accident when we were young, and our mother has always stressed the fact that our familial relationships have a kind of permanence that we will never meet with again. I don't think about the family much, but when I remember its members and the coast where they lived and the sea salt that I think is in our blood, I am happy to recall that I am a Pommeroy – that I have the nose, the coloring, and the promise of longevity – and that while we are not a distinguished family, we enjoy the illusion, when we are together, that the Pommeroys are unique. I don't say any of this because I'm interested in family history or because this sense of uniqueness is deep or important to me but in order to advance the point that we are loyal to one another in spite of our differences, and that any rupture in this loyalty is a source of confusion and pain.

We are four children; there is my sister Diana and the three men – Chaddy, Lawrence, and myself. Like most families in which the children are out of their twenties, we have been separated by business, marriage, and war. Helen and I live on Long Island now, with our four children. I teach in a secondary school, and I am past the age where I expect to be made headmaster – or principal, as we say – but I respect the work. Chaddy, who has done better than the rest of us, lives in Manhattan, with Odette and their children. Mother lives in Philadelphia, and Diana, since her divorce, has been living in France, but she comes back to the States in the summer to spend a month at Laud's Head. Laud's Head is a summer place on the shore of one of the Massachusetts islands. We used to have a cottage there, and in the twenties our father built the big house. It stands on a cliff above the sea and, excepting St Tropez and some of the Apennine villages, it is my favorite place in the world. We each have an equity in the place and we contribute some money to help keep it going.

Our youngest brother, Lawrence, who is a lawyer, got a job with a Cleveland firm after the war, and none of us saw him for four years. When he decided to leave Cleveland and go to work for a firm in Albany, he wrote Mother that he would, between jobs, spend ten days at Laud's Head, with his wife and their two children. This was when I had planned to take my vacation – I had been teaching summer school – and Helen and Chaddy and Odette and Diana were all going to be there, so the family would be together. Lawrence is the member of the family with whom the rest of us have least in common. We have never seen a great deal of him, and I suppose that's why we still call him Tifty – a nickname he was given when he was a child, because when he came down the hall toward the dining room for breakfast, his slippers made a noise that sounded like 'Tifty, tifty, tifty.' That's what Father called him, and so did everyone else. When he grew older, Diana sometimes used to call him Little Jesus, and Mother often called him the Croaker. We had disliked Lawrence, but we looked forward to his return with a mixture of apprehension and loyalty, and with some of the joy and delight of reclaiming a brother.

Lawrence crossed over from the mainland on the four-o'clock boat one afternoon late in the summer, and Chaddy and I went down to meet him. The arrivals and departures of the summer ferry have all the outward signs that suggest a voyage – whistles, bells, hand trucks, reunions, and the smell of brine – but it is a voyage of no import, and when I watched the boat come into the blue harbor that afternoon and thought that it was completing a voyage of no import, I realized that I had hit on exactly the kind of observation that Lawrence would have made. We looked for his face behind the windshields as the cars drove off the boat, and we had no trouble in recognizing him. And we ran over and shook his hand and clumsily kissed his wife and the children. 'Tifty!' Chaddy shouted. 'Tifty!' It is difficult to judge changes in the appearance of a brother, but both Chaddy and I agreed, as we drove back to Laud's Head, that Lawrence still looked very young. He got to the house first, and we took the suitcases out of his car. When I came in, he was standing in the living room, talking with Mother and Diana. They were in their best clothes and all their jewelry, and they were welcoming him extravagantly, but even then, when everyone was endeavoring to seem most affectionate and at a time when these endeavors come easiest, I was aware of a faint tension in the room. Thinking about this as I carried Lawrence's heavy suitcases up the stairs, I realized that our dislikes are as deeply ingrained as our better passions, and I remembered that once, twenty-five years ago, when I had hit Lawrence on the head with a rock, he had picked himself up and gone directly to our father to complain.

I carried the suitcases up to the third floor, where Ruth, Lawrence's wife, had begun to settle her family. She is a thin girl, and she seemed very tired from the journey, but when I asked her if she didn't want me to bring a drink upstairs to her, she said she didn't think she did.

When I got downstairs, Lawrence wasn't around, but the others were all ready for cocktails, and we decided to go ahead. Lawrence is the only member of the family who has never enjoyed drinking. We took our cocktails onto the terrace, so that we could see the bluffs and the sea and the islands in the east, and the return of Lawrence and his wife, their presence in the house, seemed to refresh our responses to the familiar view; it was as if the pleasure they would take in the sweep and the color of that coast, after such a long absence, had been imparted to us. While we were there, Lawrence came up the path from the beach.

'Isn't the beach fabulous, Tifty?' Mother asked. 'Isn't it fabulous to be back? Will you have a Martini?'

'I don't care,' Lawrence said. 'Whiskey, gin – I don't care what I drink. Give me a little rum.'

'We don't have any *rum*,' Mother said. It was the first note of asperity. She had taught us never to be indecisive, never to reply as Lawrence had. Beyond this, she is deeply concerned with the propriety of her house, and anything irregular by her standards, like drinking straight rum or bringing a beer can to the dinner table, excites in her a conflict that she cannot, even with her capacious sense of humor, surmount. She sensed the asperity and worked to repair it. 'Would you like some Irish, Tifty dear?' she said. 'Isn't Irish what you've always liked? There's some Irish on the sideboard. Why don't you get yourself some Irish?' Lawrence said that he didn't care. He poured himself a Martini, and then Ruth came down and we went in to dinner.

In spite of the fact that we had, through waiting for Lawrence, drunk too much before dinner, we were all anxious to put our best foot forward and to enjoy a peaceful time. Mother is a small woman whose face is still a striking reminder of how pretty she must have been, and whose conversation is unusually light, but she talked that evening about a soil-reclamation project that is going on up-island. Diana is as pretty as Mother must have been; she is an animated and lovely woman who likes to talk about the dissolute friends that she has made in France, but she talked that night about the school in Switzerland where she had left her two children. I could see that the dinner had been planned to please Lawrence. It was not too rich, and there was nothing to make him worry about extravagance.

After supper, when we went back onto the terrace, the clouds held that kind of light that looks like blood, and I was glad that Lawrence had such a lurid sunset for his homecoming. When we had been out there a few minutes, a man named Edward Chester came to get Diana. She had met him in France, or on the boat home, and he was staying for ten days at the inn in the village. He was introduced to Lawrence and Ruth, and then he and Diana left.

'Is that the one she's sleeping with now?' Lawrence asked.

'What a horrid thing to say!' Helen said.

'You ought to apologize for that, Tifty,' Chaddy said.

36

'I don't know,' Mother said tiredly. 'I don't know, Tifty. Diana is in a position to do whatever she wants, and I don't ask sordid questions. She's my only daughter. I don't see her often.'

'Is she going back to France?'

'She's going back the week after next.'

Lawrence and Ruth were sitting at the edge of the terrace, not in the chairs, not in the circle of chairs. With his mouth set, my brother looked to me then like a Puritan cleric. Sometimes, when I try to understand his frame of mind, I think of the beginnings of our family in this country, and his disapproval of Diana and her lover reminded me of this. The branch of the Pommeroys to which we belong was founded by a minister who was eulogized by Cotton Mather for his untiring abjuration of the Devil. The Pommeroys were ministers until the middle of the nineteenth century, and the harshness of their thought – man is full of misery, and all earthly beauty is lustful and corrupt – has been preserved in books and sermons. The temper of our family changed somewhat and became more lighthearted, but when I was of school age, I can remember a cousinage of old men and women who seemed to hark back to the dark days of the ministry and to be animated by perpetual guilt and the deification of the scourge. If you are raised in this atmosphere – and in a sense we were – I think it is a trial of the spirit to reject its habits of guilt, self-denial, taciturnity, and penitence, and it seemed to me to have been a trial of the spirit in which Lawrence had succumbed.

'Is that Cassiopeia?' Odette asked.

'No, dear,' Chaddy said. 'That isn't Cassiopeia.'

'Who was Cassiopeia?' Odette said.

'She was the wife of Cepheus and the mother of Andromeda,' I said.

'The cook is a Giants fan,' Chaddy said. 'She'll give you even money that they win the pennant.'

It had grown so dark that we could see the passage of light through the sky from the lighthouse at Cape Heron. In the dark below the cliff, the continual detonations of the surf sounded. And then, as she often does when it is getting dark and she has drunk too much before dinner, Mother began to talk about the improvements and additions that would someday be made on the house, the wings and bathrooms and gardens.

'This house will be in the sea in five years,' Lawrence said.

'Tifty the Croaker,' Chaddy said.

'Don't call me Tifty,' Lawrence said.

'Little Jesus,' Chaddy said.

'The sea wall is badly cracked,' Lawrence said. 'I looked at it this afternoon. You had it repaired four years ago, and it cost eight thousand dollars. You can't do that every four years.'

'Please, Tifty,' Mother said.

'Facts are facts,' Lawrence said, 'and it's a damned-fool idea to build a house at the edge of the cliff on a sinking coastline. In my lifetime, half the garden has washed away and there's four feet of water where we used to have a bathhouse.'

'Let's have a very *general* conversation,' Mother said bitterly. 'Let's talk about politics or the boat-club dance.'

'As a matter of fact,' Lawrence said, 'the house is probably in some danger now. If you had an unusually high sea, a hurricane sea, the wall would crumble and the house would go. We could all be drowned.'

'I can't *bear* it,' Mother said. She went into the pantry and came back with a full glass of gin.

I have grown too old now to think that I can judge the sentiments of others, but I was conscious of the tension between Lawrence and Mother, and I knew some of the history of it. Lawrence couldn't have been more than sixteen years old when he decided that Mother was frivolous, mischievous, destructive, and overly strong. When he had determined this, he decided to separate himself from her. He was at boarding school then, and I remember that he did not come home for Christmas. He spent Christmas with a friend. He came home very seldom after he had made his unfavorable judgment on Mother, and when he did come home, he always tried, in his conversation, to remind her of his estrangement. When he married Ruth, he did not tell Mother. He did not tell her when his children were born. But in spite of these principled and lengthy exertions he seemed, unlike the rest of us, never to have enjoyed any separation, and when they are together, you feel at once a tension, an unclearness.

And it was unfortunate, in a way, that Mother should have picked that night to get drunk. It's her privilege, and she doesn't get drunk often, and fortunately she wasn't bellicose, but we were all conscious of what was happening. As she quietly drank her gin, she seemed sadly to be parting from us; she seemed to be in the throes of travel. Then her mood changed from travel to injury, and the few remarks she made were petulant and irrelevant. When her glass was nearly empty, she stared angrily at the dark air in front of her nose, moving her head a little, like a fighter. I knew that there was not room in her mind then for all the injuries that were crowding into it. Her children were stupid, her husband was drowned, her servants were thieves, and the chair she sat in was uncomfortable. Suddenly she put down her empty glass and interrupted Chaddy, who was talking about baseball. 'I know one *thing*,' she said hoarsely. 'I know that if there is an afterlife, I'm going to have a very different kind of family. I'm going to have nothing but fabulously rich, witty, and enchanting children.' She got up and, starting for the door, nearly fell. Chaddy caught her and helped her up the stairs. I could hear their tender good-nights, and then Chaddy came back. I thought that Lawrence by now would be tired from his journey and his return, but he remained on the terrace, as if he were waiting to see the final malfeasance, and the rest of us left him there and went swimming in the dark.

When I woke the next morning, or half woke, I could hear the sound of someone rolling the tennis court. It is a fainter and a deeper sound than the iron buoy bells off the point – an unrhythmic iron chiming – that belongs in my mind to the beginnings of a summer day, a good portent. When I went downstairs, Lawrence's two kids were in the living room, dressed in ornate cowboy suits. They are frightened and skinny children. They told me their father was rolling the tennis court but that they did not want to go out because they had seen a snake under the doorstep. I explained to them that their cousins – all the other children – ate breakfast in the kitchen and that they'd better run along in there. At this announcement, the boy began to cry. Then his sister joined him. They cried as if to go in the kitchen and eat would destroy their most precious rights. I told them to sit down with me. Lawrence came in, and I asked him if he wanted to play some tennis. He said no, thanks, although he thought he might play some singles with Chaddy. He was in the right here, because both he and Chaddy play better tennis than I, and he did play some singles with Chaddy after breakfast, but later on, when the others came down to play family doubles, Lawrence disappeared. This made me cross – unreasonably so, I suppose – but we play darned interesting family doubles and he could have played in a set for the sake of courtesy.

Late in the morning, when I came up from the court alone, I saw Tifty on the terrace, prying up a shingle from the wall with his jack-knife. 'What's the matter, Lawrence?' I said. 'Termites?' There are termites in the wood and they've given us a lot of trouble.

He pointed out to me, at the base of each row of shingles, a faint blue line of carpenter's chalk. 'This house is about twenty-two years old,' he said. 'These shingles are about two hundred years old. Dad must have bought shingles from all the farms around here when he built the place, to make it look venerable. You can still see the carpenter's chalk put down where these antiques were nailed into place.'

It was true about the shingles, although I had forgotten it. When the house was built, our father, or his architect, had ordered it covered with lichened and weather-beaten

41

shingles. I didn't follow Lawrence's reasons for thinking that this was scandalous.

'And look at these doors,' Lawrence said. 'Look at these doors and window frames.' I followed him over to a big Dutch door that opens onto the terrace and looked at it. It was a relatively new door, but someone had worked hard to conceal its newness. The surface had been deeply scored with some metal implement, and white paint had been rubbed into the incisions to imitate brine, lichen, and weather rot. 'Imagine spending thousands of dollars to make a sound house look like a wreck,' Lawrence said. 'Imagine the frame of mind this implies. Imagine wanting to live so much in the past that you'll pay men carpenters' wages to disfigure your front door.' Then I remembered Lawrence's sensitivity to time and his sentiments and opinions about our feelings for the past. I had heard him say, years ago, that we and our friends and our part of the nation, finding ourselves unable to cope with the problems of the present, had, like a wretched adult, turned back to what we supposed was a happier and a simpler time, and that our taste for reconstruction and candlelight was a measure of this irremediable failure. The faint blue line of chalk had reminded him of these ideas, the scarified door had reinforced them, and now clue after clue presented itself to him – the stern light at the door, the bulk of the chimney, the width of the floorboards and the pieces set into them to resemble pegs. While Lawrence was lecturing me on these frailties, the others came up from the court. As soon as Mother saw Lawrence, she responded, and I saw that there was little hope of any rapport between the matriarch and the changeling. She took Chaddy's arm. 'Let's go swimming and have Martinis on the beach,' she said. 'Let's have a *fabulous* morning.'

The sea that morning was a solid color, like verd stone. Everyone went to the beach but Tifty and Ruth. 'I don't mind *him*,' Mother said. She was excited, and she tipped her glass and spilled some gin into the sand. 'I don't mind *him*. It doesn't matter to me how *rude* and *horrid* and *gloomy* he is, but what I can't bear are the faces of his wretched little children, those fabulously unhappy little children.' With the height of the cliff between us, everyone talked wrathfully about Lawrence; about how he had grown worse instead of better, how unlike the rest of us he was, how he endeavored to spoil every pleasure. We drank our gin; the abuse seemed to reach a crescendo, and then, one by one, we went swimming in the solid green water. But when we came out no one mentioned Lawrence unkindly; the line of abusive conversation had been cut, as if swimming had the cleansing force claimed for baptism. We dried our hands and lighted cigarettes, and if Lawrence was mentioned, it was only to suggest, kindly, something that might please him. Wouldn't he like to sail to Barin's cove, or go fishing?

And now I remember that while Lawrence was visiting us, we went swimming oftener than we usually do, and I think there was a reason for this. When the irritability that accumulated as a result of his company began to lessen our patience, not only with Lawrence but with one another, we would all go swimming and shed our animus in the cold water. I can see the family now, smarting from Lawrence's rebukes as they sat on the sand, and I can see them wading and diving and surface-diving and hear in their voices the restoration of patience and the rediscovery of inexhaustible good will. If Lawrence noticed this change – this illusion of purification – I suppose that he would have found in the vocabulary of psychiatry, or the mythology of the Atlantic, some circumspect name for it, but I don't think he noticed the change. He neglected to name the curative powers of the open sea, but it was one of the few chances for diminution that he missed.

The cook we had that year was a Polish woman named Anna Ostrovick, a summer cook. She was first-rate – a big, fat, hearty industrious woman who took her work seriously. She liked to cook and to have the food she cooked appreciated and eaten, and whenever we saw her, she always urged us to eat. She cooked hot bread – crescents and brioches – for breakfast two or three times a week, and she would bring these into the dining room herself and say, 'Eat, eat, eat!' When the maid took the serving dishes back into the pantry, we could sometimes hear Anna, who was standing there, say, 'Good! They eat.' She fed the garbage man, the milkman, and the gardener. 'Eat!' she told them. 'Eat, eat!' On Thursday afternoons, she went to the movies with the maid, but she didn't enjoy the movies, because the actors were all so thin. She would sit in the dark theatre for an hour and a half watching the screen anxiously for the appearance of someone who had enjoyed his food. Bette Davis merely left with Anna the impression of a woman who has not eaten well. 'They are all so skinny,' she would say when she left the movies. In the evenings, after she had gorged all of us, and washed the pots and pans, she would collect the table scraps and go out to feed the creation. We had a few chickens that year, and although they would have roosted by then, she would dump food into their troughs and urge the sleeping fowl to eat. She fed the songbirds in the orchard and the chipmunks in the yard. Her appearance at the edge of the garden and her urgent voice – we could hear her calling 'Eat, eat, eat' – had become, like the sunset gun at the boat club and the passage of light from Cape Heron, attached to that hour. 'Eat, eat, eat,' we could hear Anna say. 'Eat, eat ...' Then it would be dark.

When Lawrence had been there three days, Anna called me into the kitchen. 'You tell your mother,' she said, 'that *he* doesn't come into my kitchen. If *he* comes into my kitchen all the time, I go. *He* is always coming into my kitchen to tell me what a sad woman I am. He is always telling me that I work too hard and that I don't get paid enough and that I should belong to a union with vacations. Ha! He is so skinny but he is always coming into my kitchen when I am busy to pity me, but I am as good as him, I am as good as *anybody*, and I do not have to have people like that getting into my way all the time and feeling sorry for me. I am a famous and a wonderful cook and I have jobs everywhere and the only reason I come here to work this summer is because I was never before on an island, but I can have other jobs tomorrow, and if he is always coming into my kitchen to pity me, you tell your mother I am going. I am as good as *anybody* and I do not have to have that skinny all the time telling how poor I am.'

I was pleased to find that the cook was on our side, but I felt that the situation was delicate. If Mother asked Lawrence to stay out of the kitchen, he would make a grievance out of the request. He could make a grievance out of

45

anything, and it sometimes seemed that as he sat darkly at the dinner table, every word of disparagement, wherever it was aimed, came home to him. I didn't mention the cook's complaint to anyone, but somehow there wasn't any more trouble from that quarter.

The next cause for contention that I had from Lawrence came over our backgammon games.

When we are at Laud's Head, we play a lot of backgammon. At eight o'clock, after we have drunk our coffee, we usually get out the board. In a way, it is one of our pleasantest hours. The lamps in the room are still unlighted, Anna can be seen in the dark garden, and in the sky above her head there are continents of shadow and fire. Mother turns on the light and rattles the dice as a signal. We usually play three games apiece, each with the others. We play for money, and you can win or lose a hundred dollars on a game, but the stakes are usually much lower. I think that Lawrence used to play – I can't remember – but he doesn't play any more. He doesn't gamble. This is not because he is poor or because he has any principles about gambling but because he thinks the game is foolish and a waste of time. He was ready enough, however, to waste his time watching the rest of us play. Night after night, when the game began, he pulled a chair up beside the board, and watched the checkers and the dice. His expression was scornful, and yet he watched carefully. I wondered why he watched us night after night, and, through watching his face, I think that I may have found out.

Lawrence doesn't gamble, so he can't understand the excitement of winning and losing money. He has forgotten how to play the game, I think, so that its complex odds can't interest him. His observations were bound to include the facts that backgammon is an idle game and a game of chance, and that the board, marked with points, was a symbol of our worthlessness. And since he doesn't understand gambling or the odds of the game, I thought that what interested him must be the members of his family. One night when I was playing with Odette – I had won thirty-seven dollars from Mother and Chaddy – I think I saw what was going on in his mind.

Odette has black hair and black eyes. She is careful never to expose her white skin to the sun for long, so the striking contrast of blackness and pallor is not changed in the summer. She needs and deserves admiration – it is the element that contents her – and she will flirt, unseriously, with any man. Her shoulders were bare that night, her dress was cut to show the division of her breasts and to show her breasts when she leaned over the board to play. She kept losing and flirting and making her losses seem like a part of the flirtation. Chaddy was in the other room. She lost three games, and when the third game ended, she fell back on the sofa and, looking at me squarely, said something about going out on the dunes to settle the score. Lawrence heard her. I looked at Lawrence. He seemed shocked and gratified at the same time, as if he had suspected all along that we were not playing for anything so insubstantial as money. I may be wrong, of course, but I think that Lawrepce felt that in watching our backgammon he was observing the progress of a mordant tragedy in which the money we won and lost served as a symbol for more vital forfeits. It is like Lawrence to try to read significance and finality into every gesture that we make, and it is certain of Lawrence that when he finds the inner logic to our conduct, it will be sordid.

Chaddy came in to play with me. Chaddy and I have never liked to lose to each other. When we were younger, we used to be forbidden to play games together, because they always ended in a fight. We think we know each other's mettle intimately. I think he is prudent; he thinks I am foolish. There is always bad blood when we play anything – tennis or backgammon or softball or bridge – and it does seem at times as if we were playing for the possession of each other's liberties. When I lose to Chaddy, I can't sleep. All this is only half the truth of our competitive relationship, but it was the half-truth that would be discernible to Lawrence, and his presence at the table made me so self-conscious that I lost two games. I tried not to seem angry when I got up from the board. Lawrence was watching me. I went out onto the terrace to suffer there in the dark the anger I always feel when I lose to Chaddy.

When I came back into the room, Chaddy and Mother were playing. Lawrence was still watching. By his lights, Odette had lost her virtue to me, I had lost my self-esteem to Chaddy, and now I wondered what he saw in the present match. He watched raptly, as if the opaque checkers and the marked board served for an exchange of critical power. How dramatic the board, in its ring of light, and the quiet players and the crash of the sea outside must have seemed to him! Here was spiritual cannibalism made visible; here, under his nose, were the symbols of the rapacious use human beings make of one another.

Mother plays a shrewd, an ardent, and an interfering game. She always has her hands in her opponent's board. When she plays with Chaddy, who is her favorite, she plays intently. Lawrence would have noticed this. Mother is a sentimental woman. Her heart is good and easily moved by tears and frailty, a characteristic that, like her handsome nose, has not been changed at all by age. Grief in another provokes her deeply, and she seems at times to be trying to divine in Chaddy some grief, some loss, that she can succor and redress, and so re-establish the relationship that she enjoyed with him when he was sickly and young. She loves defending the weak and the child-like, and now that we are old, she misses it. The world of debts and business, men and war, hunting and fishing has on her an exacerbating effect. (When Father drowned, she threw away his fly rods and his guns.) She has lectured us all endlessly on self-reliance, but when we come back to her for comfort and for help – particularly Chaddy – she seems to feel most like herself. I suppose Lawrence thought that the old woman and her son were playing for each other's soul.

She lost. 'Oh *dear*,' she said. She looked stricken and bereaved, as she always does when she loses. 'Get me my glasses, get me my checkbook, get me something to drink.' Lawrence got up at last and stretched his legs. He looked at us all bleakly. The wind and the sea had risen, and I thought that if he heard the waves, he must hear them only as a dark answer to all his dark questions; that he would think that the tide had expunged the embers of our picnic fires. The company of a lie is unbearable, and he seemed like the embodiment of a lie. I couldn't explain to him the simple and intense pleasures of playing for money, and it seemed to me hideously wrong that he should have sat at the edge of the board and concluded that we were playing for one another's soul. He walked restlessly around the room two or three times and then, as usual, gave us a parting shot. 'I should think you'd go crazy,' he said, 'cooped up with one another like this, night after night. Come on, Ruth. I'm going to bed.'

That night, I dreamed about Lawrence. I saw his plain face magnified into ugliness, and when I woke in the morning, I felt sick, as if I had suffered a great spiritual loss while I slept, like the loss of courage and heart. It was foolish to let myself be troubled by my brother. I needed a vacation. I needed to relax. At school, we live in one of the dormitories, we eat at the house table, and we never get away. I not only teach English winter and summer but I work in the principal's office and fire the pistol at track meets. I needed to get away from this and from every other form of anxiety, and I decided to avoid my brother. Early that day, I took Helen and the children sailing, and we stayed out until suppertime. The next day, we went on a picnic. Then I had to go to New York for a day, and when I got back, there was the costume dance at the boat club. Lawrence wasn't going to this, and it's a party where I always have a wonderful time.

The invitations that year said to come as you wish you were. After several conversations, Helen and I had decided what to wear. The thing she most wanted to be again, she said, was a bride, and so she decided to wear her wedding dress. I thought this was a good choice – sincere, lighthearted, and inexpensive. Her choice influenced mine, and I decided to wear an old football uniform. Mother decided to go as Jenny Lind, because there was an old Jenny Lind costume in the attic. The others decided to rent costumes, and when I went to New York, I got the clothes. Lawrence and Ruth didn't enter into any of this.

Helen was on the dance committee, and she spent most of Friday decorating the club. Diana and Chaddy and I went sailing. Most of the sailing that I do these days is in Manhasset, and I am used to setting a homeward course by the gasoline barge and the tin roofs of the boat shed, and it was a pleasure that afternoon, as we returned, to keep the bow on a white church spire in the village and to find even the inshore water green and clear. At the end of our sail, we stopped at the club to get Helen. The committee had been trying to give a submarine appearance to the ballroom, and the fact that they had nearly succeeded in accomplishing this illusion made Helen very happy. We drove back to Laud's Head. It had been a brilliant afternoon, but on the way home we could smell the east wind – the dark wind, as Lawrence would have said – coming in from the sea.

My wife, Helen, is thirty-eight, and her hair would be gray, I guess, if it were not dyed, but it is dyed an unobtrusive yellow – a faded color – and I think it becomes her. I mixed cocktails that night while she was dressing, and when I took a glass upstairs to her, I saw her for the first time since our marriage in her wedding dress. There would be no point in saying that she looked to me more beautiful than she did on our wedding day, but because I have grown older and have, I think, a greater depth of feeling, and because I could see in her face that night both youth and age, both her devotion to the young woman that she had been and the positions that she had yielded graciously to time, I think I have never been so deeply moved. I had already put on the football uniform, and the weight of it, the heaviness of the pants and the shoulder guards, had worked a change in me, as if in putting on these old clothes I had put off the reasonable anxieties and troubles of my life. It felt as if we had both returned to the years before our marriage, the years before the war.

The Collards had a big dinner party before the dance, and our family – excepting Lawrence and Ruth – went to this. We drove over to the club, through the fog, at about half past nine. The orchestra was playing a waltz. While I was checking my raincoat, someone hit me on the back. It was Chucky Ewing, and the funny thing was that Chucky had on a football uniform. This seemed comical as hell to both of us. We were laughing when we went down the hall to the dance floor. I stopped at the door to look at the party, and it was beautiful. The committee had hung fish nets around the sides and over the high ceiling. The nets on the ceiling were filled with colored balloons. The light was soft and uneven, and the people – our friends and neighbors – dancing in the soft light to 'Three O'Clock in the Morning' made a pretty picture. Then I noticed the number of women dressed in white, and I realized that they, like Helen, were wearing wedding dresses. Patsy Hewitt and Mrs Gear and the Lackland girl waltzed by, dressed as brides. Then Pep Talcott came over to where Chucky and I were standing. He was dressed to be Henry VIII, but he told us that the Auerbach twins and Henry Barrett and Dwight MacGregor were all wearing football uniforms, and that by the last count there were ten brides on the floor.

This coincidence, this funny coincidence, kept everybody laughing, and made this one of the most lighthearted parties we've ever had at the club. At first I thought that the women had planned with one another to wear wedding dresses, but the ones that I danced with said it was a coincidence and I'm sure that Helen had made her decision alone. Everything went smoothly for me until a little before midnight. I saw Ruth standing at the edge of the floor. She was wearing a long red dress. It was all wrong. It wasn't the spirit of the party at all. I danced with her, but no one cut in, and I was darned if I'd spend the rest of the night dancing with her and I asked her where Lawrence was. She said he was out on the dock, and I took her over to the bar and left her and went out to get Lawrence.

The east fog was thick and wet, and he was alone on the dock. He was not in costume. He had not even bothered to get himself up as a fisherman or a sailor. He looked particularly saturnine. The fog blew around us like a cold smoke. I wished that it had been a clear night, because the easterly fog seemed to play into my misanthropic brother's hands. And I knew that the buoys – the groaners and bells that we could hear then – would sound to him like half-human, half-drowned cries, although every sailor knows that buoys are necessary and reliable fixtures, and I knew that the foghorn at the lighthouse would mean wanderings and losses to him and that he could misconstrue the vivacity of the dance music. 'Come on in, Tifty,' I said, 'and dance with your wife or get her some partners.'

'Why should I?' he said. 'Why should I?' And he walked to the window and looked in at the party. 'Look at it,' he said. 'Look at that ...'

Chucky Ewing had got hold of a balloon and was trying to organize a scrimmage line in the middle of the floor. The others were dancing a samba. And I knew that Lawrence was looking bleakly at the party as he had looked at the weather-beaten shingles on our house, as if he saw here an abuse and a distortion of time; as if in wanting to be brides and football players we exposed the fact that, the lights of youth having been put out in us, we had been unable to find other lights to go by and, destitute of faith and principle, had become foolish and sad. And that he was thinking this about so many kind and happy and generous people made me angry, made me feel for him such an unnatural abhorrence that I was ashamed, for he is my brother and a Pommeroy. I put my arm around his shoulders and tried to force him to come in, but he wouldn't.

I got back in time for the Grand March, and after the prizes had been given out for the best costumes, they let the balloons down. The room was hot, and someone opened the big doors onto the dock, and the easterly wind circled the room and went out, carrying across the dock and out onto the water most of the balloons. Chucky Ewing went running out after the balloons, and when he saw them pass the dock and settle on the water, he took off his football uniform and dove in. Then Eric Auerbach dove in and Lew Phillips dove in and I dove in, and you know how it is at a party after midnight when people start jumping into the water. We recovered most of the balloons and dried off and went on dancing, and we didn't get home until morning.

The next day was the day of the flower show. Mother and Helen and Odette all had entries. We had a pickup lunch, and Chaddy drove the women and children over to the show. I took a nap, and in the middle of the afternoon I got some trunks and a towel and, on leaving the house, passed Ruth in the laundry. She was washing clothes. I don't know why she should seem to have so much more work to do than anyone else, but she is always washing or ironing or mending clothes.

She may have been taught, when she was young, to spend her time like this, or she may be at the mercy of an expiatory passion. She seems to scrub and iron with a penitential fervor, although I can't imagine what it is that she thinks she's done wrong. Her children were with her in the laundry. I offered to take them to the beach, but they didn't want to go.

It was late in August, and the wild grapes that grow profusely all over the island made the land wind smell of wine. There is a little grove of holly at the end of the path, and then you climb the dunes, where nothing grows but that coarse grass. I could hear the sea, and I remember thinking how Chaddy and I used to talk mystically about the sea. When we were young, we had decided that we could never live in the West because we would miss the sea. 'It is very nice here,' we used to say politely when we visited people in the mountains, 'but we miss the Atlantic.' We used to look down our noses at people from Iowa and Colorado who had been denied this revelation, and we scorned the

Pacific. Now I could hear the waves, whose heaviness sounded like a reverberation, like a tumult, and it pleased me as it had pleased me when I was young, and it seemed to have a purgative force, as if it had cleared my memory of, among other things, the penitential image of Ruth in the laundry.

But Lawrence was on the beach. There he sat. I went in without speaking. The water was cold, and when I came out, I put on a shirt. I told him that I was going to walk up to Tanners Point, and he said that he would come with me. I tried to walk beside him. His legs are no longer than mine, but he always likes to stay a little ahead of his companion. Walking along behind him, looking at his bent head and his shoulders, I wondered what he could make of that landscape.

There were the dunes and cliffs, and then, where they declined, there were some fields that had begun to turn from green to brown and yellow. The fields were used for pasturing sheep, and I guess Lawrence would have noticed that the soil was eroded and that the sheep would accelerate this decay. Beyond the fields there are a few coastal farms, with square and pleasant buildings, but Lawrence could have pointed out the hard lot of an island farmer. The sea, at our other side, was the open sea. We always tell guests that there, to the east, lies the coast of Portugal, and for Lawrence it would be an easy step from the coast of Portugal to the tyranny in Spain. The waves broke with a noise like a 'hurrah, hurrah, hurrah,' but to Lawrence they would say 'Vale, vale.' I suppose it would have occurred to his baleful and incisive mind that the coast was terminal moraine, the edge of the prehistoric world, and it must have occurred to him that we walked along the edge of the known world in spirit as much as in fact. If he should otherwise have overlooked this, there were some Navy planes bombing an uninhabited island to remind him.

That beach is a vast and preternaturally clean and simple landscape. It is like a piece of the moon. The surf had pounded the floor solid, so it was easy walking, and everything left on the sand had been twice changed by the waves. There was the spine of a shell, a broomstick, part of a bottle and part of a brick, both of them milled and broken until they were nearly unrecognizable, and I suppose Lawrence's sad frame of mind – for he kept his head down – went from one broken thing to another. The company of his pessimism began to infuriate me, and I caught up with him and put a hand on his shoulder. 'It's only a summer day, Tifty,' I said. 'It's only a summer day. What's the matter? Don't you like it here?'

'I don't like it here,' he said blandly, without raising his eyes, 'I'm going to sell my equity in the house to Chaddy. I didn't expect to have a good time. The only reason I came back was to say goodbye.'

I let him get ahead again and I walked behind him, looking at his shoulders and thinking of all the goodbyes he had made. When Father drowned, he went to church and said goodbye to Father. It was only three years later that he concluded that Mother was frivolous and said goodbye to her. In his freshman year at college, he had been very good friends with his roommate, but the man drank too much, and at the beginning of the spring term Lawrence changed roommates and said goodbye to his friend. When he had been in college for two years, he concluded that the atmosphere was too sequestered and he said goodbye to Yale. He enrolled at Columbia and got his law degree there, but he found his first employer dishonest, and at the end of six months he said goodbye to a good job. He married Ruth in City Hall and said goodbye to the Protestant Episcopal Church; they went to live on a back street in Tuckahoe and said goodbye to the middle class. In 1938, he went to Washington to work as a government lawyer, saying goodbye to private enterprise, but after eight months in Washington he concluded that the Roosevelt administration was sentimental and he said goodbye to it. They left Washington for a suburb of Chicago, where he said goodbye to his neighbors, one by one, on counts of drunkenness, boorishness, and stupidity. He said goodbye to Chicago and went to Kansas; he said goodbye to Kansas and went to Cleveland. Now he had said goodbye to Cleveland and come East again, stopping at Laud's Head long enough to say goodbye to the sea.

It was elegiac and it was bigoted and narrow, it mistook circumspection for character, and I wanted to help him. 'Come out of it,' I said. 'Come out of it, Tifty.'

'Come out of what?'

'Come out of this gloominess. Come out of it. It's only a summer day. You're spoiling your own good time and you're spoiling everyone else's. We need a vacation, Tifty. I need one. I need to rest. We all do. And you've made everything tense and unpleasant. I only have two weeks in the year. Two weeks. I need to have a good time and so do all the others. We need to rest. You think that your pessimism is an advantage, but it's nothing but an unwillingness to grasp realities.'

'What are the realities?' he said. 'Diana is a foolish and a promiscuous woman. So is Odette. Mother is an alcoholic. If she doesn't discipline herself, she'll be in a hospital in a year or two. Chaddy is dishonest. He always has been. The house is going to fall into the sea.' He looked at me and added, as an afterthought, 'You're a fool.'

'You're a gloomy son of a bitch,' I said. 'You're a gloomy son of a bitch.'

'Get your fat face out of mine,' he said. He walked along.

Then I picked up a root and, coming at his back – although I have never hit a man from the back before – I swung the root, heavy with sea water, behind me, and the momentum sped my arm and I gave him, my brother, a blow on the head that forced him to his knees on the sand, and I saw the blood come out and begin to darken his hair. Then I wished that he was dead, dead and about to be buried, not buried but about to be buried, because I did not want to be denied ceremony and decorum in putting him away, in putting him out of my consciousness, and I saw the rest of us – Chaddy and Mother and Diana and Helen – in mourning in the house on Belvedere Street that was torn down twenty years ago, greeting our guests and our relatives at the door and answering their mannerly condolences with mannerly grief. Nothing decorous was lacking so that even if he had been murdered on a beach, one would feel before the tiresome ceremony ended that he had come into the winter of his life and that it was a law of nature, and a beautiful one, that Tifty should be buried in the cold, cold ground.

He was still on his knees. I looked up and down. No one had seen us. The naked beach, like a piece of the moon, reached to invisibility. The spill of a wave, in a glancing run, shot up to where he knelt. I would still have liked to end him, but now I had begun to act like two men, the murderer and the Samaritan. With a swift roar, like hollowness made sound, a white wave reached him and encircled him, boiling over his shoulders, and I held him against the undertow. Then I led him to a higher place. The blood had spread all through his hair, so that it looked black. I took off my shirt and tore it to bind up his head. He was conscious, and I didn't think he was badly hurt. He didn't speak. Neither did I. Then I left him there.

I walked a little way down the beach and turned to watch him, and I was thinking of my own skin then. He had got to his feet and he seemed steady. The daylight was still clear, but on the sea wind fumes of brine were blowing in like a light fog, and when I had walked a little way from him, I could hardly see his dark figure in this obscurity. All down the beach I could see the heavy salt air blowing in. Then I turned my back on him, and as I got near to the house, I went swimming again, as I seem to have done after every encounter with Lawrence that summer.

When I got back to the house, I lay down on the terrace. The others came back. I could hear Mother defaming the flower arrangements that had won prizes. None of ours had won anything. Then the house quieted, as it always does at that hour. The children went into the kitchen to get supper and the others went upstairs to bathe. Then I heard Chaddy making cocktails, and the conversation about the flower-show judges was resumed. Then Mother cried, 'Tifty! Tifty! Oh, Tifty!'

He stood in the door, looking half dead. He had taken off the bloody bandage and he held it in his hand. 'My brother did this,' he said. 'My brother did it. He hit me with a stone – something – on the beach.' His voice broke with self-pity. I thought he was going to cry. No one else spoke. 'Where's Ruth?' he cried. 'Where's Ruth? Where in hell is Ruth? I want her to start packing. I don't have any more time to waste here. I have important things to do. I have *important* things to do.' And he went up the stairs.

They left for the mainland the next morning, taking the six o'clock boat. Mother got up to say goodbye, but she was the only one, and it is a harsh and an easy scene to imagine – the matriarch and the changeling, looking at each other with a dismay that would seem like the powers of love reversed. I heard the children's voices and the car go down the drive, and I got up and went to the window, and what a morning that was! Jesus, what a morning! The wind was northerly. The air was clear. In the early heat, the roses in the garden smelled like strawberry jam. While I was dressing, I heard the boat whistle, first the warning signal and then the double blast, and I could see the good people on the top deck drinking coffee out of fragile paper cups, and Lawrence at the bow, saying to the sea, '*Thalassa, thalassa,*' while his timid and unhappy children watched the creation from the encirclement of their mother's arms. The buoys would toll mournfully for Lawrence, and while the grace of the light would make it an exertion not to throw out your arms and swear exultantly, Lawrence's eyes would trace the black sea as it fell astern; he would think of the bottom, dark and strange, where full fathom five our father lies.

Oh, what can you do with a man like that? What can you do? How can you dissuade his eye in a crowd from

61

seeking out the cheek with acne, the infirm hand; how can you teach him to respond to the inestimable greatness of the race, the harsh surface beauty of life; how can you put his finger for him on the obdurate truths before which fear and horror are powerless? The sea that morning was iridescent and dark. My wife and my sister were swimming – Diana and Helen – and I saw their uncovered heads, black and gold in the dark water. I saw them come out and I saw that they were naked, unshy, beautiful, and full of grace, and I watched the naked women walk out of the sea.

The Sorrows of Gin

IT WAS SUNDAY afternoon, and from her bedroom Amy could hear the Beardens coming in, followed a little while later by the Farquarsons and the Parminters. She went on reading *Black Beauty* until she felt in her bones that they might be eating something good. Then she closed her book and went down the stairs. The living-room door was shut, but through it she could hear the noise of loud talk and laughter. They must have been gossiping or worse, because they all stopped talking when she entered the room.

'Hi, Amy,' Mr Farquarson said.

'Mr Farquarson spoke to you, Amy,' her father said.

'Hello, Mr Farquarson,' she said. By standing outside the group for a minute, until they had resumed their conversation, and then by slipping past Mrs Farquarson, she was able to swoop down on the nut dish and take a handful.

'Amy!' Mr Lawton said.

'I'm sorry, Daddy,' she said, retreating out of the circle, toward the piano.

'Put those nuts back,' he said.

'I've handled them, Daddy,' she said.

'Well, pass the nuts, dear,' her mother said sweetly. 'Perhaps someone else would like nuts.'

Amy filled her mouth with the nuts she had taken, returned to the coffee table, and passed the nut dish.

'Thank you, Amy,' they said, taking a peanut or two.

'How do you like your new school, Amy?' Mrs Bearden asked.

'I like it,' Amy said. 'I like private schools better than public schools. It isn't so much like a factory.'

'What grade are you in?' Mr Bearden asked.

'Fourth,' she said.

Her father took Mr Parminter's glass and his own, and got up to go into the dining room and refill them. She fell into the chair he had left vacant.

'Don't sit in your father's chair, Amy,' her mother said, not realizing that Amy's legs were worn out from riding a bicycle, while her father had done nothing but sit down all day.

As she walked toward the French doors, she heard her mother beginning to talk about the new cook. It was a good example of the interesting things they found to talk about.

'You'd better put your bicycle in the garage,' her father said, returning with the fresh drinks. 'It looks like rain.'

Amy went out onto the terrace and looked at the sky, but it was not very cloudy, it wouldn't rain, and his advice, like all the advice he gave her, was superfluous. They were always at her. 'Put your bicycle away.' 'Open the door for Grandmother, Amy.' 'Feed the cat.' 'Do your homework.' 'Pass the nuts.' 'Help Mrs Bearden with her parcels.' 'Amy, please try and take more pains with your appearance.'

They all stood, and her father came to the door and called her. 'We're going over to the Parminters' for supper,' he said. 'Cook's here, so you won't be alone. Be sure and go to bed at eight like a good girl. And come and kiss me good night.' After their cars had driven off, Amy wandered through the kitchen to the cook's bedroom beyond it and knocked on the door. 'Come in,' a voice said, and when Amy entered, she found the cook, whose name was Rosemary, in her bathrobe, reading the Bible. Rosemary smiled at Amy. Her smile was sweet and her old eyes were blue. 'Your parents have gone out again?' she asked. Amy said that they had, and the old woman invited her to sit down. 'They do seem to enjoy themselves, don't they? During the four days I've been here, they've been out every night, or had people in.' She put the Bible face down on her lap and smiled, but not at Amy. 'Of course, the drinking that goes on here is all sociable, and what your parents do is none of my business, is it? I worry about drink more than most people, because of my poor sister. My poor sister drank too much. For ten years, I went to visit her on Sunday afternoons, and most of the time she was *non compos mentis*. Sometimes I'd find her huddled up on the floor with one or two sherry bottles empty beside her. Sometimes she'd seem sober enough to a stranger, but I could tell in a second by the way she spoke her words that she'd drunk enough not to be herself any more. Now my poor sister is gone, I don't have anyone to visit at all.'

'What happened to your sister?' Amy asked.

'She was a lovely person, with a peaches-and-cream complexion and fair hair,' Rosemary said. 'Gin makes some people gay – it makes them laugh and cry – but with my sister it only made her sullen and withdrawn. When she was drinking, she would retreat into herself. Drink made her contrary. If I'd say the weather was fine, she'd tell me I was wrong. If I'd say it was raining, she'd say it was clearing. She'd correct me about everything I said, however small it was. She died in Bellevue Hospital one summer while I was working in Maine. She was the only family I had.'

The directness with which Rosemary spoke had the effect on Amy of making her feel grown, and for once politeness came to her easily. 'You must miss your sister a great deal,' she said.

'I was just sitting here now thinking about her. She was in service, like me, and it's lonely work. You're always surrounded by a family, and yet you're never a part of it. Your pride is often hurt. The Madams seem condescending and inconsiderate. I'm not blaming the ladies I've worked for. It's just the nature of the relationship. They order chicken salad, and you get up before dawn to get ahead of yourself, and just as you've finished the chicken salad, they change their minds and want crab-meat soup.'

'My mother changes her mind all the time,' Amy said.

'Sometimes you're in a country place with nobody else in help. You're tired, but not too tired to feel lonely. You go out onto the servants' porch when the pots and pans are done, planning to enjoy God's creation, and although the front of the house may have a fine view of the lake or the mountains, the view from the back is never much. But there is the sky and the trees and the stars and the birds singing and the pleasure of resting your feet. But then you hear them in the front of the house, laughing and talking with their guests and their sons and daughters. If you're new and they whisper, you can be sure they're talking about you. That takes all the pleasure out of the evening.'

'Oh,' Amy said.

'I've worked all kinds of places – places where there were eight or nine in help and places where I was expected to burn the rubbish myself, on winter nights, and shovel the snow. In a house where there's a lot of help, there's usually some devil among them – some old butler or parlormaid – who tries to make your life miserable from the beginning. "The Madam doesn't like it this way," and "The Madam doesn't like it that way," and "I've been with the Madam for twenty years," they tell you. It takes a diplomat to get along. Then there is the rooms they give you, and every one of them I've ever seen is cheerless. If you have a bottle in your suitcase, it's a terrible temptation in the beginning not to take a drink to raise your spirits. But I have a strong character. It was different with my poor sister. She used to complain about nervousness, but, sitting here thinking about her tonight, I wonder if she suffered from nervousness at all. I wonder if she didn't make it all up. I wonder if she just wasn't meant to be in service. Toward the end, the only work she could get was out in the country, where nobody else would go, and she never lasted much more than a week or two. She'd take a little gin for her nervousness, then a little for her tiredness, and when she'd drunk her own bottle and everything she could steal, they'd hear about it in the front part of the house. There was usually a scene, and my poor sister always liked to have the last word. Oh, if I had had my way, they'd be a law against it! It's not my business to advise you to take anything from your father, but I'd be proud of you if you'd empty his gin bottle into the sink now and then – the filthy stuff! But it's made me feel better to talk with you, sweetheart. It's made me not miss my poor sister so much. Now I'll read a little more in my Bible, and then I'll get you some supper.'

The Lawtons had had a bad year with cooks – there had been five of them. The arrival of Rosemary had made Marcia Lawton think back to a vague theory of dispensations; she had suffered, and now she was being rewarded. Rosemary was clean, industrious, and cheerful, and her table – as the Lawtons said – was just like the Chambord. On Wednesday night after dinner, she took the train to New York, promising to return on the evening train Thursday. Thursday morning, Marcia went into the cook's room. It was a distasteful but a habitual precaution. The absence of anything personal in the room – a package of cigarettes, a fountain pen, an alarm clock, a radio, or anything else that could tie the old woman to the place – gave her the uneasy feeling that she was being deceived, as she had so often been deceived by cooks in the past. She opened the closet door and saw a single uniform hanging there and, on the closet floor, Rosemary's old suitcase and the white shoes she wore in the kitchen. The suitcase was locked, but when Marcia lifted it, it seemed to be nearly empty.

Mr Lawton and Amy drove to the station after dinner on Thursday to meet the eight-sixteen train. The top of the car was down, and the brisk air, the starlight, and the company of her father made the little girl feel kindly toward the world. The railroad station in Shady Hill resembled the railroad stations in old movies she had seen on television, where detectives and spies, bluebeards and their trusting victims, were met to be driven off to remote country estates. Amy liked the station, particularly toward dark. She imagined that the people who traveled on the locals were engaged on errands that were more urgent and sinister than commuting. Except when there was a heavy fog or a snowstorm, the club car that her father traveled on seemed to have the gloss and the monotony of the rest of his life. The locals that ran at odd hours belonged to a world of deeper contrasts, where she would like to live.

They were a few minutes early, and Amy got out of the car and stood on the platform. She wondered what the fringe of string that hung above the tracks at either end of the station was for, but she knew enough not to ask her father, because he wouldn't be able to tell her. She could hear the train before it came into view, and the noise excited her and made her happy. When the train drew in to the station and stopped, she looked in the lighted windows for Rosemary and didn't see her. Mr Lawton got out of the car and joined Amy on the platform. They could see the conductor bending over someone in a seat, and finally the cook arose. She clung to the conductor as he led her out to the platform of the car, and she was crying. 'Like peaches and cream,' Amy heard her sob. 'A lovely, lovely person.' The conductor spoke to her kindly, put his arm around her shoulders, and eased her down the steps. Then the train pulled out, and she stood there drying her tears. 'Don't say a word, Mr Lawton,' she said, 'and I won't say anything.' She held out a small paper bag. 'Here's a present for you, little girl.'

'Thank you, Rosemary,' Amy said. She looked into the paper bag and saw that it contained several packets of Japanese water flowers.

Rosemary walked toward the car with the caution of someone who can hardly find her way in the dim light.

A sour smell came from her. Her best coat was spotted with mud and ripped in the back. Mr Lawton told Amy to get in the back seat of the car, and made the cook sit in front, beside him. He slammed the car door shut after her angrily, and then went around to the driver's seat and drove home. Rosemary reached into her hand-bag and took out a Coca-Cola bottle with a cork stopper and took a drink. Amy could tell by the smell that the Coca-Cola bottle was filled with gin. 'Rosemary!' Mr Lawton said.

'I'm lonely,' the cook said. 'I'm lonely, and I'm afraid, and it's all I've got.'

He said nothing more until he had turned into their drive and brought the car around to the back door. 'Go and get your suitcase, Rosemary,' he said. 'I'll wait here in the car.'

As soon as the cook had staggered into the house, he told Amy to go in by the front door. 'Go upstairs to your room and get ready for bed.'

Her mother called down the stairs when Amy came in, to ask if Rosemary had returned. Amy didn't answer. She went to the bar, took an open gin bottle, and emptied it into the pantry sink. She was nearly crying when she encountered her mother in the living room, and told her that her father was taking the cook back to the station.

When Amy came home from school the next day, she found a heavy, black-haired woman cleaning the living room. The car Mr Lawton usually drove to the station was at the garage for a checkup, and Amy drove to the station with her mother to meet him. As he came across the station platform, she could tell by the lack of color in his face that he had had a hard day. He kissed her mother, touched Amy on the head, and got behind the wheel.

'You know,' her mother said, 'there's something terribly wrong with the guest-room shower.'

'Damn it, Marcia,' he said, 'I wish you wouldn't always greet me with bad news!'

His grating voice oppressed Amy, and she began to fiddle with the button that raised and lowered the window.

'Stop that, Amy!' he said.

'Oh, well, the shower isn't important,' her mother said. She laughed weakly.

'When I got back from San Francisco last week,' he said, 'you couldn't wait to tell me that we need a new oil burner.'

'Well, I've got a part-time cook. That's good news.'

'Is she a lush?' her father asked.

'Don't be disagreeable, dear. She'll get us some dinner and wash the dishes and take the bus home. We're going to the Farquarsons'.'

'I'm really too tired to go anywhere,' he said.

'Who's going to take care of me?' Amy asked.

'You always have a good time at the Farquarsons',' her mother said.

'Well, let's leave early,' he said.

'Who's going to take care of me?' Amy asked.

'Mrs Henlein,' her mother said.

When they got home, Amy went over to the piano.

Her father washed his hands in the bathroom off the hall and then went to the bar. He came into the living room holding the empty gin bottle. 'What's her name?' he asked.

'Ruby,' her mother said.

71

'She's exceptional. She's drunk a quart of gin on her first day.'

'Oh dear!' her mother said. 'Well, let's not make any trouble now.'

'Everybody is drinking my liquor,' her father shouted, 'and I am God-damned sick and tired of it!'

'There's plenty of gin in the closet,' her mother said. 'Open another bottle.'

'We paid that gardener three dollars an hour and all he did was sneak in here and drink up my Scotch. The sitter we had before we got Mrs Henlein used to water my bourbon, and I don't have to remind you about Rosemary. The cook before Rosemary not only drank everything in my liquor cabinet but she drank all the rum, kirsch, sherry, and wine that we had in the kitchen for cooking. Then, there's that Polish woman we had last summer. Even that old laundress. *And* the painters. I think they must have put some kind of a mark on my door. I think the agency must have checked me off as an easy touch.'

'Well, let's get through dinner, and then you can speak to her.'

'The hell with that!' he said 'I'm not going to encourage people to rob me. *Ruby!*' He shouted her name several times, but she didn't answer. Then she appeared in the dining-room doorway anyway, wearing her hat and coat.

'I'm sick,' she said. Amy could see that she was frightened.

I should think that you would be,' her father said.

'I'm sick,' the cook mumbled, 'and I can't find anything around here, and I'm going home.'

'Good,' he said. 'Good! I'm through with paying people to come in here and drink my liquor.'

The cook started out the front way, and Marcia Lawton followed her into the front hall to pay her something. Amy had watched this scene from the piano bench, a position that was withdrawn but that still gave her a good view. She saw her father get a fresh bottle of gin and make a shaker of Martinis. He looked very unhappy.

'Well,' her mother said when she came back into the room. 'You know, she didn't look drunk.'

'Please don't argue with me, Marcia,' her father said. He poured two cocktails, said 'Cheers,' and drank a little. 'We can get some dinner at Orpheo's,' he said.

'I suppose so,' her mother said. 'I'll rustle up something for Amy.' She went into the kitchen, and Amy opened her music to 'Reflets d'Automne.' 'COUNT,' her music teacher had written. 'COUNT and lightly, lightly ...' Amy began to play. Whenever she made a mistake, she said 'Darn it!' and started at the beginning again. In the middle of 'Reflets d'Automne' it struck her that *she* was the one who had emptied the gin bottle. Her perplexity was so intense that she stopped playing, but her feelings did not go beyond perplexity, although she did not have the strength to continue playing the piano. Her mother relieved her. 'Your supper's in the kitchen, dear,' she said. 'And you can take a popsicle out of the deep freeze for dessert. Just one.'

Marcia Lawton held her empty glass toward her husband, who filled it from the shaker. Then she went upstairs. Mr Lawton remained in the room, and, studying her father closely, Amy saw that his tense look had begun to soften. He did not seem so unhappy any more, and as she passed him on her way to the kitchen, he smiled at her tenderly and patted her on the top of the head.

When Amy had finished her supper, eaten her popsicle, and exploded the bag it came in, she returned to the piano and played 'Chopsticks' for a while. Her father came downstairs in his evening clothes, put his drink on the mantelpiece, and went to the French doors to look at his terrace and his garden. Amy noticed that the transformation that had begun with a softening of his features was even more advanced. At last, he seemed happy. Amy wondered if he was drunk, although his walk was not unsteady. If anything, it was more steady.

Her parents never achieved the kind of rolling, swinging gait that she saw impersonated by a tightrope walker in the circus each year while the band struck up 'Show Me the Way to Go Home' and that she liked to imitate herself sometimes. She liked to turn round and round and round on the lawn, until, staggering and a little sick, she would whoop, 'I'm drunk! I'm a drunken man!' and reel over the grass, righting herself as she was about to fall and finding herself not unhappy at having lost for a second her ability to see the world. But she had never seen her parents like that. She had never seen them hanging on to a lamppost and singing and reeling, but she had seen them fall down. They were never indecorous – they seemed to get more decorous and formal the more they drank – but sometimes her father would get up to fill everybody's glass and he would walk straight enough but his shoes would seem to stick to the carpet. And sometimes, when he got to the dining-room door, he would miss it by a foot or more. Once, she had seen him walk into the wall with such force that he collapsed onto the floor and broke most of the glasses he was carrying. One or two people laughed, but the laughter was not general or hearty, and most of them pretended that he had not fallen down at all. When her father got to his feet, he went right on to the bar as if nothing had happened. Amy had once seen Mrs Farquarson miss the chair she was about to sit in, by a foot, and thump down onto the floor, but nobody laughed then, and they pretended that Mrs Farquarson hadn't fallen down at all. They seemed like actors in a play. In the school play, when you knocked over a paper tree you were supposed to pick it up without showing what you were doing, so that you would not spoil the illusion of being in a deep forest, and that was the way *they* were when somebody fell down.

Now her father had that stiff, funny walk that was so different from the way he tramped up and down the station platform in the morning, and she could see that he was looking for something. He was looking for his drink. It was right on the mantelpiece, but he didn't look there. He looked on all the tables in the living room. Then he went out onto the terrace and looked there, and then he came back into the living room and looked on all the tables again. Then he went back onto the terrace, and then back over the living-room tables, looking three times in the same place, although he was always telling her to look intelligently when she lost her sneakers or her raincoat. 'Look for it, Amy,' he was always saying. 'Try and remember where you left it. I can't buy you a new raincoat every time it rains.' Finally he gave up and poured himself a cocktail in another glass. 'I'm going to get Mrs Henlein,' he told Amy, as if this were an important piece of information.

Amy's only feeling for Mrs Henlein was indifference, and when her father returned with the sitter, Amy thought of the nights, stretching into weeks – the years, almost – when she had been cooped up with Mrs Henlein. Mrs Henlein was very polite and was always telling Amy what was lady-like and what was not. Mrs Henelin also wanted to know where Amy's parents were going and what kind of a party it was, although it was none of her business. She always sat down on the sofa as if she owned the place, and talked about people she had never even been introduced to, and asked Amy to bring her the newspaper, although she had no authority at all.

When Marcia Lawton came down, Mrs Henlein wished her good evening. 'Have a lovely party,' she called after the Lawtons as they went out the door. Then she turned to Amy. 'Where are your parents going, sweetheart?

'But you must know, sweetheart. Put on your thinking cap and try and remember. Are they going to the club?'

'No,' Amy said.

'I wonder if they could be going to the Trenchers',' Mrs Henlein said. 'The Trenchers' house was lighted up when we came by.'

'They're not going to the Trenchers',' Amy said. 'They hate the Trenchers.'

'Well, where are they going, sweetheart?' Mrs Henlein asked.

'They're going to the Farquarsons',' Amy said.

'Well, that's all I wanted to know, sweetheart,' Mrs Henlein said. 'Now get me the newspaper and hand it to me politely. *Politely*,' she said, as Amy approached her with the paper. 'It doesn't mean anything when you do things for your elders unless you do them politely.' She put on her glasses and began to read the paper.

Amy went upstairs to her room. In a glass on her table were the Japanese flowers that Rosemary had brought her, blooming stalely in water that was colored pink from the dyes. Amy went down the back stairs and through the kitchen into the dining room. Her father's cocktail things were spread over the bar. She emptied the gin bottle into the pantry sink and then put it back where she had found it. It was too late to ride her bicycle and too early to go to bed, and she knew that if she got anything interesting on the television, like a murder, Mrs Henlein would make her turn it off. Then she remembered that her father had brought her home from his trip West a book about horses, and she ran cheerfully up the back stairs to read her new book.

It was after two when the Lawtons returned. Mrs Henlein, asleep on the living-room sofa dreaming about a dusty attic, was awakened by their voices in the hall. Marcia Lawton paid her, and thanked her, and asked if anyone had called, and then went upstairs. Mr Lawton was in the dining room, rattling the bottles around. Mrs Henlein, anxious to get into her own bed and back to sleep, prayed that he wasn't going to pour himself another drink, as they so often did. She was driven home night after night by drunken gentlemen. He stood in the door of the dining room, holding an empty bottle in his hand. 'You must be stinking, Mrs Henlein,' he said.

'Hmm,' she said. She didn't understand.

'You drank a full quart of gin,' he said.

The lackluster old woman – half between wakefulness and sleep – gathered together her bones and groped for her gray hair. It was in her nature to collect stray cats, pile the bathroom up to the ceiling with interesting and valuable newspapers, rouge, talk to herself, sleep in her underwear in case of fire, quarrel over the price of soup bones, and have it circulated around the neighborhood that when she finally died in her dusty junk heap, the mattress would be full of bankbooks and the pillow stuffed with hundred-dollar bills. She had resisted all these rich temptations in order to appear a lady, and she was repaid by being called a common thief. She began to scream at him.

'You take that back, Mr Lawton! You take back every one of those words you just said! I never stole anything in my whole life, and nobody in my family ever stole anything, and I don't have to stand here and be insulted by a drunk man. Why, as for drinking, I haven't drunk enough to fill an eyeglass for twenty-five years. Mr Henlein took me to a place of refreshment twenty-five years ago, and I drank two Manhattan cocktails that made me so sick and dizzy that I've never liked the stuff ever since. How dare you speak to me like this! Calling me a thief and a drunken woman! Oh, you disgust me – you disgust me in your ignorance of all the trouble I've had. Do you know what I had for Christmas dinner last year? I had a bacon sandwich. Son of a bitch!' She began to weep. 'I'm glad I said it!' she screamed. 'It's the first time I've used a dirty word in my whole life and I'm glad I said it. Son of a bitch!' A sense of liberation, as if she stood at the bow of a great ship, came over her. 'I lived in this neighborhood my whole life. I can remember when it was full of good farming people and there was fish in the rivers. My father had four acres of sweet meadowland and a name that was known far and wide, and on my mother's side I'm descended from patroons, Dutch nobility. My mother was the spit and image of Queen Wilhelmina. You think you can get away with insulting me, but you're very, very, very much mistaken.' She went to the telephone and, picking up the receiver, screamed, 'Police! Police! Police! This is Mrs Henlein, and I'm over at the Lawtons'. He's drunk, and he's calling me insulting names, and I want you to come over here and arrest him!'

The voices woke Amy, and, lying in her bed, she perceived vaguely the pitiful corruption of the adult world; how crude and frail it was, like a piece of worn burlap, patched with stupidities and mistakes, useless and ugly, and yet they never saw its worthlessness, and when you pointed it out to them, they were indignant. But as the voices went on and she heard the cry 'Police! Police!' she was frightened. She did not see how they could arrest her, although they could find her fingerprints on the empty bottle, but it was not her own danger that frightened her but the collapse, in the middle of the night, of her father's house. It was all her fault, and when she heard her father speaking into the extension telephone in the library, she felt sunk in guilt. Her father tried to be good and kind – and, remembering the expensive illustrated book about horses that he had brought her from the West, she had to set her teeth to keep from crying. She covered her head with a pillow and realized miserably that she would have to go away. She had plenty of friends from the time when they used to live in New York, or she could spend the night in the Park or hide in a museum. She would have to go away.

★

'Good morning,' her father said at breakfast. 'Ready for a good day!' Cheered by the swelling light in the sky, by the recollection of the manner in which he had handled Mrs Henlein and kept the police from coming, refreshed by his sleep, and pleased at the thought of playing golf, Mr Lawton spoke, with feeling, but the words seemed to Amy offensive and fatuous; they took away her appetite, and she slumped over her cereal bowl, stirring it with a spoon. 'Don't slump, Amy,' he said. Then she remembered the night, the screaming, the resolve to go. His cheerfulness refreshed her memory. Her decision was settled. She had a ballet lesson at ten, and she was going to have lunch with Lillian Towele. Then she would leave.

Children prepare for a sea voyage with a toothbrush and a Teddy bear; they equip themselves for a trip around the world with a pair of odd socks, a conch shell, and a thermometer; books and stones and peacock feathers, candy bars, tennis balls, soiled handkerchiefs, and skeins of old string appear to them to be the necessities of travel, and Amy packed, that afternoon, with the impulsiveness of her kind. She was late coming home from lunch, and her getaway was delayed, but she didn't mind. She could catch one of the late-afternoon locals; one of the cooks' trains. Her father was playing golf and her mother was off somewhere. A part-time worker was cleaning the living room. When Amy had finished packing, she went into her parents' bedroom and flushed the toilet. While the water murmured, she took a twenty-dollar bill from her mother's desk. Then she went downstairs and left the house and walked around Blenhollow Circle and down Alewives Lane to the station. No regrets or goodbyes formed in her mind. She went over the names of the friends she had in the city, in case she decided not to spend the night in a museum. When she opened the door of the waiting room, Mr Flanagan, the stationmaster, was poking his coal fire.

'I want to buy a ticket to New York,' Amy said.

'One-way or round-trip?'

'One-way, please.'

Mr Flanagan went through the door into the ticket office and raised the glass window. 'I'm afraid I haven't got a half-fare ticket for you, Amy,' he said. 'I'll have to write one.'

'That's all right,' she said. She put the twenty-dollar bill on the counter.

'And in order to change that,' he said, 'I'll have to go over to the other side. Here's the four-thirty-two coming in now, but you'll be able to get the five-ten.' She didn't protest, and went and sat beside her cardboard suitcase, which was printed with European hotel and place names. When the local had come and gone, Mr Flanagan shut his glass window and walked over the footbridge to the northbound platform and called the Lawtons'. Mr Lawton had just come in from his game and was mixing himself a cocktail. 'I think your daughter's planning to take some kind of a trip,' Mr Flanagan said.

It was dark by the time Mr Lawton got down to the station. He saw his daughter through the station window. The girl sitting on the bench, the rich names on her paper suitcase, touched him as it was in her power to touch him only when she seemed helpless or when she was very sick. Someone had walked over his grave! He shivered with longing, he felt his skin coarsen as when, driving home late and alone, a shower of leaves on the wind crossed the beam of his headlights, liberating him for a second at the most from the literal symbols of his life – the buttonless shirts, the vouchers and bank statements, the order blanks, and the empty glasses. He seemed to listen – God knows for what. Commands, drums, the crackle of signal fires, the music of the glockenspiel – how sweet it sounds on the Alpine air – singing from a tavern in the pass, the honking of wild swans; he seemed to smell the salt air in the churches of Venice. Then, as it was with the leaves, the power of the figure to trouble him was ended; his gooseflesh vanished. He was himself. Oh, why should she want to run away? Travel – and who knew better than a man who spent three days of every fortnight on the road – was a world of overheated plane cabins and repetitious magazines, where even the coffee, even the champagne, tasted of plastics. How could he teach her that home sweet home was the best place of all?

O Youth and Beauty!

AT THE TAG end of nearly every long, large Saturday-night party in the suburb of Shady Hill, when almost everybody who was going to play golf or tennis in the morning had gone home hours ago and the ten or twelve people remaining seemed powerless to bring the evening to an end although the gin and whiskey were running low, and here and there a woman who was sitting out her husband would have begun to drink milk; when everybody had lost track of time, and the baby-sitters who were waiting at home for these diehards would have long since stretched out on the sofa and fallen into a deep sleep, to dream about cooking-contest prizes, ocean voyages, and romance; when the bellicose drunk, the crapshooter, the pianist, and the woman faced with the expiration of her hopes had all expressed themselves; when every proposal – to go to the Farquarsons' for breakfast, to go swimming, to go and wake up the Townsends, to go here and go there – died as soon as it was made, then Trace Bearden would begin to chide Cash Bentley about his age and thinning hair. The chiding was preliminary to moving the living-room furniture. Trace and Cash moved the tables and the chairs, the sofas and the fire screen, the woodbox and the footstool; and when they had finished, you wouldn't know the place. Then if the host had a revolver, he would be asked to produce it. Cash would take off his shoes and assume a starting crouch behind a sofa. Trace would fire the weapon out of an open window, and if you were new to the community and had not understood what the preparations were about, you would then realize that you were watching a hurdle race. Over the sofa went Cash, over the tables, over the fire screen and the woodbox. It was not exactly a race, since Cash ran it alone, but it was extraordinary to see this man of forty surmount so many obstacles so gracefully. There was not a piece of furniture in Shady Hill that Cash could not take in his stride. The race ended with cheers, and presently the party would break up.

Cash was, of course, an old track star, but he was never aggressive or tiresome about his brilliant past. The college where he had spent his youth had offered him a paying job on the alumni council, but he had refused it, realizing that that part of his life was ended. Cash and his wife, Louise, had two children, and they lived in a medium-cost ranch house on Alewives Lane. They belonged to the country club, although they could not afford it, but in the case of the Bentleys nobody ever pointed this out, and Cash was one of the best-liked men in Shady Hill. He was still slender – he was careful about his weight – and he walked to the train in the morning with a light and vigorous step that marked him as an athlete. His hair was thin, and there were mornings when his eyes looked bloodshot, but this did not detract much from a charming quality of stubborn youthfulness.

In business Cash had suffered reverses and disappointments, and the Bentleys had many money worries. They were always late with their tax payments and their mortgage

84

payments, and the drawer of the hall table was stuffed with unpaid bills; it was always touch and go with the Bentleys and the bank. Louise looked pretty enough on Saturday night, but her life was exacting and monotonous. In the pockets of her suits, coats, and dresses there were little wads and scraps of paper on which was written: 'Oleomargarine, frozen spinach, Kleenex, dog biscuit, hamburger, pepper, lard ...' When she was still half awake in the morning, she was putting on the water for coffee and diluting the frozen orange juice. Then she would be wanted by the children. She would crawl under the bureau on her hands and knees to find a sock for Toby. She would lie flat on her belly and wiggle under the bed (getting dust up her nose) to find a shoe for Rachel. Then there were the housework, the laundry, and the cooking, as well as the demands of the children. There always seemed to be shoes to put on and shoes to take off, snowsuits to be zipped and unzipped, bottoms to be wiped, tears to be dried, and when the sun went down (she saw it set from the kitchen window) there was the supper to be cooked, the baths, the bedtime story, and the Lord's Prayer. With the sonorous words of the Our Father in a darkened room the children's day was over, but the day was far from over for Louise Bentley. There were the darning, the mending, and some ironing to do, and after sixteen years of housework she did not seem able to escape her chores even while she slept. Snowsuits, shoes, baths, and groceries seemed to have permeated her subconscious. Now and then she would speak in her sleep – so loudly that she woke her husband. 'I can't *afford* veal cutlets,' she said one night. Then she sighed uneasily and was quiet again.

By the standards of Shady Hill, the Bentleys were a happily married couple, but they had their ups and downs.
Cash could be very touchy at times. When he came home
after a bad day at the office and found that Louise, for some
good reason, had not started supper, he would be ugly. 'Oh,
for Christ sake!' he would say, and go into the kitchen and
heat up some frozen food. He drank some whiskey to relax
himself during this ordeal, but it never seemed to relax him,
and he usually burned the bottom out of a pan, and when
they sat down for supper the dining space would be full of
smoke. It was only a question of time before they were
plunged into a bitter quarrel. Louise would run upstairs,
throw herself onto the bed and sob. Cash would grab the
whiskey bottle and dose himself. These rows, in spite of the
vigor with which Cash and Louise entered into them, were
the source of a great deal of pain for both of them. Cash
would sleep downstairs on the sofa, but sleep never repaired
the damage, once the trouble had begun, and if they met in
the morning, they would be at one another's throats in a
second. Then Cash would leave for the train, and, as soon as
the children had been taken to nursery school, Louise
would put on her coat and cross the grass to the Beardens'
house. She would cry into a cup of warmed-up coffee and
tell Lucy Bearden her troubles. What was the meaning of
marriage? What was the meaning of love? Lucy always suggested that Louise get a job. It would give her emotional
and financial independence, and that, Lucy said, was what
she needed.

The next night, things would get worse. Cash would not
come home for dinner at all, but would stumble in at about
eleven, and the whole sordid wrangle would be repeated,

with Louise going to bed in tears upstairs and Cash again stretching out on the living-room sofa. After a few days and nights of this, Louise would decide that she was at the end of her rope. She would decide to go and stay with her married sister in Mamaroneck. She usually chose a Saturday, when Cash would be at home, for her departure. She would pack a suitcase and get her War Bonds from the desk. Then she would take a bath and put on her best slip. Cash, passing the bedroom door, would see her. Her slip was transparent, and suddenly he was all repentance, tenderness, charm, wisdom, and love. 'Oh, my darling!' he would groan, and when they went downstairs to get a bite to eat about an hour later, they would be sighing and making cow eyes at one another; they would be the happiest married couple in the whole eastern United States. It was usually at about this time that Lucy Bearden turned up with the good news that she had found a job for Louise. Lucy would ring the doorbell, and Cash, wearing a bathrobe, would let her in. She would be brief with Cash, naturally, and hurry into the dining room to tell poor Louise the good news. 'Well, that's very nice of you to have looked,' Louise would say wanly, 'but I don't think that I want a job any more. I don't think that Cash wants me to work, do you, sweetheart?' Then she would turn her big dark eyes on Cash, and you could practically smell smoke. Lucy would excuse herself hurriedly from this scene of depravity, but never left with any hard feelings, because she had been married for nineteen years herself and she knew that every union has its ups and downs. She didn't seem to leave any wiser, either; the next time the Bentleys quarreled she would be just as intent as ever on getting Louise a job. But these quarrels and reunions, like the hurdle race, didn't seem to lose their interest through repetition.

On a Saturday night in the spring, the Farquarsons gave the Bentleys an anniversary party. It was their seventeenth anniversary. Saturday afternoon, Louise Bentley put herself through preparations nearly as arduous as the Monday wash. She rested for an hour, by the clock, with her feet high in the air, her chin in a sling, and her eyes bathed in some astringent solution. The clay packs, the too tight girdle, and the plucking and curling and painting that went on were all aimed at rejuvenation. Feeling in the end that she had not been entirely successful, she tied a piece of veiling over her eyes – but she was a lovely woman, and all the cosmetics that she had struggled with seemed, like her veil, to be drawn transparently over a face where mature beauty and a capacity for wit and passion were undisguisable. The Farquarsons' party was nifty, and the Bentleys had a wonderful time. The only person who drank too much was Trace Bearden. Late in the party, he began to chide Cash about his thinning hair and Cash good-naturedly began to move the furniture around. Harry Farquarson had a pistol, and Trace went out onto the terrace to fire it up at the sky. Over the sofa went Cash, over the end table, over the arms of the wing chair and the fire screen. It was a piece of carving on a chest that brought him down, and down he came like a ton of bricks.

Louise screamed and ran to where he lay. He had cut a gash in his forehead, and someone made a bandage to stop the flow of blood. When he tried to get up, he stumbled and fell again, and his face turned a terrible green. Harry telephoned Dr Parminter, Dr Hopewell, Dr Altman, and Dr Barnstable, but it was two in the morning and none of them answered. Finally, a Dr Yerkes – a total stranger – agreed to come. Yerkes was a young man – he did not seem old enough to be a doctor – and he looked around at the disordered room and the anxious company as if there was something weird about the scene. He got off on the wrong foot with Cash. 'What seems to be the matter, old-timer?' he asked.

Cash's leg was broken. The doctor put a splint on it, and Harry and Trace carried the injured man out to the doctor's car. Louise followed them in her own car to the hospital, where Cash was bedded down in a ward. The doctor gave Cash a sedative, and Louise kissed him and drove home in the dawn.

Cash was in the hospital for two weeks, and when he came home he walked with a crutch and his broken leg was in a heavy cast. It was another ten days before he could limp to the morning train. 'I won't be able to run the hurdle race any more, sweetheart,' he told Louise sadly. She said that it didn't matter, but while it didn't matter to her, it seemed to matter to Cash. He had lost weight in the hospital. His spirits were low. He seemed discontented. He did not himself understand what had happened. He, or everything around him, seemed subtly to have changed for the worse. Even his senses seemed to conspire to damage the ingenuous world that he had enjoyed for so many years. He went into the kitchen late one night to make himself a sandwich, and when he opened the icebox door he noticed a rank smell. He dumped the spoiled meat into the garbage, but the smell clung to his nostrils. A few days later he was in the attic, looking for his varsity sweater. There were no windows in the attic and his flashlight was dim. Kneeling on the floor to unlock a trunk, he broke a spider web with his lips. The frail web covered his mouth as if a hand had been put over it. He wiped it impatiently, but also with the feeling of having been gagged. A few nights later, he was walking down a New York side street in the rain and saw an old whore standing in a doorway. She was so sluttish and ugly that she looked like a cartoon of Death, but before he could appraise her – the instant his eyes took an impression of her crooked figure – his lips swelled, his breathing quickened, and he experienced all the other symptoms of erotic excitement. A few nights later, while he was reading *Time* in the living room, he noticed that the faded roses Louise had brought in from the garden smelled more of earth than of anything else. It was a putrid, compelling smell. He dropped the roses into a wastebasket, but not before they had reminded him of the spoiled meat, the whore, and the spider web.

He had started going to parties again, but without the hurdle race to run, the parties of his friends and neighbors seemed to him interminable and stale. He listened to their dirty jokes with an irritability that was hard for him to conceal. Even their countenances discouraged him, and, slumped in a chair, he could regard their skin and their teeth narrowly, as if he were himself a much younger man.

The brunt of his irritability fell on Louise, and it seemed to her that Cash, in losing the hurdle race, had lost the thing that had preserved his equilibrium. He was rude to his friends when they stopped in for a drink. He was rude and gloomy when he and Louise went out. When Louise asked him what was the matter, he only murmured, 'Nothing, nothing, nothing,' and poured himself some bourbon. May and June passed, and then the first part of July, without his showing any improvement.

Then it is a summer night, a wonderful summer night. The passengers on the eight-fifteen see Shady Hill – if they notice it at all – in a bath of placid golden light. The noise of the train is muffled in the heavy foliage, and the long car windows look like a string of lighted aquarium tanks before they flicker out of sight. Up on the hill, the ladies say to one another, 'Smell the grass! Smell the trees!' The Farquarsons are giving another party, and Harry has hung a sign, WHIS-KEY GULCH, from the rose arbor, and is wearing a chef's white hat and an apron. His guests are still drinking, and the smoke from his meat fire rises, on this windless evening, straight up into the trees.

In the clubhouse on the hill, the first of the formal dances for the young people begins around nine. On Alewives Lane sprinklers continue to play after dark. You can smell the water. The air seems as fragrant as it is dark – it is a delicious element to walk through – and most of the windows on Alewives Lane are open to it. You can see Mr and Mrs Bearden, as you pass, looking at their television. Joe Lockwood, the young lawyer who lives on the corner, is practicing a speech to the jury before his wife. 'I intend to show you,' he says, 'that a man of probity, a man whose reputation for honesty and reliability ...' He waves his bare arms as he speaks. His wife goes on knitting. Mrs Carver – Harry Farquarson's mother-in-law – glances up at the sky and asks, '*Where* did all the stars come from?' She is old and foolish, and yet she is right:

Last night's stars seem to have drawn to themselves a new range of galaxies, and the night sky is not dark at all, except where there is a tear in the membrane of light. In the unsold house lots near the track a hermit thrush is singing.

The Bentleys are at home. Poor Cash has been so rude and gloomy that the Farquarsons have not asked him to their party. He sits on the sofa beside Louise, who is sewing elastic into the children's underpants. Through the open window he can hear the pleasant sounds of the summer night. There is another party, in the Rogerses' garden, behind the Bentleys'. The music from the dance drifts down the hill. The band is sketchy – saxophone, drums, and piano – and all the selections are twenty years old. The band plays 'Valencia,' and Cash looks tenderly toward Louise, but Louise, tonight, is a discouraging figure. The lamp picks out the gray in her hair. Her apron is stained. Her face seems colorless and drawn. Suddenly, Cash begins frenziedly to beat his feet in time to the music. He sings some gibberish – Jabajabajabajaba – to the distant saxophone. He sighs and goes into the kitchen.

Here a faint, stale smell of cooking clings to the dark. From the kitchen window Cash can see the lights and figures of the Rogerses' party. It is a young people's party. The Rogers girl has asked some friends in for dinner before the dance, and now they seem to be leaving. Cars are driving away. 'I'm covered with grass stains,' a girl says. 'I hope the old man remembered to buy gasoline,' a boy says, and a girl laughs. There is nothing on their minds but the passing summer nights. Taxes and the elastic in underpants – all the unbeautiful facts of life that threaten to crush the breath out of Cash – have not touched a single figure in this garden. Then jealousy seizes him – such savage and bitter jealousy that he feels ill.

He does not understand what separates him from these children in the garden next door. He has been a young man. He has been a hero. He has been adored and happy and full of animal spirits, and now he stands in a dark kitchen, deprived of his athletic prowess, his impetuousness, his good looks – of everything that means anything to him. He feels as if the figures in the next yard are the specters from some party in that past where all his tastes and desires lie, and from which he has been cruelly removed. He feels like a ghost of the summer evening. He is sick with longing. Then he hears voices in the front of the house. Louise turns on the kitchen light. 'Oh, here you are,' she says. 'The Beardens stopped in. I think they'd like a drink.'

Cash went to the front of the house to greet the Beardens. They wanted to go up to the club, for one dance. They saw, at a glance, that Cash was at loose ends, and they urged the Bentleys to come. Louise got someone to stay with the children and then went upstairs to change.

When they got to the club, they found a few friends of their age hanging around the bar, but Cash did not stay in the bar. He seemed restless and perhaps drunk. He banged into a table on his way through the lounge to the ballroom. He cut in on a young girl. He seized her too vehemently and jigged her off in an ancient two-step. She signaled openly for help to a boy in the stag line, and Cash was cut out. He walked angrily off the dance floor onto the terrace. Some young couples there withdrew from one another's arms as he pushed open the screen door. He walked to the end of the terrace, where he hoped to be alone, but here he surprised another young couple, who got up from the lawn, where they seemed to have been lying, and walked off in the dark toward the pool.

Louise remained in the bar with the Beardens. 'Poor Cash is tight,' she said. And then, 'He told me this afternoon that he was going to paint the storm windows,' she said. 'Well, he mixed the paint and washed the brushes and put on some old fatigues and went into the cellar. There was a telephone call for him at around five, and when I went down to tell him, do you know what he was doing? He was just sitting there in the dark with a cocktail shaker. He hadn't touched the storm windows. He was just sitting there in the dark, drinking Martinis.'

'Poor Cash,' Trace said.

'You ought to get a job,' Lucy said. 'That would give you emotional and financial independence.' As she spoke, they all heard the noise of furniture being moved around in the lounge.

'Oh, my God!' Louise said. 'He's going to run the race. Stop him, Trace, stop him! He'll hurt himself. He'll kill himself!'

They all went to the door of the lounge. Louise again asked Trace to interfere, but she could see by Cash's face that he was way beyond remonstrating with. A few couples left the dance floor and stood watching the preparations. Trace didn't try to stop Cash – he helped him. There was no pistol, so he slammed a couple of books together for the start.

Over the sofa went Cash, over the coffee table, the lamp table, the fire screen, and the hassock. All his grace and strength seemed to have returned to him. He cleared the big sofa at the end of the room and instead of stopping there, he turned and started back over the course. His face was strained. His mouth hung open. The tendons of his neck protruded hideously. He made the hassock, the fire screen, the lamp table, and the coffee table. People held their breath when he approached the final sofa, but he cleared it and landed on his feet. There was some applause. Then he groaned and fell. Louise ran to his side. His clothes were soaked with sweat and he gasped for breath. She knelt down beside him and took his head in her lap and stroked his thin hair.

Cash had a terrible hangover on Sunday, and Louise let him sleep until it was nearly time for church. The family went off to Christ Church together at eleven, as they always did. Cash sang, prayed, and got to his knees, but the most he ever felt in church was that he stood outside the realm of God's infinite mercy, and, to tell the truth, he no more believed in the Father, the Son, and the Holy Ghost than does my bull terrier. They returned home at one to eat the overcooked meat and stony potatoes that were their customary Sunday lunch. At around five, the Parminters called up and asked them over for a drink. Louise didn't want to go, so Cash went alone. (Oh, those suburban Sunday nights, those Sunday-night blues! Those departing weekend guests, those stale cocktails, those half-dead flowers, those trips to Harmon to catch the Century, those postmortems and pickup suppers!) It was sultry and overcast. The dog days were beginning. He drank gin with the Parminters for an hour or two and then went over to the Townsends' for a drink. The Farquarsons called up the Townsends and asked them to come over and bring Cash with them, and at the Farquarsons' they had some more drinks and ate the left-over party food. The Farquarsons were glad to see that Cash seemed like himself again. It was half past ten or eleven when he got home. Louise was upstairs, cutting out of the current copy of *Life* those scenes of mayhem, disaster, and violent death that she felt might corrupt her children. She always did this. Cash came upstairs and spoke to her and then went down again. In a little while, she heard him moving the living-room furniture around. Then he called to her, and when she went down, he was standing at the foot of the stairs in his stocking feet, holding the pistol out to her. She had never fired it before, and the directions he gave her were not much help.

'Hurry up,' he said, 'I can't wait all night.'

He had forgotten to tell her about the safety, and when she pulled the trigger nothing happened.

'It's that little lever,' he said. 'Press that little lever.' Then, in his impatience, he hurdled the sofa anyhow.

The pistol went off and Louise got him in midair. She shot him dead.

The Five-Forty-Eight

WHEN BLAKE STEPPED out of the elevator, he saw her. A few people, mostly men waiting for girls, stood in the lobby watching the elevator doors. She was among them. As he saw her, her face took on a look of such loathing and purpose that he realized she had been waiting for him. He did not approach her. She had no legitimate business with him. They had nothing to say. He turned and walked toward the glass doors at the end of the lobby, feeling that faint guilt and bewilderment we experience when we bypass some old friend or classmate who seems threadbare, or sick, or miserable in some other way. It was five-eighteen by the clock in the Western Union office. He could catch the express. As he waited his turn at the revolving doors, he saw that it was still raining. It had been raining all day, and he noticed now how much louder the rain made the noises of the street. Outside, he started walking briskly east toward Madison Avenue. Traffic was tied up, and horns were blowing urgently on a crosstown street in the distance. The sidewalk was crowded. He wondered what she had hoped to gain by a glimpse of him coming out of the office building at the end of the day. Then he wondered if she was following him.

Walking in the city, we seldom turn and look back. The habit restrained Blake. He listened for a minute – foolishly

– as he walked, as if he could distinguish her footsteps from the worlds of sound in the city at the end of a rainy day. Then he noticed, ahead of him on the other side of the street, a break in the wall of buildings. Something had been torn down; something was being put up, but the steel structure had only just risen above the sidewalk fence and daylight poured through the gap. Blake stopped opposite here and looked into a store window. It was a decorator's or an auctioneer's. The window was arranged like a room in which people live and entertain their friends. There were cups on the coffee table, magazines to read, and flowers in the vases, but the flowers were dead and the cups were empty and the guests had not come. In the plate glass, Blake saw a clear reflection of himself and the crowds that were passing, like shadows, at his back. Then he saw her image – so close to him that it shocked him. She was standing only a foot or two behind him. He could have turned then and asked her what she wanted, but instead of recognizing her, he shied away abruptly – from the reflection of her contorted face and went along the street. She might be meaning to do him harm – she might be meaning to kill him.

The suddenness with which he moved when he saw the reflection of her face tipped the water out of his hat brim in such a way that some of it ran down his neck. It felt unpleasantly like the sweat of fear. Then the cold water falling into his face and onto his bare hands, the rancid smell of the wet gutters and paving, the knowledge that his feet were beginning to get wet and that he might catch cold – all the common discomforts of walking in the rain – seemed to heighten the menace of his pursuer and to give him a morbid consciousness of his own physicalness and of the ease with which he could be hurt. He could see ahead of him the corner of Madison Avenue, where the lights were brighter. He felt that if he could get to Madison Avenue he would be all right. At the corner, there was a bakery shop with two entrances, and he went in by the door on the crosstown street, bought a coffee ring, like any other commuter, and went out the Madison Avenue door. As he started down Madison Avenue, he saw her waiting for him by a hut where newspapers were sold.

She was not clever. She would be easy to shake. He could get into a taxi by one door and leave by the other. He could speak to a policeman. He could run – although he was afraid that if he did run, it might precipitate the violence he now felt sure she had planned. He was approaching a part of the city that he knew well and where the maze of street-level and underground passages, elevator banks, and crowded lobbies made it easy for a man to lose a pursuer. The thought of this, and a whiff of sugary warmth from the coffee ring, cheered him. It was absurd to imagine being harmed on a crowded street. She was foolish, misled, lonely perhaps – that was all it could amount to. He was an insignificant man, and there was no point in anyone's following him from his office to the station. He knew no secrets of any consequence. The reports in his briefcase had no bearing on war, peace, the dope traffic, the hydrogen bomb, or any of the other international skulduggeries that he associated with pursuers, men in trench coats, and wet sidewalks. Then he saw ahead of him the door of a men's bar. Oh, it was so simple!

He ordered a Gibson and shouldered his way in between two other men at the bar, so that if she should be watching from the window she would lose sight of him. The place was crowded with commuters putting down a drink before the ride home. They had brought in on their clothes – on their shoes and umbrellas – the rancid smell of the wet dusk outside, but Blake began to relax as soon as he tasted his Gibson and looked around at the common, mostly not-young faces that surrounded him and that were worried, if they were worried at all, about tax rates and who would be put in charge of merchandising. He tried to remember her name – Miss Dent, Miss Bent, Miss Lent – and he was surprised to find that he could not remember it, although he was proud of the retentiveness and reach of his memory and it had only been six months ago.

Personnel had sent her up one afternoon – he was looking for a secretary. He saw a dark woman – in her twenties, perhaps – who was slender and shy. Her dress was simple, her figure was not much, one of her stockings was crooked, but her voice was soft and he had been willing to try her out. After she had been working for him a few days, she told him that she had been in the hospital for eight months and that it had been hard after this for her to find work, and she wanted to thank him for giving her a chance. Her hair was dark, her eyes were dark; she left with him a pleasant impression of darkness. As he got to know her better, he felt that she was oversensitive and, as a consequence, lonely. Once, when she was speaking to him of what she imagined his life to be – full of friend-ships, money, and a large and loving family – he had thought he recognized a peculiar feeling of deprivation. She seemed to imagine the lives of the rest of the world to be more brilliant than they were. Once, she had put a rose on his desk, and he had dropped it into the waste basket. 'I don't like roses,' he told her.

She had been competent, punctual, and a good typist, and he had found only one thing in her that he could object to – her handwriting. He could not associate the crudeness of her handwriting with her appearance. He would have expected her to write a rounded backhand, and in her writing there were intermittent traces of this, mixed with clumsy printing. Her writing gave him the feeling that she had been the victim of some inner – some emotional – conflict that had in its violence broken the continuity of the lines she was able to make on paper. When she had been working for him three weeks – no longer – they stayed late one night and he offered, after work, to buy her a drink. 'If you really want a drink,' she said, 'I have some whiskey at my place.'

She lived in a room that seemed to him like a closet. There were suit boxes and hatboxes piled in a corner, and although the room seemed hardly big enough to hold the bed, the dresser, and the chair he sat in, there was an upright piano against one wall, with a book of Beethoven sonatas on the rack. She gave him a drink and said that she was going to put on something more comfortable. He urged her to; that was, after all, what he had come for. If he had any qualms, they would have been practical. Her diffidence, the feeling of deprivation in her point of view, promised to protect him from any consequences. Most of the many women he had known had been picked for their lack of self-esteem.

When he put on his clothes again, an hour or so later, she was weeping. He felt too contented and warm and sleepy

101

to worry much about her tears. As he was dressing, he noticed on the dresser a note she had written to a cleaning woman. The only light came from the bathroom – the door was ajar – and in this half light the hideously scrawled letters again seemed entirely wrong for her, and as if they must be the handwriting of some other and very gross woman. The next day, he did what he felt was the only sensible thing. When she was out for lunch, he called personnel and asked them to fire her. Then he took the afternoon off. A few days later, she came to the office, asking to see him. He told the switchboard girl not to let her in. He had not seen her again until this evening.

Blake drank a second Gibson and saw by the clock that he had missed the express. He would get the local – the five-forty-eight. When he left the bar the sky was still light; it was still raining. He looked carefully up and down the street and saw that the poor woman had gone. Once or twice, he looked over his shoulder, walking to the station, but he seemed to be safe. He was still not quite himself, he realized, because he had left his coffee ring at the bar, and he was not a man who forgot things. This lapse of memory pained him.

He bought a paper. The local was only half full when he boarded it, and he got a seat on the river side and took off his raincoat. He was a slender man with brown hair – undistinguished in every way, unless you could have divined in his pallor or his gray eyes his unpleasant tastes. He dressed – like the rest of us – as if he admitted the existence of sumptuary laws. His raincoat was the pale buff color of a mushroom. His hat was dark brown; so was his suit. Except

for the few bright threads in his necktie, there was a scru-
pulous lack of color in his clothing that seemed protective.

He looked around the car for neighbors. Mrs Compton
was several seats in front of him, to the right. She smiled,
but her smile was fleeting. It died swiftly and horribly. Mr
Watkins was directly in front of Blake. Mr Watkins needed
a haircut, and he had broken the sumptuary laws; he was
wearing a corduroy jacket. He and Blake had quarreled, so
they did not speak.

The swift death of Mrs Compton's smile did not affect
Blake at all. The Comptons lived in the house next to the
Blakes, and Mrs Compton had never understood the
importance of minding her own business. Louise Blake
took her troubles to Mrs Compton, Blake knew, and instead
of discouraging her crying jags, Mrs Compton had come to
imagine herself a sort of confessor and had developed a
lively curiosity about the Blakes' intimate affairs. She had
probably been given an account of their most recent quarrel. Blake had come home one night, overworked and tired,
and had found that Louise had done nothing about getting
supper. He had gone into the kitchen, followed by Louise,
and had pointed out to her that the date was the fifth. He
had drawn a circle around the date on the kitchen calendar.
'One week is the twelfth,' he had said. 'Two weeks will be
the nineteenth.' He drew a circle around the nineteenth.
'I'm not going to speak to you for two weeks,' he had said.
'That will be the nineteenth.' She had wept, she had pro-
tested, but it had been eight or ten years since she had been
able to touch him with her entreaties. Louise had got old.
Now the lines in her face were ineradicable, and when she
clapped her glasses onto her nose to read the evening paper,

she looked to him like an unpleasant stranger. The physical charms that had been her only attraction were gone. It had been nine years since Blake had built a bookshelf in the doorway that connected their rooms and had fitted into the bookshelf wooden doors that could be locked, since he did not want the children to see his books. But their prolonged estrangement didn't seem remarkable to Blake. He had quarreled with his wife, but so did every other man born of woman. It was human nature. In any place where you can hear their voices – a hotel courtyard, an air shaft, a street on a summer evening – you will hear harsh words.

The hard feeling between Blake and Mr Watkins also had to do with Blake's family, but it was not as serious or as troublesome as what lay behind Mrs Compton's fleeting smile. The Watkinses rented. Mr Watkins broke the sumptuary laws day after day – he once went to the eight-fourteen in a pair of sandals – and he made his living as a commercial artist. Blake's oldest son – Charlie was fourteen – had made friends with the Watkins boy. He had spent a lot of time in the sloppy rented house where the Watkinses lived. The friendship had affected his manners and his neatness. Then he had begun to take some meals with the Watkinses, and to spend Saturday nights there. When he had moved most of his possessions over to the Watkinses' and had begun to spend more than half his nights there, Blake had been forced to act. He had spoken not to Charlie but to Mr Watkins, and had, of necessity, said a number of things that must have sounded critical. Mr Watkins' long and dirty hair and his corduroy jacket reassured Blake that he had been in the right.

But Mrs Compton's dying smile and Mr Watkins' dirty hair did not lessen the pleasure Blake took in setting himself in an uncomfortable seat on the five-forty-eight deep underground. The coach was old and smelled oddly like a bomb shelter in which whole families had spent the night. The light that spread from the ceiling down onto their heads and shoulders was dim. The filth on the window glass was streaked with rain from some other journey, and clouds of rank pipe and cigarette smoke had begun to rise from behind each newspaper, but it was a scene that meant to Blake that he was on a safe path, and after his brush with danger he even felt a little warmth toward Mrs Compton and Mr Watkins.

The train traveled up from underground into the weak daylight, and the slums and the city reminded Blake vaguely of the woman who had followed him. To avoid speculation or remorse about her, he turned his attention to the evening paper. Out of the corner of his eye he could see the landscape. It was industrial and, at that hour, sad. There were machine sheds and warehouses, and above these he saw a break in the clouds – a piece of yellow light. 'Mr Blake,' someone said. He looked up. It was she. She was standing there holding one hand on the back of the seat to steady herself in the swaying coach. He remembered her name then – Miss Dent. 'Hello, Miss Dent,' he said.

'Do you mind if I sit here?'

'I guess not.'

'Thank you. It's very kind of you. I don't like to inconvenience you like this. I don't want to ...' He had been frightened when he looked up and saw her, but her timid voice rapidly reassured him. He shifted his hams – that futile and reflexive gesture of hospitality – and she sat down. She sighed. He smelled her wet clothing. She wore a formless black hat with a cheap crest stitched onto it. Her coat was thin cloth, he saw, and she wore gloves and carried a large pocketbook.

'Are you living out in this direction now, Miss Dent?'

'No.'

She opened her purse and reached for her handkerchief. She had begun to cry. He turned his head to see if anyone in the car was looking, but no one was. He had sat beside a thousand passengers on the evening train. He had noticed their clothes, the holes in their gloves; and if they fell asleep and mumbled he had wondered what their worries were. He had classified almost all of them briefly before he buried his nose in the paper. He had marked them as rich, poor, brilliant or dull, neighbors or strangers, but no one of the thousand had ever wept. When she opened her purse, he remembered her perfume. It had clung to his skin the night he went to her place for a drink.

'I've been very sick,' she said. 'This is the first time I've been out of bed in two weeks. I've been terribly sick.'

'I'm sorry that you've been sick, Miss Dent,' he said in a voice loud enough to be heard by Mr Watkins and Mrs Compton. 'Where are you working now?'

'What?'

'Where are you working now?'

'Oh, don't make me laugh,' she said softly.

'I don't understand.'

'You poisoned their minds.'

He straightened his neck and braced his shoulders. These wrenching movements expressed a brief – and hopeless – longing to be in some other place. She meant trouble. He took a breath. He looked with deep feeling at the half-filled, half-lighted coach to affirm his sense of actuality, of a world in which there was not very much bad trouble after all. He was conscious of her heavy breathing and the smell of her rain-soaked coat. The train stopped. A nun and a man in overalls got off. When it started again, Blake put on his hat and reached for his raincoat.

'Where are you going?' she said.

'I'm going to the next car.'

'Oh, no,' she said. 'No, no, no.' She put her white face so close to his ear that he could feel her warm breath on his cheek. 'Don't do that,' she whispered. 'Don't try and escape me. I have a pistol and I'll have to kill you and I don't want to. All I want to do is to talk with you. Don't move or I'll kill you. Don't, don't, don't!'

Blake sat back abruptly in his seat. If he had wanted to stand and shout for help, he would not have been able to. His tongue had swelled to twice its size, and when he tried to move it, it stuck horribly to the roof of his mouth. His legs were limp. All he could think of to do then was to wait for his heart to stop its hysterical beating, so that he could judge the extent of his danger. She was sitting a little side-wise, and in her pocketbook was the pistol, aimed at his belly.

'You understand me now, don't you?' she said. 'You understand that I'm serious?' He tried to speak but he was still mute. He nodded his head. 'Now we'll sit quietly for a little while,' she said. 'I got so excited that my thoughts are all confused. We'll sit quietly for a little while, until I can get my thoughts in order again.'

Help would come, Blake thought. It was only a question of minutes. Someone, noticing the look on his face or her peculiar posture, would stop and interfere, and it would all be over. All he had to do was to wait until someone noticed his predicament. Out of the window he saw the river and the sky. The rain clouds were rolling down like a shutter, and while he watched, a streak of orange light on the horizon became brilliant. Its brilliance spread – he could see it move – across the waves until it raked the banks of the river with a dim firelight. Then it was put out. Help would come in a minute, he thought. Help would come before they stopped again; but the train stopped, there were some comings and goings, and Blake still lived on, at the mercy of the woman beside him. The possibility that help might not come was one that he could not face. The possibility that his predicament was not noticeable, that Mrs Compton would guess that he was taking a poor relation out to dinner at Shady Hill, was something he would think about later. Then the saliva came back into his mouth and he was able to speak.

'Miss Dent?'

'Yes.'

'What do you want?'

I want to talk to you.'

'You can come to my office.'

'Oh, no. I went there every day for two weeks.'

'You could make an appointment.'

'No,' she said, 'I think we can talk here. I wrote you a letter but I've been too sick to go out and mail it. I've put down all my thoughts. I like to travel. I like trains. One of my troubles has always been that I could never afford to travel. I suppose you see this scenery every night and don't notice it any more, but it's nice for someone who's been in

108

bed a long time. They say that He's not in the river and the hills but I think He is. "Where shall wisdom be found?" it says. "Where is the place of understanding? The depth saith it is not in me; the sea saith it is not with me. Destruction and death say we have heard the force with our ears."

'Oh, I know what you're thinking,' she said. 'You're thinking that I'm crazy, and I have been very sick again but I'm going to be better. It's going to make me better to talk with you. I was in the hospital all the time before I came to work for you but they never tried to cure me, they only wanted to take away my self-respect. I haven't had any work now for three months. Even if I did have to kill you, they wouldn't be able to do anything to me except put me back in the hospital, so you see I'm not afraid. But let's sit quietly for a little while longer. I have to be calm.'

The train continued its halting progress up the bank of the river, and Blake tried to force himself to make some plans for escape, but the immediate threat to his life made this difficult, and instead of planning sensibly, he thought of the many ways in which he could have avoided her in the first place. As soon as he had felt these regrets, he realized their futility. It was like regretting his lack of suspicion when she first mentioned her months in the hospital. It was like regretting his failure to have been warned by her shyness, her diffidence, and the handwriting that looked like the marks of a claw. There was no way of rectifying his mistakes, and he felt – for perhaps the first time in his mature life – the full force of regret. Out of the window, he saw some men fishing on the nearly dark river, and then a ramshackle boat club that seemed to have been nailed together out of scraps of wood that had been washed up on the shore.

Mr Watkins had fallen asleep. He was snoring. Mrs Compton read her paper. The train creaked, slowed, and halted infirmly at another station. Blake could see the southbound platform, where a few passengers were waiting to go into the city. There was a workman with a lunch pail, a dressed-up woman, and a woman with a suitcase. They stood apart from one another. Some advertisements were posted on the wall behind them. There was a picture of a couple drinking a toast in wine, a picture of a Cat's Paw rubber heel, and a picture of a Hawaiian dancer. Their cheerful intent seemed to go no farther than the puddles of water on the platform and to expire there. The platform and the people on it looked lonely. The train drew away from the station into the scattered lights of a slum and then into the darkness of the country and the river.

'I want you to read my letter before we get to Shady Hill,' she said. 'It's on the seat. Pick it up. I would have mailed it to you, but I've been too sick to go out. I haven't gone out for two weeks. I haven't had any work for three months. I haven't spoken to anybody but the landlady. Please read my letter.'

He picked up the letter from the seat where she had put it. The cheap paper felt abhorrent and filthy to his fingers. It was folded and refolded. 'Dear Husband,' she had written, in that crazy, wandering hand, 'they say that human love leads us to divine love, but is this true? I dream about you every night. I have such terrible desires. I have always had a gift for dreams. I dreamed on Tuesday of a volcano erupting with blood. When I was in the hospital they said they wanted to cure me but they only wanted to take away my self-respect. They only wanted me to dream about sewing

110

and basketwork but I protected my gift for dreams. I'm clairvoyant. I can tell when the telephone is going to ring. I've never had a true friend in my whole life ...'

The train stopped again. There was another platform, another picture of the couple drinking a toast, the rubber heel, and the Hawaiian dancer. Suddenly she pressed her face close to Blake's again and whispered in his ear. 'I know what you're thinking. I can see it in your face. You're thinking you can get away from me in Shady Hill, aren't you? Oh, I've been planning this for weeks. It's all I've had to think about. I won't harm you if you'll let me talk. I've been thinking about devils. I mean, if there are devils in the world, if there are people in the world who represent evil, is it our duty to exterminate them? I know that you always prey on weak people. I can tell. Oh, sometimes I think I ought to kill you. Sometimes I think you're the only obstacle between me and my happiness. Sometimes ...'

She touched Blake with the pistol. He felt the muzzle against his belly. The bullet, at that distance, would make a small hole where it entered, but it would rip out of his back a place as big as a soccer ball. He remembered the unburied dead he had seen in the war. The memory came in a rush; entrails, eyes, shattered bone, ordure, and other filth.

'All I've ever wanted in life is a little love,' she said. She lightened the pressure of the gun. Mr Watkins still slept. Mrs Compton was sitting calmly with her hands folded in her lap. The coach rocked gently, and the coats and mushroom-colored raincoats that hung between the windows swayed a little as the car moved. Blake's elbow was on the window sill and his left shoe was on the guard above the steampipe. The car smelled like some dismal classroom. The passengers seemed asleep and apart, and Blake felt that he might never escape the smell of heat and wet clothing and the dimness of the light. He tried to summon the calculated self-deceptions with which he sometimes cheered himself, but he was left without any energy for hope of self-deception.

The conductor put his head in the door and said, 'Shady Hill, next, Shady Hill.'

'Now,' she said. 'Now you get out ahead of me.'

Mr Watkins waked suddenly, put on his coat and hat, and smiled at Mrs Compton, who was gathering her parcels to her in a series of maternal gestures. They went to the door. Blake joined them, but neither of them spoke to him or seemed to notice the woman at his back. The conductor threw open the door, and Blake saw on the platform of the next car a few other neighbors who had missed the express, waiting patiently and tiredly in the wan light for their trip to end. He raised his head to see through the open door the abandoned mansion out of town, a NO TRESPASSING sign nailed to a tree, and then the oil tanks. The concrete abutments of the bridge passed, so close to the open door that he could have touched them. Then he saw the first of the lamp-posts on the northbound platform, the sign SHADY HILL in black and gold, and the little lawn and flower bed kept up by the Improvement Association, and then the cab stand and a corner of the old-fashioned depot. It was raining again; it was pouring. He could hear the splash of water and see the lights reflected in puddles and in the shining pavement, and the idle sound of splashing and dripping formed in his mind a conception of shelter, so light and strange that it seemed to belong to a time of his life that he could not remember.

He went down the steps with her at his back. A dozen or so cars were waiting by the station with their motors running. A few people got off from each of the other coaches; he recognized most of them, but none of them offered to give him a ride. They walked separately or in pairs – purposefully out of the rain to the shelter of the platform, where the car horns called to them. It was time to go home, time for a drink, time for love, time for supper, and he could see the lights on the hill – lights by which children were being bathed, meat cooked, dishes washed – shining in the rain. One by one, the cars picked up the heads of families, until there were only four left. Two of the stranded passengers drove off in the only taxi the village had. 'I'm sorry, darling,' a woman said tenderly to her husband when she drove up a few minutes later. 'All our clocks are slow.' The last man looked at his watch, looked at the rain, and then walked off into it, and Blake saw him go as if they had some reason to say goodbye – not as we say goodbye to friends after a party but as we say goodbye when we are faced with an inexorable and unwanted parting of the spirit and the heart. The man's footsteps sounded as he crossed the parking lot to the sidewalk, and then they were lost. In the station, a telephone began to ring. The ringing was loud, evenly spaced, and unanswered. Someone wanted to know about the next train to Albany, but Mr Flanagan, the stationmaster, had gone home an hour ago. He had turned on all his lights before he went away. They burned in the empty waiting room. They burned, tin-shaded, at intervals up and down the platform and with the peculiar sadness of dim and purposeless lights. They lighted the Hawaiian dancer, the couple drinking a toast, the rubber heel.

'I've never been here before,' she said. 'I thought it would look different. I didn't think it would look so shabby. Let's get out of the light. Go over there.'

His legs felt sore. All his strength was gone. 'Go on,' she said.

North of the station there were a freight house and a coalyard and an inlet where the butcher and the baker and the man who ran the service station moored the dinghies, from which they fished on Sundays, sunk now to the gunwales with the rain. As he walked toward the freight house, he saw a movement on the ground and heard a scraping sound, and then he saw a rat take its head out of a paper bag and regard him. The rat seized the bag in its teeth and dragged it into a culvert.

'Stop,' she said. 'Turn around. Oh, I ought to feel sorry for you. Look at your poor face. But you don't know what I've been through. I'm afraid to go out in the daylight. I'm afraid the blue sky will fall down on me. I'm like poor Chicken-Licken. I only feel like myself when it begins to get dark. But still and all I'm better than you. I still have good dreams sometimes. I dream about picnics and heaven and the brotherhood of man, and about castles in the moonlight and a river with willow trees all along the edge of it and foreign cities, and after all I know more about love than you.'

He heard from off the dark river the drone of an outboard motor, a sound that drew slowly behind it across the dark water such a burden of clear, sweet memories of gone summers and gone pleasures that it made his flesh crawl, and he thought of dark in the mountains and the children singing. 'They never wanted to cure me,' she said.

'They ...' The noise of a train coming down from the north drowned out her voice, but she went on talking. The noise filled his ears, and the windows where people ate, drank, slept, and read flew past. When the train had passed beyond the bridge, the noise grew distant, and he heard her screaming at him, '*Kneel down!* Kneel down! Do what I say. *Kneel down!*'

He got to his knees. He bent his head. 'There,' she said. 'You see, if you do what I say, I won't harm you, because I really don't want to harm you, I want to help you, but when I see your face it sometimes seems to me that I can't help you. Sometimes it seems to me that if I were good and loving and sane – oh, much better than I am – sometimes it seems to me that if I were all these things and young and beautiful, too, and if I called to show you the right way, you wouldn't heed me. Oh, I'm better than you, I'm better than you, and I shouldn't waste my time or spoil my life like this. Put your face in the dirt. *Put your face in the dirt!* Do what I say. Put your face in the dirt.'

He fell forward in the filth. The coal skinned his face. He stretched out on the ground, weeping. 'Now I feel better,' she said. 'Now I can wash my hands of you, I can wash my hands of all this, because you see there is some kindness, some saneness in me that I can find and use. I can wash my hands.' Then he heard her footsteps go away from him, over the rubble. He heard the clearer and more distant sound they made on the hard surface of the platform. He heard them diminish. He raised his head. He saw her climb the stairs of the wooden footbridge and cross it and go down to the other platform, where her figure in the dim light looked small, common, and harmless. He raised himself out of the dust – warily at first, until he saw by her attitude, her looks, that she had forgotten him; that she had completed what she had wanted to do, and that he was safe. He got to his feet and picked up his hat from the ground where it had fallen and walked home.

The Country Husband

TO BEGIN AT the beginning, the airplane from Minneapolis in which Francis Weed was traveling East ran into heavy weather. The sky had been a hazy blue, with the clouds below the plane lying so close together that nothing could be seen of the earth. Then mist began to form outside the windows, and they flew into a white cloud of such density that it reflected the exhaust fires. The color of the cloud darkened to gray, and the plane began to rock. Francis had been in heavy weather before, but he had never been shaken up so much. The man in the seat beside him pulled a flask out of his pocket and took a drink. Francis smiled at his neighbor, but the man looked away; he wasn't sharing his pain killer with anyone. The plane began to drop and flounder wildly. A child was crying. The air in the cabin was overheated and stale, and Francis' left foot went to sleep. He read a little from a paperback that he had bought at the airport, but the violence of the storm divided his attention. It was black outside the ports. The exhaust fires blazed and shed sparks in the dark, and, inside, the shaded lights, the stuffiness, and the window curtains gave the cabin an atmosphere of intense and misplaced domesticity. Then the lights flickered and went out. 'You know what I've always wanted to do?' the man beside Francis said suddenly. 'I've always wanted to buy a farm in New Hampshire and raise beef cattle.' The stewardess announced that they were going to make an emergency landing. All but the children saw in their minds the spreading wings of the Angel of Death. The pilot could be heard singing faintly, 'I've got sixpence, jolly, jolly sixpence. I've got sixpence to last me all my life ...' There was no other sound.

The loud groaning of the hydraulic valves swallowed up the pilot's song, and there was a shrieking high in the air, like automobile brakes, and the plane hit flat on its belly in a cornfield and shook them so violently that an old man up forward howled, 'Me kidneys! Me kidneys!' The stewardess flung open the door, and someone opened an emergency door at the back, letting in the sweet noise of their continuing mortality – the idle splash and smell of a heavy rain. Anxious for their lives, they filed out of the doors and scattered over the corn-field in all directions, praying that the thread would hold. It did. Nothing happened. When it was clear that the plane would not burn or explode, the crew and the stewardess gathered the passengers together and led them to the shelter of a barn. They were not far from Philadelphia, and in a little while a string of taxis took them into the city. 'It's just like the Marne,' someone said, but there was surprisingly little relaxation of that suspiciousness with which many Americans regard their fellow travelers.

In Philadelphia, Francis Weed got a train to New York. At the end of that journey, he crossed the city and caught just as it was about to pull out the commuting train that he took five nights a week to his home in Shady Hill.

He sat with Trace Bearden. 'You know, I was in that plane that just crashed outside Philadelphia,' he said. 'We came down in a field ...' He had traveled faster than the newspapers or the rain, and the weather in New York was sunny and mild. It was a day in late September, as fragrant and shapely as an apple. Trace listened to the story, but how could he get excited? Francis had no powers that would let him re-create a brush with death – particularly in the atmosphere of a commuting train, journeying through a sunny countryside where already, in the slum gardens, there were signs of harvest. Trace picked up his newspaper, and Francis was left alone with his thoughts. He said good night to Trace on the platform at Shady Hill and drove in his secondhand Volkswagen up to the Blenhollow neighborhood, where he lived.

The Weeds' Dutch Colonial house was larger than it appeared to be from the driveway. The living room was spacious and divided like Gaul into three parts. Around an ell to the left as one entered from the vestibule was the long table, laid for six, with candles and a bowl of fruit in the center. The sounds and smells that came from the open kitchen door were appetizing, for Julia Weed was a good cook. The largest part of the living room centered on a fireplace. On the right were some bookshelves and a piano. The room was polished and tranquil, and from the windows that opened to the west there was some late-summer sunlight, brilliant and as clear as water. Nothing here was neglected; nothing had not been burnished. It was not the kind of household where, after prying open a stuck cigarette box, you would find an old shirt button and a tarnished nickel. The hearth was swept, the roses on the piano were

119

reflected in the polish of the broad top, and there was an album of Schubert waltzes on the rack. Louisa Weed, a pretty girl of nine, was looking out the western windows. Her younger brother Henry was standing beside her. Her still younger brother, Toby, was studying the figures of some tonsured monks drinking beer on the polished brass of the woodbox. Francis, taking off his hat and putting down his paper, was not consciously pleased with the scene; he was not that reflective. It was his element, his creation, and he returned to it with that sense of lightness and strength with which any creature returns to his home. 'Hi, everybody,' he said. 'The plane from Minneapolis . . .'

Nine times out of ten, Francis would be greeted with affection, but tonight the children are absorbed in their own antagonisms. Francis had not finished his sentence about the plane crash before Henry plants a kick in Louisa's behind. Louisa swings around, saying, '*Damn* you!' Francis makes the mistake of scolding Louisa for bad language before he punishes Henry. Now Louisa turns on her father and accuses him of favoritism. Henry is always right; she is persecuted and lonely; her lot is hopeless. Francis turns to his son, but the boy has justification for the kick – she hit him first; she hit him on the ear, which is dangerous. Louisa agrees with this passionately. She hit him on the ear, and she *meant* to hit him on the ear, because he messed up her china collection. Henry says that this is a lie. Little Toby turns away from the woodbox to throw in some evidence for Louisa. Henry claps his hand over little Toby's mouth. Francis separates the two boys but accidentally pushes Toby into the woodbox. Toby begins to cry. Louisa is already crying. Just then, Julia Weed comes into that part of the room where the table is laid. She is a pretty, intelligent woman, and the white in her hair is premature. She does not seem to notice the fracas. 'Hello, darling,' she says serenely to Francis. 'Wash your hands, everyone. Dinner is ready.' She strikes a match and lights the six candles in this vale of tears.

This simple announcement, like the war cries of the Scottish chieftains, only refreshes the ferocity of the combatants. Louisa gives Henry a blow on the shoulder. Henry, although he seldom cries, has pitched nine innings and is tired. He bursts into tears. Little Toby discovers a splinter in his hand and begins to howl. Francis says loudly that he has been in a plane crash and that he is tired. Julia appears again from the kitchen and, still ignoring the chaos, asks Francis to go upstairs and tell Helen that everything is ready. Francis is happy to go; it is like getting back to headquarters company. He is planning to tell his oldest daughter about the airplane crash, but Helen is lying on her bed reading a *True Romance* magazine, and the first thing Francis does is to take the magazine from her hand and remind Helen that he has forbidden her to buy it. She did not buy it, Helen replies. It was given to her by her best friend, Bessie Black. Everybody reads *True Romance*. Bessie Black's father reads *True Romance*. There isn't a girl in Helen's class who doesn't read *True Romance*. Francis expresses his detestation of the magazine and then tells her that dinner is ready – although from the sounds downstairs it doesn't seem so. Helen follows him down the stairs. Julia has seated herself in the candlelight and spread a napkin over her lap. Neither Louisa nor Henry has come to the table. Little Toby is still howling, lying face down on the floor. Francis speaks to him gently: 'Daddy was in a plane crash this afternoon,

121

Toby. Don't you want to hear about it?' Toby goes on crying. 'If you don't come to the table now, Toby,' Francis says, 'I'll have to send you to bed without any supper.' The little boy rises, gives him a cutting look, flies up the stairs to his bedroom, and slams the door. 'Oh dear,' Julia says, and starts to go after him. Francis says that she will spoil him. Julia says that Toby is ten pounds underweight and has to be encouraged to eat. Winter is coming, and he will spend the cold months in bed unless he has his dinner. Julia goes upstairs. Francis sits down at the table with Helen. Helen is suffering from the dismal feeling of having read too intently on a fine day, and she gives her father and the room a jaded look. She doesn't understand about the plane crash, because there wasn't a drop of rain in Shady Hill.

Julia returns with Toby, and they all sit down and are served. 'Do I have to look at that big, fat slob?' Henry says, of Louisa. Everybody but Toby enters into this skirmish, and it rages up and down the table for five minutes. Toward the end, Henry puts his napkin over his head and, trying to eat that way, spills spinach all over his shirt. Francis asks Julia if the children couldn't have their dinner earlier. Julia's guns are loaded for this. She can't cook two dinners and lay two tables. She paints with lightning strokes that panorama of drudgery in which her youth, her beauty, and her wit have been lost. Francis says that he must be understood; he was nearly killed in an airplane crash, and he doesn't like to come home every night to a battlefield. Now Julia is deeply concerned. Her voice trembles. He doesn't come home every night to a battlefield. The accusation is stupid and mean. Everything was tranquil until he arrived. She stops speaking, puts down her knife and fork, and looks into her plate as if it is a gulf. She begins to cry. 'Poor Mummy!' Toby says, and when Julia gets up from the table, drying her tears with a napkin, Toby goes to her side. 'Poor Mummy,' he says. 'Poor Mummy!' And they climb the stairs together. The other children drift away from the battlefield, and Francis goes into the back garden for a cigarette and some air.

It was a pleasant garden, with walks and flower beds and places to sit. The sunset had nearly burned out, but there was still plenty of light. Put into a thoughtful mood by the crash and the battle, Francis listened to the evening sounds of Shady Hill. 'Varmints! Rascals!' old Mr Nixon shouted to the squirrels in his bird-feeding station. 'Avaunt and quit my sight!' A door slammed. Someone was cutting grass. Then Donald Goslin, who lived at the corner, began to play the 'Moonlight Sonata'. He did this nearly every night. He threw the tempo out the window and played it *rubato* from beginning to end, like an outpouring of tearful petulance, lonesomeness, and self-pity – of everything it was Beethoven's greatness not to know. The music rang up and down the street beneath the trees like an appeal for love, for tenderness, aimed at some lovely housemaid – some fresh-faced, homesick girl from Galway, looking at old snapshots in her third-floor room. 'Here, Jupiter, here, Jupiter,' Francis called to the Mercers' retriever. Jupiter crashed through the tomato vines with the remains of a felt hat in his mouth.

Jupiter was an anomaly. His retrieving instincts and his high spirits were out of place in Shady Hill. He was as black as coal, with a long, alert, intelligent, rakehell face. His eyes gleamed with mischief, and he held his head high. It was the fierce, heavily collared dog's head that appears in heraldry, in tapestry, and that used to appear on umbrella handles and walking sticks. Jupiter went where he pleased, ransacking wastebaskets, clotheslines, garbage pails, and shoe bags. He broke up garden parties and tennis matches, and got mixed up in the processional at Christ Church on Sunday, barking at the men in red dresses. He crashed through old Mr Nixon's rose garden two or three times a day, cutting a wide swath through the Condesa de Sastagos, and as soon as Donald Goslin lighted his barbecue fire on Thursday nights, Jupiter would get the scent. Nothing the Goslins did could drive him away. Sticks and stones and rude commands only moved him to the edge of the terrace, where he remained, with his gallant and heraldic muzzle, waiting for Donald Goslin to turn his back and reach for the salt. Then he would spring onto the terrace, lift the steak lightly off the fire, and run away with the Goslins' dinner. Jupiter's days were numbered. The Wrightsons' German gardener or the Farquarsons' cook would soon poison him. Even old Mr Nixon might put some arsenic in the garbage that Jupiter loved. 'Here, Jupiter, Jupiter!' Francis called, but the dog pranced off, shaking the hat in his white teeth. Looking at the windows of his house, Francis saw that Julia had come down and was blowing out the candles.

Julia and Francis Weed went out a great deal. Julia was well liked and gregarious, and her love of parties sprang from a most natural dread of chaos and loneliness. She went through her morning mail with real anxiety, looking for invitations, and she usually found some, but she was insatiable, and if she had gone out seven nights a week, it would not have cured her of a reflective look – the look of someone who hears distant music – for she would always suppose that there was a more brilliant party somewhere else. Francis limited her to two week-night parties, putting a flexible interpretation on Friday, and rode through the weekend like a dory in a gale. The day after the airplane crash, the Weeds were to have dinner with the Farquarsons.

Francis got home late from town, and Julia got the sitter while he dressed, and then hurried him out of the house. The party was small and pleasant, and Francis settled down to enjoy himself. A new maid passed the drinks. Her hair was dark, and her face was round and pale and seemed familiar to Francis. He had not developed his memory as a sentimental faculty. Wood smoke, lilac, and other such perfumes did not stir him, and his memory was something like his appendix – a vestigial repository. It was not his limitation at all to be unable to escape the past; it was perhaps his limitation that he had escaped it so successfully. He might have seen the maid at other parties, he might have seen her taking a walk on Sunday afternoons, but in either case he would not be searching his memory now. Her face was, in a wonderful way, a moon face – Norman or Irish – but it was not beautiful enough to account for his feeling that he had seen her before, in circumstances that he ought to be able to remember. He asked Nellie Farquarson who she was. Nellie said that the maid had come through an agency, and that her home was Trenon, in Normandy – a small place with a church and a restaurant that Nellie had once visited. While Nellie talked on about her travels abroad, Francis realized where he had seen the woman before. It had been at the end of the war. He had left a replacement depot with some other men and taken a three-day pass in Trenon. On their second day, they had walked out to a

125

crossroads to see the public chastisement of a young woman who had lived with the German commandant during the Occupation.

It was a cool morning in the fall. The sky was overcast, and poured down onto the dirt crossroads a very discouraging light. They were on high land and could see how like one another the shapes of the clouds and the hills were as they stretched off toward the sea. The prisoner arrived sitting on a three-legged stool in a farm cart. She stood by the cart while the Mayor read the accusation and the sentence. Her head was bent and her face was set in that empty half smile behind which the whipped soul is suspended. When the Mayor was finished, she undid her hair and let it fall across her back. A little man with a gray mustache cut off her hair with shears and dropped it on the ground. Then, with a bowl of soapy water and a straight razor, he shaved her skull clean. A woman approached and began to undo the fastenings of her clothes, but the prisoner pushed her aside and undressed herself. When she pulled her chemise over her head and threw it on the ground, she was naked. The women jeered; the men were still. There was no change in the falseness or the plaintiveness of the prisoner's smile. The cold wind made her white skin rough and hardened the nipples of her breasts. The jeering ended gradually, put down by the recognition of their common humanity. One woman spat on her, but some inviolable grandeur in her nakedness lasted through the ordeal. When the crowd was quiet, she turned – she had begun to cry – and, with nothing on but a pair of worn black shoes and stockings, walked down the dirt road alone away from the village. The round white face had aged a little, but there was no question but that the maid who passed his cocktails and later served Francis his dinner was the woman who had been punished at the crossroads.

The war seemed now so distant and that world where the cost of partisanship had been death or torture so long ago. Francis had lost track of the men who had been with him in Vesey. He could not count on Julia's discretion. He could not tell anyone. And if he had told the story now, at the dinner table, it would have been a social as well as a human error. The people in the Farquarsons' living room seemed united in their tacit claim that there had been no past, no war – that there was no danger or trouble in the world. In the recorded history of human arrangements, this extraordinary meeting would have fallen into place, but the atmosphere of Shady Hill made the memory unseemly and impolite. The prisoner withdrew after passing the coffee, but the encounter left Francis feeling languid; it had opened his memory and his senses, and left them dilated. Julia went into the house. Francis stayed in the car to take the sitter home.

Expecting to see Mrs Henlein, the old lady who usually stayed with the children, he was surprised when a young girl opened the door and came out onto the lighted stoop. She stayed in the light to count her textbooks. She was frowning and beautiful. Now, the world is full of beautiful young girls, but Francis saw here the difference between beauty and perfection. All those endearing flaws, moles, birthmarks, and healed wounds were missing, and he experienced in his consciousness that moment when music breaks glass, and felt a pang of recognition as strange, deep, and wonderful as anything in his life. It hung from her

127

frown, from an impalpable darkness in her face – a look that impressed him as a direct appeal for love. When she had counted her books, she came down the steps and opened the car door. In the light, he saw that her cheeks were wet. She got in and shut the door.

'You're new,' Francis said.

'Yes. Mrs Henlein is sick. I'm Anne Murchison.'

'Did the children give you any trouble?'

'Oh, no, no.' She turned and smiled at him unhappily in the dim dashboard light. Her light hair caught on the collar of her jacket, and she shook her head to set it loose.

'You've been crying.'

'Yes.'

'I hope it was nothing that happened in our house.'

'No, no, it was nothing that happened in your house.' Her voice was bleak. 'It's no secret. Everybody in the village knows. Daddy's an alcoholic, and he just called me from some saloon and gave me a piece of his mind. He thinks I'm immoral. He called just before Mrs Weed came back.'

'I'm sorry.'

'Oh, *Lord!*' She gasped and began to cry. She turned toward Francis, and he took her in his arms and let her cry on his shoulder. She shook in his embrace, and this movement accentuated his sense of the fineness of her flesh and bone. The layers of their clothing felt thin, and when her shuddering began to diminish, it was so much like a paroxysm of love that Francis lost his head and pulled her roughly against him. She drew away. 'I live on Belleview Avenue,' she said. 'You go down Lansing Street to the railroad bridge.'

'All right.' He started the car.

'You turn left at that traffic light ... Now you turn right here and go straight on toward the tracks.'

The road Francis took brought him out of his own neighborhood, across the tracks, and toward the river, to a street where the near-poor lived, in houses whose peaked gables and trimmings of wooden lace conveyed the purest feelings of pride and romance, although the houses themselves could not have offered much privacy or comfort, they were all so small. The street was dark, and, stirred by the grace and beauty of the troubled girl, he seemed, in turning into it, to have come into the deepest part of some submerged memory. In the distance, he saw a porch light burning. It was the only one, and she said that the house with the light was where she lived. When he stopped the car, he could see beyond the porch light into a dimly lighted hallway with an old-fashioned clothes tree. 'Well, here we are,' he said, conscious that a young man would have said something different.

She did not move her hands from the books, where they were folded, and she turned and faced him. There were tears of lust in his eyes. Determinedly – not sadly – he opened the door on his side and walked around to open hers. He took her free hand, letting his fingers in between hers, climbed at her side the two concrete steps, and went up a narrow walk through a front garden where dahlias, marigolds, and roses – things that had withstood the light frosts – still bloomed, and made a bittersweet smell in the night air. At the steps, she freed her hand and then turned and kissed him swiftly. Then she crossed the porch and shut the door. The porch light went out, then the light in the hall. A second later, a light went on upstairs at the side of the house, shining into a tree that was still covered with leaves. It took her only a few minutes to undress and get into bed, and then the house was dark.

Julia was asleep when Francis got home. He opened a second window and got into bed to shut his eyes on that night, but as soon as they were shut – as soon as he had dropped off to sleep – the girl entered his mind, moving with perfect freedom through its shut doors and filling chamber after chamber with her light, her perfume, and the music of her voice. He was crossing the Atlantic with her on the old *Mauretania* and, later, living with her in Paris. When he woke from his dream, he got up and smoked a cigarette at the open window. Getting back into bed, he cast around in his mind for something he desired to do that would injure no one, and he thought of skiing. Up through the dimness in his mind rose the image of a mountain deep in snow. It was late in the day. Wherever his eyes looked, he saw broad and heartening things. Over his shoulder, there was a snow-filled valley, rising into wooded hills where the trees dimmed the whiteness like a sparse coat of hair. The cold deadened all sound but the loud, iron clanking of the lift machinery. The light on the trails was blue, and it was harder than it had been a minute or two earlier to pick the turns, harder to judge – now that the snow was all deep blue – the crust, the ice, the bare spots, and the deep piles of dry powder. Down the mountain he swung, matching his speed against the contours of a slope that had been formed in the first ice age, seeking with ardor some simplicity of feeling and circumstance. Night fell then, and he drank a Martini with some old friend in a dirty country bar.

In the morning, Francis' snow-covered mountain was gone, and he was left with his vivid memories of Paris and the *Mauretania*. He had been bitten gravely. He washed his body, shaved his jaws, drank his coffee, and missed the seven-thirty-one. The train pulled out just as he brought his car to the station, and the longing he felt for the coaches as they drew stubbornly away from him reminded him of the humors of love. He waited for the eight-two, on what was now an empty platform. It was a clear morning; the morning seemed thrown like a gleaming bridge of light over his mixed affairs. His spirits were feverish and high. The image of the girl seemed to put him into a relationship to the world that was mysterious and enthralling. Cars were beginning to fill up the parking lot, and he noticed that those that had driven down from the high land above Shady Hill were white with hoarfrost. This first clear sign of autumn thrilled him. An express train – a night train from Buffalo or Albany – came down the tracks between the platforms, and he saw that the roofs of the foremost cars were covered with a skin of ice. Struck by the miraculous physicalness of everything, he smiled at the passengers in the dining car, who could be seen eating eggs and wiping their mouths with napkins as they traveled. The sleeping-car compartments, with their soiled bed linen, trailed through the fresh morning like a string of rooming-house windows. Then he saw an extraordinary thing; at one of the bedroom windows sat an unclothed woman of exceptional beauty, combing her golden hair. She passed like an apparition through Shady Hill, combing and combing her hair, and Francis followed her with his eyes until she was out of sight. Then old Mrs Wrightson joined him on the platform and began to talk.

'Well, I guess you must be surprised to see me here the third morning in a row,' she said, 'but because of my window curtains I'm becoming a regular commuter. The curtains I bought on Monday I returned on Tuesday, and the curtains I bought Tuesday I'm returning today. On Monday, I got exactly what I wanted – it's a wool tapestry with roses and birds – but when I got them home, I found they were the wrong length. Well, I exchanged them yesterday, and when I got them home, I found they were still the wrong length. Now I'm praying to high heaven that the decorator will have them in the right length, because you know my house, you *know* my living-room windows, and you can imagine what a problem they present. I don't know what to do with them.'

'I know what to do with them,' Francis said.

'What?'

'Paint them black on the inside, and shut up.'

There was a gasp from Mrs Wrightson, and Francis looked down at her to be sure that she knew he meant to be rude. She turned and walked away from him, so damaged in spirit that she limped. A wonderful feeling enveloped him, as if light were being shaken about him, and he thought again of Venus combing and combing her hair as she drifted through the Bronx. The realization of how many years had passed since he had enjoyed being deliberately impolite sobered him. Among his friends and neighbors, there were brilliant and gifted people – he saw that – but many of them, also, were bores and fools, and he had made the mistake of listening to them all with equal attention. He had confused a lack of discrimination with Christian love, and the confusion seemed general and destructive. He was grateful to the girl for this bracing sensation of independence. Birds were singing – cardinals and the last of the robins. The sky shone like enamel. Even the smell of ink from his morning paper honed his appetite for life, and the world that was spread out around him was plainly a paradise.

If Francis had believed in some hierarchy of love – in spirits armed with hunting bows, in the capriciousness of Venus and Eros – or even in magical potions, philters, and stews, in scapulae and quarters of the moon, it might have explained his susceptibility and his feverish high spirits. The autumnal loves of middle age are well publicized, and he guessed that he was face to face with one of these, but there was not a trace of autumn in what he felt. He wanted to sport in the green woods, scratch where he itched, and drink from the same cup.

His secretary, Miss Rainey, was late that morning – she went to a psychiatrist three mornings a week – and when she came in, Francis wondered what advice a psychiatrist would have for him. But the girl promised to bring back into his life something like the sound of music. The realization that this music might lead him straight to a trial for statutory rape at the county courthouse collapsed his happiness. The photograph of his four children laughing into the camera on the beach at Gay Head reproached him. On the letterhead of his firm there was a drawing of the Laocoon, and the figure of the priest and his sons in the coils of the snake appeared to him to have the deepest meaning.

He had lunch with Pinky Trabert. At a conversational level, the mores of his friends were robust and elastic, but he knew that the moral card house would come down on them all – on Julia and the children as well – if he got caught taking advantage of a baby-sitter. Looking back over the recent history of Shady Hill for some precedent, he found there was none. There was no turpitude; there had not been a divorce since he lived there; there had not even been a breath of scandal. Things seemed arranged with more propriety even than in the Kingdom of Heaven. After leaving Pinky, Francis went to a jeweler's and bought the girl a bracelet. How happy this clandestine purchase made him, how stuffy and comical the jeweler's clerks seemed, how sweet the women who passed at his back smelled! On Fifth Avenue, passing Atlas with his shoulders bent under the weight of the world, Francis thought of the strenuousness of containing his physicalness within the patterns he had chosen.

He did not know when he would see the girl next. He had the bracelet in his inside pocket when he got home. Opening the door of his house, he found her in the hall. Her back was to him, and she turned when she heard the door close. Her smile was open and loving. Her perfection stunned him like a fine day – a day after a thunderstorm. He seized her and covered her lips with his, and she struggled but she did not have to struggle for long, because just then little Gertrude Flannery appeared from somewhere and said, 'Oh, Mr Weed ...'

Gertrude was a stray. She had been born with a taste for exploration, and she did not have it in her to center her life with her affectionate parents. People who did not know the Flannerys concluded from Gertrude's behavior that she was the child of a bitterly divided family, where drunken quarrels were the rule. This was not true. The fact that little Gertrude's clothing was ragged and thin was her own triumph over her mother's struggle to dress her warmly and neatly. Garrulous, skinny, and unwashed, she drifted from house to house around the Blenhollow neighborhood, forming and breaking alliances based on an attachment to babies, animals, children her own age, adolescents, and sometimes adults. Opening your front door in the morning, you would find Gertrude sitting on your stoop. Going into the bathroom to shave, you would find Gertrude using the toilet. Looking into your son's crib, you would find it empty, and, looking further, you would find that Gertrude had pushed him in his baby carriage into the next village. She was helpful, pervasive, honest, hungry, and loyal. She never went home of her own choice. When the time to go arrived, she was indifferent to all its signs. 'Go home, Gertrude,' people could be heard saying in one house or another, night after night. 'Go home, Gertrude. It's time for you to go home now, Gertrude.' 'You had better go home and get your supper, Gertrude.' 'I told you to go home twenty minutes ago, Gertrude.' 'Your mother will be worrying about you, Gertrude.' 'Go home, Gertrude, go home.'

There are times when the lines around the human eye seem like shelves of eroded stone and when the staring eye itself strikes us with such a wilderness of animal feeling that we are at a loss. The look Francis gave the little girl was ugly and queer, and it frightened her. He reached into his pockets – his hands were shaking – and took out a quarter. 'Go home, Gertrude, go home, and don't tell anyone, Gertrude. Don't –' He choked and ran into the living room as Julia called down to him from upstairs to hurry and dress.

The thought that he would drive Anne Murchison home later that night ran like a golden thread through the events of the party that Francis and Julia went to, and he laughed uproariously at dull jokes, dried a tear when Mabel Mercer told him about the death of her kitten, and stretched, yawned, sighed, and grunted like any other man with a rendezvous at the back of his mind. The bracelet was in his pocket. As he sat talking, the smell of grass was in his nose, and he was wondering where he would park the car. Nobody lived in the old Parker mansion, and the driveway was used as a lovers' lane. Townsend Street was a dead end, and he could park there, beyond the last house. The old lane that used to connect Elm Street to the riverbanks was overgrown, but he had walked there with his children, and he could drive his car deep enough into the brushwoods to be concealed.

The Weeds were the last to leave the party, and their host and hostess spoke of their own married happiness while they all four stood in the hallway saying good night. 'She's my girl,' their host said, squeezing his wife. 'She's my blue sky. After sixteen years, I still bite her shoulders. She makes me feel like Hannibal crossing the Alps.'

The Weeds drove home in silence. Francis brought the car up the driveway and sat still, with the motor running. 'You can put the car in the garage,' Julia said as she got out. 'I told the Murchison girl she could leave at eleven. Someone drove her home.' She shut the door, and Francis sat in the dark. He would be spared nothing then, it seemed, that a fool was not spared: ravening lewdness, jealousy, this hurt to his feelings that put tears in his eyes, even scorn – for he could see clearly the image he now presented, his arms

136

spread over the steering wheel and his head buried in them for love.

Francis had been a dedicated Boy Scout when he was young, and, remembering the precepts of his youth, he left his office early the next afternoon and played some round-robin squash, but, with his body toned up by exercise and a shower, he realized that he might better have stayed at his desk. It was a frosty night when he got home. The air smelled sharply of change. When he stepped into the house, he sensed an unusual stir. The children were in their best clothes, and when Julia came down, she was wearing a lavender dress and her diamond sunburst. She explained the stir: Mr Hubber was coming at seven to take their photograph for the Christmas card. She had put out Francis' blue suit and a tie with some color in it, because the picture was going to be in color this year. Julia was lighthearted at the thought of being photographed for Christmas. It was the kind of ceremony she enjoyed.

Francis went upstairs to change his clothes. He was tired from the day's work and tired with longing, and sitting on the edge of the bed had the effect of deepening his weariness. He thought of Anne Murchison, and the physical need to express himself, instead of being restrained by the pink lamps of Julia's dressing table, engulfed him. He went to Julia's desk, took a piece of writing paper, and began to write on it. 'Dear Anne, I love you, I love you, I love you ...' No one would see the letter, and he used no restraint. He used phrases like 'heavenly bliss,' and 'love nest'. He salivated, sighed, and trembled. When Julia called him to come down, the abyss between his fantasy and the practical world opened so wide that he felt it affected the muscles of his heart.

Julia and the children were on the stoop, and the photographer and his assistant had set up a double battery of floodlights to show the family and the architectural beauty of the entrance to their house. People who had come home on a late train slowed their cars to see the Weeds being photographed for their Christmas card. A few waved and called to the family. It took half an hour of smiling and wetting their lips before Mr Hubber was satisfied. The heat of the lights made an unfresh smell in the frosty air, and when they were turned off, they lingered on the retina of Francis' eyes.

Later that night, while Francis and Julia were drinking their coffee in the living room, the doorbell rang. Julia answered the door and let in Clayton Thomas. He had come to pay for some theatre tickets that she had given his mother some time ago, and that Helen Thomas had scrupulously insisted on paying for, though Julia had asked her not to. Julia invited him in to have a cup of coffee. 'I won't have any coffee,' Clayton said, 'but I will come in for a minute.' He followed her into the living room, said good evening to Francis, and sat awkwardly in a chair.

Clayton's father had been killed in the war, and the young man's fatherlessness surrounded him like an element. This may have been conspicuous in Shady Hill because the Thomases were the only family that lacked a piece; all the other marriages were intact and productive. Clayton was in his second or third year of college, and he and his mother lived alone in a large house, which she hoped to sell. Clayton had once made some trouble. Years ago, he had stolen some money and run away; he had got to California before they caught up with him. He was tall and homely, wore horn-rimmed glasses, and spoke in a deep voice.

'When do you go back to college, Clayton?' Francis asked.

'I'm not going back,' Clayton said, 'Mother doesn't have the money, and there's no sense in all this pretense. I'm going to get a job, and if we sell the house, we'll take an apartment in New York.'

'Won't you miss Shady Hill?' Julia asked.

'No,' Clayton said. 'I don't like it.'

'Why not?' Francis asked.

'Well, there's a lot here I don't approve of,' Clayton said gravely. 'Things like the club dances. Last Saturday night, I looked in toward the end and saw Mr Granner trying to put Mrs Minot into the trophy case. They were both drunk. I disapprove of so much drinking.'

'It was Saturday night,' Francis said.

'And all the dovecotes are phony,' Clayton said. 'And the way people clutter up their lives. I've thought about it a lot, and what seems to me to be really wrong with Shady Hill is that it doesn't have any future. So much energy is spent in perpetuating the place – in keeping out undesirables, and so forth – that the only idea of the future anyone has is just more and more commuting trains and more parties. I don't think that's healthy. I think people ought to be able to dream big dreams about the future. I think people ought to be able to dream great dreams.'

'It's too bad you couldn't continue with college,' Julia said.

'I wanted to go to divinity school,' Clayton said.

'What's your church?' Francis asked.

'Unitarian, Theosophist, Transcendentalist, Humanist,' Clayton said.

'Wasn't Emerson a transcendentalist?' Julia asked.

'I mean the English transcendentalists,' Clayton said. 'All the American transcendentalists were goops.'

'What kind of job do you expect to get?' Francis asked.

'Well, I'd like to work for a publisher,' Clayton said, 'but everyone tells me there's nothing doing. But it's the kind of thing I'm interested in. I'm writing a long verse play about good and evil. Uncle Charlie might get me into a bank, and that would be good for me. I need the discipline. I have a long way to go in forming my character. I have some terrible habits. I talk too much. I think I ought to take vows of silence. I ought to try not to speak for a week, and discipline myself. I've thought of making a retreat at one of the Episcopalian monasteries, but I don't like Trinitarianism.'

'Do you have any girl friends?' Francis asked.

'I'm engaged to be married,' Clayton said. 'Of course, I'm not old enough or rich enough to have my engagement observed or respected or anything, but I bought a simulated emerald for Anne Murchison with the money I made cutting lawns this summer. We're going to be married as soon as she finishes school.'

Francis recoiled at the mention of the girl's name. Then a dingy light seemed to emanate from his spirit, showing everything – Julia, the boy, the chairs – in their true colorlessness. It was like a bitter turn of the weather.

'We're going to have a large family,' Clayton said. 'Her father's a terrible rummy, and I've had my hard times, and we want to have lots of children. Oh, she's wonderful, Mr and Mrs Weed, and we have so much in common. We like all the same things. We sent out the same Christmas card last year without planning it, and we both have an allergy to tomatoes, and our eyebrows grow together in the middle. Well, goodnight.'

Julia went to the door with him. When she returned, Francis said that Clayton was lazy, irresponsible, affected, and smelly. Julia said that Francis seemed to be getting intolerant; the Thomas boy was young and should be given a chance. Julia had noticed other cases where Francis had been short-tempered. 'Mrs Wrightson has asked everyone in Shady Hill to her anniversary party but us,' she said.

'I'm sorry, Julia.'

'Do you know why they didn't ask us?'

'Why?'

'Because you insulted Mrs Wrightson.'

'Then you know about it?'

'June Masterson told me. She was standing behind you.'

Julia walked in front of the sofa with a small step that expressed, Francis knew, a feeling of anger.

'I did insult Mrs Wrightson, Julia, and I meant to. I've never liked her parties, and I'm glad she's dropped us.'

'What about Helen?'

'How does Helen come into this?'

'Mrs Wrightson's the one who decides who goes to the assemblies.'

'You mean she can keep Helen from going to the dances?'

'Yes.'

'I hadn't thought of that.'

'Oh. I knew you hadn't thought of it,' Julia cried, thrusting hilt-deep into this chink of his armor. 'And it makes me furious to see this kind of stupid thoughtlessness wreck everyone's happiness.'

'I don't think I've wrecked anyone's happiness.'

'Mrs Wrightson runs Shady Hill and has run it for the last forty years. I don't know what makes you think that in a community like this you can indulge every impulse you have to be insulting, vulgar, and offensive.'

'I have very good manners,' Francis said, trying to give the evening a turn toward the light.

'Damn you, Francis Weed!' Julia cried, and the spit of her words struck him in the face. 'I've worked hard for the social position we enjoy in this place, and I won't stand by and see you wreck it. You must have understood when you settled here that you couldn't expect to live like a bear in a cave.'

'I've got to express my likes and dislikes.'

'You can conceal your dislikes. You don't have to meet everything head on, like a child. Unless you're anxious to be a social leper. It's no accident that we get asked out a great deal! It's no accident that Helen has so many friends. How would you like to spend your Saturday nights at the movies? How would you like to spend your Sundays raking up dead leaves? How would you like it if your daughter spent the assembly nights sitting at her window, listening to the music from the club? How would you like it –' He did something then that was, after all, not so unaccountable, since her words seemed to raise up between them a wall so deadening that he gagged. He struck her full in the face. She staggered and then, a moment later, seemed composed. She went up the stairs to their room. She didn't slam the door. When Francis followed, a few minutes later, he found her packing a suitcase.

'Julia, I'm very sorry.'

142

'It doesn't matter,' she said. She was crying.

'Where do you think you're going?'

'I don't know. I just looked at a timetable. There's an eleven-sixteen into New York. I'll take that.'

'You can't go, Julia.'

'I can't stay. I know that.'

'I'm sorry about Mrs Wrightson, Julia, and I'm –'

'It doesn't matter about Mrs Wrightson. That isn't the trouble.'

'What is the trouble?'

'You don't love me.'

'I do love you, Julia.'

'No, you don't.'

'Julia, I do love you, and I would like to be as we were – sweet and bawdy and dark – but now there are so many people.'

'You hate me.'

'I don't hate you, Julia.'

'You have no idea of how much you hate me. I think it's subconscious. You don't realize the cruel things you've done.'

'What cruel things, Julia?'

'The cruel acts your subconscious drives you to in order to express your hatred of me.'

'What, Julia?'

'I've never complained.'

'Tell me.'

'You don't know what you're doing.'

'Tell me.'

'Your clothes.'

'What do you mean?'

'I mean the way you leave your dirty clothes around in order to express your subconscious hatred of me.'

'I don't understand.'

'I mean your dirty socks and your dirty pajamas and your dirty underwear and your dirty shirts!' She rose from kneeling by the suitcase and faced him, her eyes blazing and her voice ringing with emotion. 'I'm talking about the fact that you've never learned to hang up anything. You just leave your clothes all over the floor where they drop, in order to humiliate me. You do it on purpose!' She fell on the bed, sobbing.

'Julia, darling!' he said, but when she felt his hand on her shoulder she got up.

'Leave me alone,' she said. 'I have to go.' She brushed past him to the closet and came back with a dress. 'I'm not taking any of the things you've given me,' she said. 'I'm leaving my pearls and the fur jacket.'

'Oh, Julia!' Her figure, so helpless in its self-deceptions, bent over the suitcase made him nearly sick with pity. She did not understand how desolate her life would be without him. She didn't understand the hours that working women have to keep. She didn't understand that most of her friendships existed within the framework of their marriage, and that without this she would find herself alone. She didn't understand about travel, about hotels, about money. 'Julia, I can't let you go! What you don't understand, Julia, is that you've come to be dependent on me.'

She tossed her head back and covered her face with her hands. 'Did you say that *I* was dependent on *you*?' she asked. 'Is that what you said? And who is it that tells you what time to get up in the morning and when to go to bed at night? Who is it that prepares your meals and picks up your dirty clothes and invites your friends to dinner? If it weren't for me, your neckties would be greasy and your clothing would be full of moth holes. You were alone when I met you, Francis Weed, and you'll be alone when I leave. When Mother asked you for a list to send out invitations to our wedding, how many names did you have to give her? Fourteen!'

'Cleveland wasn't my home, Julia.'

'And how many of your friends came to the church? Two!'

'Cleveland wasn't my home, Julia.'

'Since I'm not taking the fur jacket,' she said quietly, 'you'd better put it back into storage. There's an insurance policy on the pearls that comes due in January. The name of the laundry and the maid's telephone number – all those things are in my desk. I hope you won't drink too much, Francis. I hope that nothing bad will happen to you. If you do get into serious trouble, you can call me.'

'Oh, my darling, I can't let you go!' Francis said. 'I can't let you go, Julia!' He took her in his arms.

'I guess I'd better stay and take care of you for a little while longer,' she said.

Riding to work in the morning, Francis saw the girl walk down the aisle of the coach. He was surprised; he hadn't realized that the school she went to was in the city, but she was carrying books, she seemed to be going to school. His surprise delayed his reaction, but then he got up clumsily and stepped into the aisle. Several people had come between them, but he could see her ahead of him, waiting for some-one to open the car door, and then, as the train swerved, putting out her hand to support herself as she crossed the platform into the next car. He followed her through that car and halfway through another before calling her name – 'Anne! Anne!' – but she didn't turn. He followed her into still another car, and she sat down in an aisle seat. Coming up to her, all his feelings warm and bent in her direction, he put his hand on the back of her seat – even this touch warmed him – and leaning down to speak to her, he saw that it was not Anne. It was an older woman wearing glasses. He went on deliberately into another car, his face red with embarrassment and the much deeper feeling of having his good sense challenged; for if he couldn't tell one person from another, what evidence was there that his life with Julia and the children had as much reality as his dreams of iniquity in Paris or the litter, the grass smell, and the cave-shaped trees in Lovers' Lane.

Late that afternoon, Julia called to remind Francis that they were going out for dinner. A few minutes later, Trace Bearden called. 'Look, fellar,' Trace said. 'I'm calling for Mrs Thomas. You know? Clayton, that boy of hers, doesn't seem able to get a job, and I wondered if you could help. If you'd call Charlie Bell – I know he's indebted to you – and say a good word for the kid, I think Charlie would –'

'Trace, I hate to say this,' Francis said, 'but I don't feel that I can do anything for that boy. The kid's worthless. I know it's a harsh thing to say, but it's a fact. Any kindness done for him would backfire in everybody's face. He's just a worthless kid, Trace, and there's nothing to be done about it. Even if we got him a job, he wouldn't be able to keep it for a week. I know that to be a fact. It's an awful thing, Trace, and I know it is, but instead of recommending that kid, I'd feel obligated to warn people against him – people who knew his father and would naturally want to step in and do something. I'd feel obliged to warn them. He's a thief ...'

The moment this conversation was finished, Miss Rainey came in and stood by his desk. 'I'm not going to be able to work for you any more, Mr Weed,' she said. 'I can stay until the seventeenth if you need me, but I've been offered a whirlwind of a job, and I'd like to leave as soon as possible.'

She went out, leaving him to face alone the wickedness of what he had done to the Thomas boy. His children in their photograph laughed and laughed, glazed with all the bright colors of summer, and he remembered that they had met a bagpiper on the beach that day and he had paid the piper a dollar to play them a battle song of the Black Watch. The girl would be at the house when he got home. He would spend another evening among his kind neighbors, picking and choosing dead-end streets, cart tracks, and the driveways of abandoned houses. There was nothing to mitigate his feeling – nothing that laughter or a game of softball with the children would change – and, thinking back over the plane crash, the Farquarsons' new maid, and Anne Murchison's difficulties with her drunken father, he wondered how he could have avoided arriving at just where he was. He was in trouble. He had been lost once in his life, coming back from a trout stream in the north woods, and he had now the same bleak realization that no amount of cheerfulness or hopefulness or valor or perseverance could help him find, in the gathering dark, the path that he'd lost. He smelled the forest. The feeling of bleakness was intolerable, and he saw clearly that he had reached the point where he would have to make a choice.

He could go to a psychiatrist, like Miss Rainey; he could go to church and confess his lusts; he could go to a Danish massage parlor in the West Seventies that had been recommended by a salesman; he could rape the girl or trust that he would somehow be prevented from doing this; or he could get drunk. It was his life, his boat, and, like every other man, he was made to be the father of thousands, and what harm could there be in a tryst that would make them both feel more kindly toward the world? This was the wrong train of thought, and he came back to the first, the psychiatrist. He had the telephone number of Miss Rainey's doctor, and he called and asked for an immediate appointment. He was insistent with the doctor's secretary – it was his manner in business – and when she said that the doctor's schedule was full for the next few weeks, Francis demanded an appointment that day and was told to come at five.

The psychiatrist's office was in a building that was used mostly by doctors and dentists, and the hallways were filled with the candy smell of mouthwash and memories of pain. Francis' character had been formed upon a series of private resolves – resolves about cleanliness, about going off the high diving board or repeating any other feat that challenged his courage, about punctuality, honesty, and virtue. To abdicate the perfect loneliness in which he had made his most vital decisions shattered his concept of character and left him now in a condition that felt like shock. He was stupefied. The scene for his *miserere mei Deus* was, like the waiting room of so many doctors' offices, a crude token gesture toward the sweets of domestic bliss: a place arranged with antiques, coffee tables, potted plants, and etchings of snow-covered bridges and geese in flight, although there were no children, no marriage bed, no stove, even, in this travesty of a house, where no one had ever spent the night and where the curtained windows looked straight onto a dark air shaft. Francis gave his name and address to a secretary and then saw, at the side of the room, a policeman moving toward him. 'Hold it, hold it,' the policeman said. 'Don't move. Keep your hands where they are.'

'I think it's all right, Officer,' the secretary began. 'I think it will be —'

'Let's make sure,' the policeman said, and he began to slap Francis' clothes, looking for what — pistols, knives, an icepick? Finding nothing, he went off and the secretary began a nervous apology: 'When you called on the telephone, Mr Weed, you seemed very excited, and one of the doctor's patients has been threatening his life, and we have to be careful. If you want to go in now?' Francis pushed open a door connected to an electrical chime, and in the doctor's lair sat down heavily, blew his nose into a handkerchief, searched in his pockets for cigarettes, for matches, for something, and said hoarsely, with tears in his eyes, 'I'm in love, Dr Herzog.'

It is a week or ten days later in Shady Hill. The seven-fourteen has come and gone, and here and there dinner is finished and the dishes are in the dish-washing machine. The village hangs, morally and economically, from a thread; but it hangs by its thread in the evening light. Donald Goslin has begun to worry the 'Moonlight Sonata' again. *Marcato ma sempre pianissimo!* He seems to be wringing out a wet bath towel, but the housemaid does not heed him. She is writing a letter to Arthur Godfrey. In the cellar of his house,

Francis Weed is building a coffee table. Dr Herzog recommends woodwork as a therapy, and Francis finds some true consolation in the simple arithmetic involved and in the holy smell of new wood. Francis is happy. Upstairs, little Toby is crying, because he is tired. He puts off his cowboy hat, gloves, and fringed jacket, unbuckles the belt studded with gold and rubies, the silver bullets and holsters, slips off his suspenders, his checked shirt, and Levi's, and sits on the edge of his bed to pull off his high boots. Leaving this equipment in a heap, he goes to the closet and takes his space suit off a nail. It is a struggle for him to get into the long tights, but he succeeds. He loops the magic cape over his shoulders and, climbing onto the footboard of his bed, he spreads his arms and flies the short distance to the floor, landing with a bump that is audible to everyone in the house but himself.

'Go home, Gertrude, go home,' Mrs Masterson says. 'I told you to go home an hour ago, Gertrude. It's way past your suppertime, and your mother will be worried. Go home!' A door on the Babcocks' terrace flies open, and out comes Mrs Babcock without any clothes on, pursued by a naked husband. (Their children are away at boarding school, and their terrace is screened by a hedge.) Over the terrace they go and in at the kitchen door, as passionate and handsome a nymph and satyr as you will find on any wall in Venice. Cutting the last of the roses in her garden, Julia hears old Mr Nixon shouting at the squirrels in his bird-feeding station. 'Rapscallions! Varmints! Avaunt and quit my sight!' A miserable cat wanders into the garden, sunk in spiritual and physical discomfort. Tied to its head is a small straw hat – a doll's hat – and it is securely buttoned into a doll's dress, from the skirts of which protrudes its long, hairy tail. As it walks, it shakes its feet, as if it had fallen into water.

'Here, pussy, pussy, pussy!' Julia calls.

'Here, pussy, here, poor pussy!' But the cat gives her a skeptical look and stumbles away in its skirts. The last to come is Jupiter. He prances through the tomato vines, holding his generous mouth the remains of an evening slipper. Then it is dark; it is a night where kings in golden suits ride elephants over the mountains.

The Death of Justina

So HELP ME God it gets more and more preposterous, it corresponds less and less to what I remember and what I expect as if the force of life were centrifugal and threw one further and further away from one's purest memories and ambitions; and I can barely recall the old house where I was raised, where in midwinter Parma violets bloomed in a cold frame near the kitchen door, and down the long corridor, past the seven views of Rome – up two steps and down three – one entered the library, where all the books were in order, the lamps were bright, where there was a fire and a dozen bottles of good bourbon locked in a cabinet with a veneer like tortoiseshell whose silver key my father wore on his watch chain. Fiction is art and art is the triumph over chaos (no less) and we can accomplish this only by the most vigilant exercise of choice, but in a world that changes more swiftly than we can perceive there is always the danger that our powers of selection will be mistaken and that the vision we serve will come to nothing. We admire decency and we despise death but even the mountains seem to shift in the space of a night and perhaps the exhibitionist at the corner of Chestnut and Elm streets is more significant than the lovely woman with a bar of sunlight in her hair, putting a fresh piece of cuttlebone in the nightingale's cage. Just let

me give you one example of chaos and if you disbelieve me
look honestly into your own past and see if you can't find a
comparable experience ...

On Saturday the doctor told me to stop smoking and
drinking and I did. I won't go into the commonplace symptoms of withdrawal but I would like to point out that,
standing at my window in the evening, watching the brilliant afterlight and the spread of darkness, I felt, through the
lack of these humble stimulants, the force of some primitive
memory in which the coming of night with its stars and its
moon was apocalyptic. I thought suddenly of the neglected
graves of my three brothers on the mountainside and that
death is a loneliness much crueler than any loneliness hinted
at in life. The soul (I thought) does not leave the body but
lingers with it through every degrading stage of decompos-
ition and neglect, through heat, through cold, through the
long winter nights when no one comes with a wreath or a
plant and no one says a prayer. This unpleasant premonition
was followed by anxiety. We were going out for dinner and
I thought that the oil burner would explode in our absence
and burn the house. The cook would get drunk and attack
my daughter with a carving knife or my wife and I would
be killed in a collision on the main highway, leaving our
children bewildered orphans with nothing in life to look
forward to but sadness. I was able to observe, along with
these foolish and terrifying anxieties, a definite impairment
of my discretionary poles. I felt as if I were being lowered
by ropes into the atmosphere of my childhood. I told my
wife – when she passed through the living room – that I
had stopped smoking and drinking but she didn't seem to

care and who would reward me for my privations? Who cared about the bitter taste in my mouth and that my head seemed to be leaving my shoulders? It seemed to me that men had honored one another with medals, statuary, and cups for much less and that abstinence is a social matter. When I abstain from sin it is more often a fear of scandal than a private resolve to improve on the purity of my heart, but here was a call for abstinence without the worldly enforcement of society, and death is not the threat that scandal is. When it was time for us to go out I was so light-headed that I had to ask my wife to drive the car. On Sunday I sneaked seven cigarettes in various hiding places and drank two Martinis in the downstairs coat closet. At breakfast on Monday my English muffin stared up at me from the plate. I mean I *saw* a face there in the rough, toasted surface. The moment of recognition was fleeting, but it was deep, and I wondered who it had been. Was it a friend, an aunt, a sailor, a ski instructor, a bartender, or a conductor on a train? The smile faded off the muffin but it had been there for a second – the sense of a person, a life, a pure force of gentleness and censure – and I am convinced that the muffin had contained the presence of some spirit. As you can see, I was nervous.

On Monday my wife's old cousin, Justina, came to visit her. Justina was a lively guest although she must have been crowding eighty. On Tuesday my wife gave her a lunch party. The last guest left at three and a few minutes later Cousin Justina, sitting on the living-room sofa with a glass of good brandy, breathed her last. My wife called me at the office and I said that I would be right out. I was clearing my desk when my boss, MacPherson, came in.

'Spare me a minute,' he asked. 'I've been bird-dogging all over the place, trying to track you down. Pierce had to leave early and I want you to write the last Elixircol commercial.'

'Oh, I can't, Mac,' I said. 'My wife just called. Cousin Justina is dead.'

'You write that commercial,' he said. His smile was satanic. 'Pierce had to leave early because his grandmother fell off a stepladder.'

Now, I don't like fictional accounts of office life. It seems to me that if you're going to write fiction you should write about mountain climbing and tempests at sea, and I will go over my predicament with MacPherson briefly, aggravated as it was by his refusal to respect and honor the death of dear old Justina. It was like MacPherson. It was a good example of the way I've been treated. He is, I might say, a tall, splendidly groomed man of about sixty who changes his shirt three times a day, romances his secretary every afternoon between two and two-thirty, and makes the habit of continuously chewing gum seem hygienic and elegant. I write his speeches for him and it has not been a happy arrangement for me. If the speeches are successful MacPherson takes all the credit. I can see that his presence, his tailor, and his fine voice are all a part of the performance but it makes me angry never to be given credit for what was said. On the other hand, if the speeches are unsuccessful – if his presence and his voice can't carry the hour – his threatening and sarcastic manner is surgical and I am obliged to contain myself in the role of a man who can do no good in spite of the piles of congratulatory mail that my eloquence sometimes brings in. I must pretend – I must, like an actor, study and improve on my pretension – to have nothing to do with his triumphs, and I must bow my head gracefully in shame when we have both failed. I am forced to appear grateful for injuries, to lie, to smile falsely, and to play out a role as inane and as unrelated to the facts as a minor prince in an operetta, but if I speak the truth it will be my wife and my children who will pay in hardships for my outspokenness. Now he refused to respect or even to admit the solemn fact of a death in our family and if I couldn't rebel it seemed as if I could at least hint at it.

The commercial he wanted me to write was for a tonic called Elixircol and was to be spoken on television by an actress who was neither young nor beautiful but who had an appearance of ready abandon and who was anyhow the mistress of one of the sponsor's uncles. *Are you growing old?* I wrote. *Are you falling out of love with your image in the looking glass? Does your face in the morning seem rucked and seamed with alcoholic and sexual excesses and does the rest of you appear to be a grayish-pink lump, covered all over with brindle hair? Walking in the autumn woods do you feel that a subtle distance has come between you and the smell of wood smoke? Have you drafted your obituary? Are you easily winded? Do you wear a girdle? Is your sense of smell fading, is your interest in gardening waning, is your fear of heights increasing, and are your sexual drives as ravening and intense as ever and does your wife look more and more to you like a stranger with sunken cheeks who has wandered into your bedroom by mistake? If this or any of this is true you need Elixircol, the true juice of youth. The small economy size (business with the bottle) costs seventy-five dollars and the giant family bottle comes at two hundred and fifty. It's a lot of scratch, God knows, but these are inflationary times and who can put a price on youth? If*

*you don't have the cash borrow it from your neighborhood loan
shark or hold up the local bank. The odds are three to one that with
a ten-cent water pistol and a slip of paper you can shake ten thousand out of any fainthearted teller. Everybody's doing it. (Music up
and out.)* I sent this in to MacPherson via Ralphie, the messenger boy, and took the 4:16 home, traveling through a
landscape of utter desolation.

Now, my journey is a digression and has no real connection to Justina's death but what followed could only have
happened in my country and in my time and since I was an
American traveling across an American landscape the trip
may be part of the sum. There are some Americans who,
although their fathers emigrated from the Old World three
centuries ago, never seem to have quite completed the voyage and I am one of these. I stand, figuratively, with one wet
foot on Plymouth Rock, looking with some delicacy, not
into a formidable and challenging wilderness but onto a
half-finished civilization embracing glass towers, oil derricks, suburban continents, and abandoned movie houses
and wondering why, in this most prosperous, equitable, and
accomplished world – where even the cleaning women
practice the Chopin preludes in their spare time – everyone
should seem to be disappointed.

At Proxmire Manor I was the only passenger to get off
the random, meandering, and profitless local that carried its
shabby lights off into the dusk like some game-legged
watchman or beadle making his appointed rounds. I went
around to the front of the station to wait for my wife and
to enjoy the traveler's fine sense of crisis. Above me on the
hill were my home and the homes of my friends, all lighted
and smelling of fragrant wood smoke like the temples in a

sacred grove, dedicated to monogamy, feckless childhood, and domestic bliss but so like a dream that I felt the lack of viscera with much more than poignance – the absence of that inner dynamism we respond to in some European landscapes. In short, I was disappointed. It was my country, my beloved country, and there have been mornings when I could have kissed the earth that covers its many provinces and states. There was a hint of bliss; romantic and domestic bliss. I seemed to hear the jinglebells of the sleigh that would carry me to Grandmother's house although in fact Grandmother spent the last years of her life working as a hostess on an ocean liner and was lost in the tragic sinking of the S.S. *Lorelei* and I was responding to a memory that I had not experienced. But the hill of light rose like an answer to some primitive dream of homecoming. On one of the highest lawns I saw the remains of a snowman who still smoked a pipe and wore a scarf and a cap but whose form was wasting away and whose anthracite eyes stared out at the view with terrifying bitterness. I sensed some disappointing greenness of spirit in the scene although I knew in my bones, no less, how like yesterday it was that my father left the Old World to found a new; and I thought of the forces that had brought stamina to the image: the cruel towns of Calabria and their cruel princes, the badlands northwest of Dublin, ghettos, despots, whorehouses, bread lines, the graves of children, intolerable hunger, corruption, persecution, and despair had generated these faint and mellow lights and wasn't it all a part of the great migration that is the life of man?

My wife's cheeks were wet with tears when I kissed her. She was distressed, of course, and really quite sad.

She had been attached to Justina. She drove me home, where Justina was still sitting on the sofa. I would like to spare you the unpleasant details but I will say that both her mouth and her eyes were wide open. I went into the pantry to telephone Dr Hunter. His line was busy. I poured myself a drink – the first since Sunday – and lighted a cigarette. When I called the doctor again he answered and I told him what had happened. 'Well, I'm awfully sorry to hear about it, Moses,' he said. 'I can't get over until after six and there isn't much that I can do. This sort of thing has come up before and I'll tell you all I know. You see, you live in Zone B – two-acre lots, no commercial enterprises and so forth. A couple of years ago some stranger bought the old Plewett mansion and it turned out that he was planning to operate it as a funeral home. We didn't have any zoning provision at the time that would protect us and one was rushed through the Village Council at midnight and they overdid it. It seems that you not only can't have a funeral home in Zone B – you can't bury anything there and you can't die there. Of course it's absurd, but we all make mistakes, don't we? Now there are two things you can do. I've had to deal with this before. You can take the old lady and put her into the car and drive her over to Chestnut Street, where Zone C begins. The boundary is just beyond the traffic light by the high school. As soon as you get her over to Zone C, it's all right. You can just say she died in the car. You can do that or if this seems distasteful you can call the Mayor and ask him to make an exception to the zoning laws. But I can't write you out a death certificate until you get her out of that neighborhood and of

159

course no undertaker will touch her until you get a death certificate.'

'I don't understand,' I said, and I didn't, but then the possibility that there was some truth in what he had just told me broke against me or over me like a wave, exciting mostly indignation. 'I've never heard such a lot of damned foolishness in my life,' I said. 'Do you mean to tell me that I can't die in one neighborhood and that I can't fall in love in another and that I can't eat ...'

'Listen. Calm down, Moses. I'm not telling you anything but the facts and I have a lot of patients waiting. I don't have the time to listen to you fulminate. If you want to move her, call me as soon as you get her over to the traffic light. Otherwise, I'd advise you to get in touch with the Mayor or someone on the Village Council.' He cut the connection. I was outraged but this did not change the fact that Justina was still sitting on the sofa. I poured a fresh drink and lit another cigarette.

Justina seemed to be waiting for me and to be changing from an inert into a demanding figure. I tried to imagine carrying her out to the station wagon but I couldn't complete the task in my imagination and I was sure that I couldn't complete it in fact. I then called the Mayor but this position in our village is mostly honorary and as I might have known he was in his New York law office and was not expected home until seven. I could cover her, I thought, that would be a decent thing to do, and I went up the back stairs to the linen closet and got a sheet. It was getting dark when I came back into the living room but this was no merciful twilight. Dusk seemed to be playing directly into her hands and she gained power and stature with the dark. I covered her with a sheet and turned on a lamp at the other end of the room but the rectitude of the place with its old furniture, flowers, paintings, etc., was demolished by her monumental shape. The next thing to worry about was the children, who would be home in a few minutes. Their knowledge of death, excepting their dreams and intuitions of which I know nothing, is zero and the bold figure in the parlor was bound to be traumatic. When I heard them coming up the walk I went out and told them what had happened and sent them up to their rooms. At seven I drove over to the Mayor's.

He had not come home but he was expected at any minute and I talked with his wife. She gave me a drink. By this time I was chainsmoking. When the Mayor came in we went into a little office or library, where he took up a position behind a desk, putting me in the low chair of a supplicant. 'Of course I sympathize with you, Moses,' he said, 'it's an awful thing to have happened, but the trouble is that we can't give you a zoning exception without a majority vote of the Village Council and all the members of the Council happen to be out of town. Pete's in California and Jack's in Paris and Larry won't be back from Stowe until the end of the week.'

I was sarcastic. 'Then I suppose Cousin Justina will have to gracefully decompose in my parlor until Jack comes back from Paris.'

'Oh no,' he said, 'oh *no*. Jack won't be back from Paris for another month but I think you might wait until Larry comes from Stowe. Then we'd have a majority, assuming of course that they would agree to your appeal.'

'For Christ's sake,' I snarled.

'Yes, yes,' he said, 'it is difficult, but after all you must realize that this is the world you live in and the importance of

161

zoning can't be overestimated. Why, if a single member of the Council could give out zoning exceptions, I could give you permission right now to open a saloon in your garage, put up neon lights, hire an orchestra, and destroy the neighborhood and all the human and commercial values we've worked so hard to protect.'

'I don't want to open a saloon in my garage,' I howled. 'I don't want to hire an orchestra. I just want to bury Justina.'

'I know, Moses, I know,' he said. 'I understand that. But it's just that it happened in the wrong zone and if I make an exception for you I'll have to make an exception for everyone and this kind of morbidity, when it gets out of hand, can be very depressing. People don't like to live in a neighborhood where this sort of thing goes on all the time.'

'Listen to me,' I said. 'You give me an exception and you give it to me now or I'm going home and dig a hole in my garden and bury Justina myself.'

'But you can't do that, Moses. You can't bury anything in Zone B. You can't even bury a cat.'

'You're mistaken,' I said. 'I can and I will. I can't function as a doctor and I can't function as an undertaker, but I can dig a hole in the ground and if you don't give me my exception, that's what I'm going to do.'

'Come back, Moses, come back,' he said. 'Please come back. Look, I'll give you an exception if you'll promise not to tell anyone. It's breaking the law, it's a forgery but I'll do it if you promise to keep it a secret.'

I promised to keep it a secret, he gave me the documents, and I used his telephone to make the arrangements. Justina was removed a few minutes after I got home but that night I had the strangest dream. I dreamed that I was in a crowded supermarket. It must have been night because the windows were dark. The ceiling was paved with fluorescent light – brilliant, cheerful but, considering our prehistoric memories, a harsh link in the chain of light that binds us to the past. Music was playing and there must have been at least a thousand shoppers pushing their wagons among the long corridors of comestibles and victuals. Now is there – or isn't there – something about the posture we assume when we push a wagon that unsexes us? Can it be done with gallantry? I bring this up because the multitude of shoppers seemed that evening, as they pushed their wagons, penitential and unsexed. There were all kinds, this being my beloved country. There were Italians, Finns, Jews, Negroes, Shropshiremen, Cubans – anyone who had heeded the voice of liberty – and they were dressed with that sumptuary abandon that European caricaturists record with such bitter disgust. Yes, there were grandmothers in shorts, big-butted women in knitted pants, and men wearing such an assortment of clothing that it looked as if they had dressed hurriedly in a burning building. But this, as I say, is my own country and in my opinion the caricaturist who vilifies the old lady in shorts vilifies himself. I am a native and I was wearing buckskin jump boots, chino pants cut so tight that my sexual organs were discernible, and a rayon-acetate pajama top printed with representations of the *Pinta*, the *Niña*, and the *Santa Maria* in full sail. The scene was strange – the strangeness of a dream where we see familiar objects in an unfamiliar light – but as I looked more closely I saw that there were some irregularities. Nothing was labeled. Nothing was identified or known. The cans and boxes were all bare. The frozen-food bins were full of brown parcels but they were such odd shapes that you couldn't tell if they contained a frozen turkey or a Chinese dinner. All the goods at the vegetable and the bakery counters were concealed in brown bags and even the books for sale had no titles. In spite of the fact that the contents of nothing was known, my companions of the dream – my thousands of bizarrely dressed compatriots – were deliberating gravely over these mysterious containers as if the choices they made were critical. Like any dreamer, I was omniscient, I was with them and I was withdrawn, and stepping above the scene for a minute I noticed the men at the check-out counters. They were brutes. Now, sometimes in a crowd, in a bar or a street, you will see a face so full-blown in its obdurate resistance to the appeals of love, reason, and decency, so lewd, so brutish and unregenerate, that you turn away. Men like these were stationed at the only way out and as the shoppers approached them they tore their packages open – I still couldn't see what they contained – but in every case the customer, at the sight of what he had chosen, showed all the symptoms of the deepest guilt; that force that brings us to our knees. Once their choice had been opened to their shame they were pushed – in some cases kicked – toward the door and beyond the door I saw dark water and heard a terrible noise of moaning and crying in the air. They waited at the door in groups to be taken away in some conveyance that I couldn't see. As I watched, thousands and thousands pushed their wagons through the market, made their careful and mysterious choices, and were reviled and taken away. What could be the meaning of this?

★

We buried Justina in the rain the next afternoon. The dead are not, God knows, a minority, but in Proxmire Manor their unexalted kingdom is on the outskirts, rather like a dump, where they are transported furtively as knaves and scoundrels and where they lie in an atmosphere of perfect neglect. Justina's life had been exemplary, but by ending it she seemed to have disgraced us all. The priest was a friend and a cheerful sight, but the undertaker and his helpers, hiding behind their limousines, were not; and aren't they at the root of most of our troubles, with their claim that death is a violet-flavored kiss? How can a people who do not mean to understand death hope to understand love, and who will sound the alarm?

I went from the cemetery back to my office. The commercial was on my desk and MacPherson had written across it in grease pencil: *Very funny, you broken-down bore. Do again.* I was tired but unrepentant and didn't seem able to force myself into a practical posture of usefulness and obedience. I did another commercial. *Don't lose your loved ones,* I wrote, *because of excessive radioactivity. Don't be a wall-flower at the dance because of strontium 90 in your bones. Don't be a victim of fallout. When the tart on Thirty-sixth Street gives you the big eye does your body stride off in one direction and your imagination in another? Does your mind follow her up the stairs and taste her wares in revolting detail while your flesh goes off to Brooks Brothers or the foreign exchange desk of the Chase Manhattan Bank? Haven't you noticed the size of the ferns, the lushness of the grass, the bitterness of the string beans, and the brilliant markings on the new breeds of butterflies? You have been inhaling lethal atomic waste for the last twenty-five years and only Elixircol can save you.* I gave this to Ralphie and waited perhaps ten minutes, when it was returned, marked again with grease pencil. *Do,* he wrote, *or you'll be dead.* I felt very tired. I put another piece of paper into the machine and wrote: *The Lord is my shepherd; therefore can I lack nothing. He shall feed me in a green pasture and lead me forth beside the waters of comfort. He shall convert my soul and bring me forth in the paths of righteousness for his Name's sake. Yea, though I walk through the valley of the shadow of death I will fear no evil for thou art with me; thy rod and thy staff comfort me. Thou shalt prepare a table before me in the presence of them that trouble me; thou hast anointed my head with oil and my cup shall be full. Surely thy loving-kindness and mercy shall follow me all the days of my life and I will dwell in the house of the Lord for ever.* I gave this to Ralphie and went home.

A Miscellany of Characters
That Will Not Appear

1. THE PRETTY GIRL at the Princeton—Dartmouth Rugby game. She wandered up and down behind the crowd that was ranged along the foul line. She seemed to have no date, no particular companion but to be known to everyone. Everyone called her name (Florrie), everyone was happy to see her, and, as she stopped to speak with friends, one man put his hand flat on the small of her back, and at this touch (in spite of the fine weather and the green of the playing field) a dark and thoughtful look came over his face, as if he felt immortal longings. Her hair was a fine dark gold, and she pulled a curl down over her eyes and peered through it. Her nose was a little too quick, but the effect was sensual and aristocratic, her arms and legs were round and fine but not at all womanly, and she squinted her violet eyes. It was the first half, there was no score, and Dartmouth kicked the ball offside. It was a muffed kick, and it went directly into her arms. The catch was graceful; she seemed to have been chosen to receive the ball and stood there for a second, smiling, bowing, observed by everyone, before she tossed it charmingly and clumsily back into play. There was some applause. Then everyone turned their attention from Florrie back to the field, and a second later she dropped to her

knees, covering her face with her hands, recoiling violently from the excitement. She seemed very shy. Someone opened a can of beer and passed it to her, and she stood and wandered again along the foul line and out of the pages of my novel because I never saw her again.

2. All parts for Marlon Brando.

3. All scornful descriptions of American landscapes with ruined tenements, automobile dumps, polluted rivers, jerry-built ranch houses, abandoned miniature golf links, cinder deserts, ugly hoardings, unsightly oil derricks, diseased elm trees, eroded farmlands, gaudy and fanciful gas stations, unclean motels, candlelit tearooms, and streams paved with beer cans, for these are not, as they might seem to be, the ruins of our civilization but are the temporary encampments and outposts of the civilization that we – you and I – shall build.

4. All such scenes as the following: 'Clarissa stepped into the room and then _____,' Out with this and all other explicit descriptions of sexual commerce, for how can we describe the most exalted experience of our physical lives, as if – jack, wrench, hubcap, and nuts – we were describing the changing of a flat tire?

5. All lushes. For example: The curtain rises on the copy office of a Madison Avenue advertising agency, where X, our principal character, is working out the exploitation plans for a new brand of rye whiskey. On a drafting table to the right of his fruitwood desk is a pile of suggestions from the art department. Monarchal and baronial crests and escutcheons have been suggested for the label. For advertising there is a suggested scene of plantation life where the long-gone cotton aristocracy drink whiskey on a magnificent porch. X

is not satisfied with this and examines next a watercolor of pioneer America. How fresh, cold, and musical is the stream that pours through the forest. The tongues of the brook speak into the melancholy silence of a lost wilderness, and what is that in the corner of the blue sky but a flight of carrier pigeons. On a rock in the foreground a wiry young man, in rude leather clothing and a coonskin hat, is drinking rye from a stone jug. This prospect seems to sadden X, and he goes on to the next suggestion, which is that one entertain with rye; that one invite to one's house one exploded literary celebrity, one unemployed actress, the grandniece of a President of the United States, one broken-down bore, and one sullen and wicked literary critic. They stand grouped around an enormous bottle of rye. This picture disgusts X, and he goes on to the last, where a fair young couple in evening dress stand at dusk on a medieval battlement (aren't those the lights and towers of Siena in the distance?) toasting what must be a seduction of indescribable prowess and duration in the rye that is easy on your dollar.

X is not satisfied. He turns away from the drafting table and walks toward his desk. He is a slender man of indiscernible age, although time seems to have seized upon his eye sockets and the scruff of his neck. This last is seamed and scored as wildly as some disjointed geodetic survey. There is a cut as deep as a saber scar running diagonally from the left to the right of his neck with so many deep and numerous branches and tributaries that the effect is discouraging. But it is in his eyes that the recoil of time is most noticeable. Here we see, as on a sandy point we see the working of two tides, how the powers of his exaltation and his misery, his lusts and his aspirations, have stamped a wilderness of wrinkles onto the dark and pouchy skin. He may have tired his eyes looking at Vega through a telescope or reading Keats by a dim light, but his gaze seems hangdog and impure. These details would lead you to believe that he was a man of some age, but suddenly he drops his left shoulder very gracefully and shoots the cuff of his silk shirt as if he were eighteen – nineteen at the most. He glances at his Italian calendar watch. It is ten in the morning. His office is soundproofed and preternaturally still. The voice of the city comes faintly to his high window. He stares at his dispatch case, darkened by the rains of England, France, Italy, and Spain. He is in the throes of a gruelling melancholy that makes the painted walls of his office (pale yellow and pale blue) seem like fabrications of paper put up to conceal the volcanos and floodwaters that are the terms of his misery. He seems to be approaching the moment of his death, the moment of his conception, some critical point in time. His head, his shoulders, and his hands begin to tremble. He opens his dispatch case, takes out a bottle of rye, gets to his knees, and thirstily empties the bottle.

He is on the skids, of course, and we will bother with only one more scene. After having been fired from the office where we last saw him he is offered a job in Cleveland, where the rumors of his weakness seem not to have reached. He has gone to Cleveland to settle the arrangements and rent a house for his family. Now they are waiting at the railroad station for him to return with good news. His pretty wife, his three children, and the two dogs have all come down to welcome Daddy. It is dusk in the suburb where they live. They are, by this time, a family that have received more than their share of discouragements, but in having been recently denied the common promises and rewards of their way of life – the new car and the new bicycle – they have discovered a melancholy but steady quality of affection that has nothing to do with acquisitions. They have glimpsed, in their troubled love for Daddy, the thrill of a destiny. The local rattles into view. A soft spray of golden sparks falls from the brake box as the train slows and halts. They all feel, in the intensity of their anticipation, nearly incorporeal. Seven men and two women leave the train, but where is Daddy? It takes two conductors to get him down the stairs. He has lost his hat, his necktie, and his topcoat, and someone has blacked his right eye. He still holds the dispatch case under one arm. No one speaks, no one weeps as they get him into the car and drive him out of our sight, out of our jurisdiction and concern. Out they go, male and female, all the lushes; they throw so little true light on the way we live.

6. And while we are about it, out go all those homosexuals who have taken such a dominating position in recent fiction. Isn't it time that we embraced the indiscretion and inconstancy of the flesh and moved on? The scene this time is Hewitt's Beach on the afternoon of the Fourth of July. Mrs Ditmar, the wife of the Governor, and her son Randall have carried their picnic lunch up the beach to a deserted cove, although the American flag on the clubhouse can be seen flying beyond the dunes. The boy is sixteen, well formed, his skin the fine gold of youth, and he seems to his lonely mother so beautiful that she admires him with trepidation. For the last ten years her husband, the Governor, has neglected her in favor of his intelligent and pretty executive secretary. Mrs Ditmar has absorbed, with the extraordinary

commodiousness of human nature, a nearly daily score of wounds. Of course she loves her son. She finds nothing of her husband in his appearance. He has the best qualities of *her* family, she thinks, and she is old enough to think that such things as a slender foot and fine hair are marks of breeding, as indeed they may be. His shoulders are square. His body is compact. As he throws a stone into the sea, it is not the force with which he throws the stone that absorbs her but the fine grace with which his arm completes the circular motion once the stone has left his hand – as if every gesture he made were linked, one to the other. Like any lover, she is immoderate and does not want the afternoon with him to end. She does not dare wish for an eternity, but she wishes the day had more hours than is possible. She fingers her pearls in her worn hands, and admires their sea lights, and wonders how they would look against his golden skin.

He is a little bored. He would rather be with men and girls his own age, but his mother has supported him and defended him so he finds some security in her company. She has been a staunch and formidable protector. She can and has intimidated the headmaster and most of the teachers at his school. Offshore he sees the sails of the racing fleet and wishes briefly that he were with them, but he refused an invitation to crew and has not enough self-confidence to skipper, so in a sense he chose to be alone on the beach with his mother. He is timid about competitive sports, about the whole appearance of organized society, as if it concealed a force that might tear him to pieces; but why is this? Is he a coward, and is there such a thing? Is one born a coward, as one is born dark or fair? Is his mother's surveillance excessive; has she gone so far in protecting him that he has become vulnerable and morbid? But considering how intimately he knows the depth of her unhappiness, how can he forsake her until she has found other friends?

He thinks of his father with pain. He has tried to know and love his father, but all their plans come to nothing. The fishing trip was canceled by the unexpected arrival of the Governor of Massachusetts. At the ball park a messenger brought him a note saying that his father would be unable to come. When he fell out of the pear tree and broke his arm, his father would undoubtedly have visited him in the hospital had he not been in Washington. He learned to cast with a fly rod, feeling that, cast by cast, he might work his way into the terrain of his father's affection and esteem, but his father had never found time to admire him. He can grasp the power of his own disappointment. This emotion surrounds him like a mass of energy, but an energy that has no wheels to drive, no stones to move. These sad thoughts can be seen in his posture. His shoulders droop. He looks childish and forlorn, and his mother calls him to her.

He sits in the sand at her feet, and she runs her fingers through his light hair. Then she does something hideous. One wants to look away but not before we have seen her undo her pearls and fasten them around his golden neck. 'See how they shine,' says she, doing the clasp as irrevocably as the manacle is welded to the prisoner's shin.

Out they go; out they go; for, like Clarissa and the lush, they shed too little light.

7. In closing – in closing, that is, for this afternoon (I have to go to the dentist and then have my hair cut), I would like to consider the career of my laconic old friend

Royden Blake. We can, for reasons of convenience, divide his work into four periods. First there were the bitter moral anecdotes – he must have written a hundred – that proved that most of our deeds are sinful. This was followed, as you will remember, by nearly a decade of snobbism, in which he never wrote of characters who had less than sixty-five thousand dollars a year. He memorized the names of the Groton faculty and the bartenders at '21'. All of his characters were waited on hand and foot by punctilious servants, but when you went to his house for dinner you found the chairs held together with picture wire, you ate fried eggs from a cracked plate, the doorknobs came off in your hand, and if you wanted to flush the toilet you had to lift the lid off the water tank, roll up a sleeve, and reach deep into the cold and rusty water to manipulate the valves. When he had finished with snobbism, he made the error I have mentioned in Item 4 and then moved on into his romantic period, where he wrote 'The Necklace of Malvio d'Alfi' (with that memorable scene of childbirth on a mountain pass), 'The Wreck of the S.S. *Lorelei*,' 'The King of the Trojans,' and 'The Lost Girdle of Venus,' to name only a few. He was quite sick at the time, and his incompetence seemed to be increasing. His work was characterized by everything that I have mentioned. In his pages one found alcoholics, scarifying descriptions of the American landscape, and fat parts for Marlon Brando. You might say that he had lost the gift of evoking the perfumes of life: sea water, the smoke of burning hemlock, and the breasts of women. He had damaged, you might say, the ear's innermost chamber, where we hear the heavy noise of the dragon's tail moving over the dead leaves. I never liked him, but he was a colleague and a drinking companion, and when I heard, in my home in Kitzbühel, that he was dying, I drove to Innsbruck and took the express to Venice, where he then lived. It was in the late autumn. Cold and brilliant. The boarded-up palaces of the Grand Canal — gaunt, bedizened, and crowned — looked like the haggard faces of that grade of nobility that shows up for the royal weddings in Hesse. He was living in a *pensione* on a back canal. There was a high tide, the reception hall was flooded, and I got to the staircase over an arrangement of duckboards. I brought him a bottle of Turinese gin and a package of Austrian cigarettes, but he was too far gone for these, I saw when I sat down in a painted chair (broken) beside his bed. 'I'm working,' he exclaimed. 'I'm working. I can see it all. Listen to me!'

'Yes,' I said.

'It begins like this,' he said, and changed the level of his voice to correspond, I suppose, to the gravity of his narrative. 'The Transalpini stops at Kirchbach at midnight,' he said, looking in my direction to make sure that I had received the full impact of this poetic fact.

'Yes,' I said.

'Here the passengers for Vienna continue on,' he said sonorously, 'while those for Padua must wait an hour. The station is kept open and heated for their convenience, and there is a bar where one may buy coffee and wine. One snowy night in March, three strangers at this bar fell into a conversation. The first was a tall, bald-headed man, wearing a sable-lined coat that reached to his ankles. The second was a beautiful American woman going to Isvia to attend funeral services for her only son, who had been killed in a mountain-climbing accident. The third was a white-haired, heavy Italian woman in a black shawl, who was treated with great deference by the waiter. He bowed from the waist when he poured her a glass of cheap wine, and addressed her as "Your Majesty." Avalanche warnings had been posted earlier in the day ...' Then he put his head back on the pillow and died – indeed, these were his dying words, and the dying words, it seemed to me, of generations of storytellers, for how could this snowy and trumped-up pass, with its trio of travelers, hope to celebrate a world that lies spread out around us like a bewildering and stupendous dream?

The Brigadier and
the Golf Widow

I WOULD NOT want to be one of those writers who begin each morning by exclaiming, 'O Gogol, O Chekhov, O Thackeray and Dickens, what would you have made of a bomb shelter ornamented with four plaster-of-Paris ducks, a birdbath, and three composition gnomes with long beards and red mobcaps?' As I say, I wouldn't want to begin a day like this, but I often wonder what the dead would have done. But the shelter is as much a part of my landscape as the beech and horse-chestnut trees that grow on the ridge. I can see it from this window where I write. It was built by the Pasterns, and stands on the acre of ground that adjoins our property. It bulks under a veil of thin, new grass, like some embarrassing fact of physicalness, and I think Mrs Pastern set out the statuary to soften its meaning. It would have been like her. She was a pale woman. Sitting on her terrace, sitting in her parlor, sitting anywhere, she ground an ax of self-esteem. Offer her a cup of tea and she would say, 'Why, these cups look just like a set I gave to the Salvation Army last year.' Show her the new swimming pool and she would say, slapping her ankle, 'I suppose this must be where you breed your gigantic mosquitoes.' Hand her a chair and she would say, 'Why, it's a nice imitation of those Queen

Anne chairs I inherited from Grandmother Delaney.' These trumps were more touching than they were anything else, and seemed to imply that the nights were long, her children ungrateful, and her marriage bewilderingly threadbare. Twenty years ago, she would have been known as a golf widow, and the sum of her manner was perhaps one of bereavement. She usually wore weeds, and a stranger watching her board a train might have guessed that Mr Pastern was dead, but Mr Pastern was far from dead. He was marching up and down the locker room of the Grassy Brae Golf Club shouting, 'Bomb Cuba! Bomb Berlin! Let's throw a little nuclear hardware at them and show them who's boss.' He was brigadier of the club's locker-room light infantry, and at one time or another declared war on Russia, Czechoslovakia, Yugoslavia, and China.

It all began on an autumn afternoon – and who, after all these centuries, can describe the fineness of an autumn day? One might pretend never to have seen one before, or, to more purpose, that there would never be another like it. The clear and searching sweep of sun on the lawns was like a climax of the year's lights. Leaves were burning somewhere and the smoke smelled, for all its ammoniac acidity, of beginnings. The boundless blue air was stretched over the zenith like the skin of a drum. Leaving her house one late afternoon, Mrs Pastern stopped to admire the October light. It was the day to canvass for infectious hepatitis. Mrs Pastern had been given sixteen names, a bundle of literature, and a printed book of receipts. It was her work to go among her neighbors and collect their checks. Her house stood on a rise of ground, and before she got into her car she looked at the houses below.

Charity as she knew it was complex and reciprocal, and almost every roof she saw signified charity. Mrs Balcolm worked for the brain. Mrs Ten Eyke did mental health. Mrs Trenchard worked for the blind. Mrs Horowitz was in charge of diseases of the nose and throat. Mrs Trempler was tuberculosis, Mrs Surcliffe was Mothers' March of Dimes, Mrs Craven was cancer, and Mrs Gilkson did the kidney. Mrs Hewlitt led the birth-control league, Mrs Ryerson was arthritis, and way in the distance could be seen the slate roof of Ethel Littleton's house, a roof that signified gout.

Mrs Pastern undertook the work of going from house to house with the thoughtless resignation of an honest and traditional laborer. It was her destiny; it was her life. Her mother had done it before her, and even her old grand-mother had collected money for smallpox and unwed mothers. Mrs Pastern had telephoned most of her neigh-bors in advance, and most of them were ready for her. She experienced none of the suspense of some poor stranger selling encyclopedias. Here and there she stayed to visit and drink a glass of sherry. The contributions were ahead of what she had got the previous year, and while the money, of course, was not hers, it excited her to stuff her kit with big checks. She stopped at the Surcliffes' after dusk, and had a Scotch and soda. She stayed too late, and when she left it was dark and time to go home and cook supper for her husband. 'I got a hundred and sixty dollars for the hepatitis fund,' she said excitedly when he walked in. 'I did every-body on my list but the Blevins and the Flannagans. I want to get my kit in tomorrow morning – would you mind doing them while I cook the dinner?' 'But I don't know the

Flannagans,' Charlie Pastern said. 'Nobody does, but they gave me ten last year.'

He was tired, he had his business worries, and the sight of his wife arranging pork chops in the broiler only seemed like an extension of a boring day. He was happy enough to take the convertible and race up the hill to the Blevins', thinking that they might give him a drink. But the Blevins were away; their maid gave him an envelope with a check in it and shut the door. Turning in at the Flannagans' drive-way, he tried to remember if he had ever met them. The name encouraged him, because he always felt that he could *handle* the Irish. There was a glass pane in the front door, and through this he could see into a hallway where a plump woman with red hair was arranging flowers.

'Infectious hepatitis,' he shouted heartily.

She took a good look at herself in the mirror before she turned and, walking with very small steps, started toward the door. 'Oh, please come in,' she said. The girlish voice was nearly a whisper. She was not a girl, he could see. Her hair was dyed, and her bloom was fading, and she must have been crowding forty, but she seemed to be one of those women who cling to the manners and graces of a pretty child of eight. 'Your wife just called,' she said, separating one word from another, exactly like a child. 'And I am not sure that I have any cash – any *money*, that is – but if you will wait just a minute I will write you out a check if I can find my checkbook. Won't you step into the living room, where it's cozier?'

A fire had just been lighted, he saw, and things had been set out for drinks, and, like any stray, his response to these comforts was instantaneous. Where was *Mr* Flannagan? he wondered. Traveling home on a late train? Changing his clothes upstairs? Taking a shower? At the end of the room there was a desk heaped with papers, and she began to riffle these, making sighs and noises of girlish exasperation. 'I am terribly sorry to keep you waiting,' she said, 'but won't you make yourself a little drink while you wait? Everything's on the table.'

'What train does Mr Flannagan come out on?'

'Mr Flannagan is away,' she said. Her voice dropped. 'Mr Flannagan has been away for six weeks. ...

'I'll have a drink, then, if you'll have one with me.'

'If you will promise to make it weak.'

'Sit down,' he said, 'and enjoy your drink and look for your checkbook later. The only way to find things is to relax.'

All in all, they had six drinks. She described herself and her circumstances unhesitatingly. Mr Flannagan manufactured plastic tongue depressors. He traveled all over the world. She didn't like to travel. Planes made her feel faint, and in Tokyo, where she had gone that summer, she had been given raw fish for breakfast and so she had come straight home. She and her husband had formerly lived in New York, where she had many friends, but Mr Flannagan thought the country would be safer in case of war. She would rather live in danger than die of loneliness and boredom. She had no children; she had made no friends. 'I've seen you, though, before,' she said with enormous coyness, patting his knee. 'I've seen you walking your dogs on Sunday and driving by in the convertible ... .'

The thought of this lonely woman sitting at her window touched him, although he was even more touched by her plumpness. Sheer plumpness, he knew, is not a vital part of the body and has no procreative functions. It serves merely as an excess cushion for the rest of the carcass. And knowing its humble place in the scale of things, why did he, at this time of life, seem almost ready to sell his soul for plumpness? The remarks she made about the sufferings of a lonely woman seemed so broad at first that he didn't know what to make of them, but after the sixth drink he put his arm around her and suggested that they go upstairs and look for her checkbook there.

'I've never done this before,' she said later, when he was arranging himself to leave. Her voice shook with feeling, and he thought it lovely. He didn't doubt her truthfulness, although he had heard the words a hundred times. 'I've never done this before,' they always said, shaking their dresses down over their white shoulders. 'I've never done this before,' they always said, waiting for the elevator in the hotel corridor. 'I've never done this before,' they always said, pouring another whiskey. 'I've never done this before,' they always said, putting on their stockings. On ships at sea, on railroad trains, in summer hotels with mountain views, they always said. 'I've never done this before.'

'Where have you been?' Mrs Pastern asked sadly, when he came in. 'It's after eleven.'

'I had a drink with the Flannagans.'

'She told me he was in Germany.'

'He came home unexpectedly.'

Charlie ate some supper in the kitchen and went into the TV room to hear the news. 'Bomb them!' he shouted. 'Throw a little nuclear hardware at them! Show them who's boss!' But in bed he had trouble sleeping. He thought first of his son and daughter, away at college. He loved them. It was the only meaning of the word that he had ever known. Then he played nine imaginary holes of golf, choosing his handicap, his irons, his stance, his opponents, and his weather in detail, but the green of the links seemed faded in the light of his business worries. His money was tied up in a Nassau hotel, an Ohio pottery works, and a detergent for window washing, and luck had been running against him. His worries harried him up out of bed, and he lighted a cigarette and went to the window. In the starlight he could see the trees stripped of their leaves. During the summer he had tried to repair some of his losses at the track, and the bare trees reminded him that his pari-mutuel tickets would still be lying, like leaves, in the gutters near Belmont and Saratoga. Maple and ash, beech and elm, one hundred to win on Three in the fourth, fifty to win on Six in the third, one hundred to win on Two in the eighth. Children walking home from school would scuff through what seemed to be his foliage. Then, getting back into bed, he thought unashamedly of Mrs Flannagan, planning where they would next meet and what they would do. There are, he thought, so few true means of forgetfulness in this life that why should he shun the medicine even when the medicine seemed, as it did, a little crude?

A new conquest always had a wonderful effect on Charlie. He became overnight generous, understanding, inexhaustibly good-humored, relaxed, kind to cats, dogs, and strangers, expansive, and compassionate. There was, of course, the reproachful figure of Mrs Pastern waiting for him in the evenings, but he had served her well, he thought, for twenty-five years, and if he were to touch her tenderly these days she would likely say, 'Ouch. That's where I bruised myself in the garden.' On the evenings that they spent together, she seemed to choose to display the roughest angles of her personality; to grind her ax. 'You know,' she said, 'Mary Quested cheats at cards.' Her remarks fell a good deal short of where he sat. If these were indirect expressions of disappointment, it was a disappointment that no longer touched him.

He met Mrs Flannagan for lunch in the city, and they spent the afternoon together. Leaving the hotel, Mrs Flannagan stopped at a display of perfume. She said that she liked perfume, worked her shoulders, and called him 'Monkey.' Considering her girlishness and her claims to fidelity, there was, he thought, a distinct atmosphere of practice about her request, but he bought her a bottle of perfume. The second time they met, she admired a peignoir in a store window and he bought this. On their third meeting, she got a silk umbrella. Waiting for her in the restaurant for their fourth meeting, he hoped that she wasn't going to ask for jewelry, because his reserves of cash were low. She had promised to meet him at one, and he basked in his circumstances and the smells of sauce, gin, and red floor carpets. She was always late, and at half past one he ordered a second drink. At a quarter to two, he saw his waiter whispering to another waiter – whispering, laughing, and nodding his head in Charlie's direction. It was his first intimation of the chance that she might stand him up. But who was she – who did she think she was that she could do this to him? She was nothing but a lonely housewife; she was nothing but that. At two, he ordered his lunch. He was crushed. What had his emotional life been these last years but a series of sometimes shabby one-night stands, but without them his life would be unendurable.

There is something universal about being stood up in a city restaurant between one and two – a spiritual no-man's-land, whose blasted trees, entrenchments, and ratholes we all share, disarmed by the gullibility of our hearts. The waiter knew, and the laughter and lighthearted conversations at the tables around Charlie honed his feelings. He seemed to be helplessly elevated on his disappointment like a flagpole sitter, his aloneness looming larger and larger in the crowded room. Then he saw his own swollen image in a mirror, his gray hair clinging to his pate like the remains of a romantic landscape, his heavy body shaped a little like a firehouse Santa Claus, the paunch enlarged by one or two of Mrs Kelly's second-best sofa cushions. He pushed his table away and started for a telephone booth in the hall.

'Is there anything wrong with your lunch, monsieur?' the waiter asked.

She answered the phone, and in her most girlish voice said, 'We cannot go on like this. I have thought it over, and we cannot go on. It is not because I do not want to, because you are a very virile man, but my conscience will not let me.'

'Can I stop by tonight and talk it over?'

'Well ...' she said.

'I'll come straight up from the station.'

'If you'll do me a favor.'

'What?'

'I will tell you when I see you tonight. But please park your car behind the house and come in the back door. I do not want to give these old gossips here anything to talk about. You must remember that I have never done this before.'

Of course she was right, he thought. She had her self-esteem to maintain. Her pride, he thought, was so childish, so sterling! Sometimes, driving through a New Hampshire mill town late in the day, he thought, you will see in some alley or driveway, down by the river, a child dressed in a tablecloth, sitting on a broken stool, waving her scepter over a kingdom of weeds and cinders and a few skinny chickens. It is the purity and the irony of their pride that touches one; and he felt that way about Mrs Flannagan.

She let him in at the back door that night, but in the living room the scene was the same. The fire was burning, she made him a drink, and in her company he felt as if he had just worked his shoulders free of a heavy pack. But she was coy, in and out of his arms, tickling him and then tripping across the room to look at herself in the mirror. 'I want my favor first,' she said.

'What is it?'

'Guess.'

'I can't give you money. I'm not rich, you know.'

'Oh, I wouldn't think of taking money.' She was indignant.

'Then what is it?'

'Something you wear.'

'But my watch is worthless, my cuff links are brass.'

'Something else.'

'But what?'

'I won't tell you unless you promise to give it to me.'

186

He pushed her away from him then, knowing that he could easily be made a fool of. 'I can't make a promise unless I know what it is you want.'

'It's something very small.'

'How small?'

'Tiny. Weeny.'

'Please tell me what it is.' Then he seized her in his arms, and this was the moment he felt most like himself: solemn, virile, wise, and imperturbable.

'I won't tell you unless you promise.'

'But I can't promise.'

'Then go away,' she said. 'Go away and never, never, come back.'

She was too childish to give the command much force, and yet it was not wasted on him. Could he go back to his own house, empty but for his wife, who would be grinding her ax? Go there and wait until time and chance turned up another friend?

'Please tell me.'

'Promise.'

'I promise.'

'I want,' she said, 'a key to your bomb shelter.'

The demand struck at him like a sledge-hammer blow, and suddenly he felt in all his parts the enormous weight of chagrin. All his gentle speculations on her person – the mill-town girl ruling her chickens – backfired bitterly. This must have been on her mind from the beginning, when she first lit the fire, lost her checkbook, and gave him a drink. The demand abraded his lust, but only for a moment, for now she was back in his arms, marching her fingers up and down his rib cage, saying, 'Creepy, creepy, creepy mouse, come to live in Charlie's house.' His need for her was crippling; it seemed like a cruel blow at the back of his knees. And yet in some chamber of his thick head he could see the foolishness and the obsolescence of his hankering skin. But how could he reform his bone and muscle to suit this new world; instruct his meandering and greedy flesh in politics, geography, holocausts, and cataclysms? Her front was round, fragrant, and soft, and he took the key off its ring – a piece of metal one and one-half inches long, warmed by the warmth of his hands, a genuine talisman of salvation, a defense against the end of the world – and dropped it into the neck of her dress.

The Pasterns' bomb shelter had been completed that spring. They would have liked to keep it a secret; would have liked at least to softpedal its existence; but the trucks and bulldozers going in and out of their driveway had informed everyone. It had cost thirty-two thousand dollars, and it had two chemical toilets, an oxygen supply, and a library, compiled by a Columbia professor, consisting of books meant to inspire hopefulness, humor, and tranquillity. There were stores of survival food to last three months, and several cases of hard liquor. Mrs Pastern had bought the plaster-of-Paris ducks, the birdbath, and the gnomes in an attempt to give the lump in her garden a look of innocence; to make it acceptable – at least to herself. For, bulking as it did in so pretty and domestic a scene and signifying as it must the death of at least half the world's population, she had found it, with its grassy cover, impossible to reconcile with the blue sky and the white clouds. She liked to keep the curtains drawn at that side of the house, and they were drawn the next afternoon, when she served gin to the bishop.

The bishop had come unexpectedly. Her minister had telephoned and said that the bishop was in the neighborhood and would like to thank her for her services to the church, and could he bring the bishop over now? She threw together some things for tea, changed her dress, and came down into the hall just as they rang the bell.

'How do you do, Your Grace,' she said. 'Won't you come in, Your Grace? Would you like some tea, Your Grace – or would you sooner have a drink, Your Grace?'

'I would like a Martini,' said the bishop.

He had the gift of a clear and carrying voice. He was a well-built man, with hair as black as dye, firm and sallow skin deeply creased around a wide mouth, and eyes as glittering and haggard, she thought, as someone drugged. 'If you'll excuse me, Your Grace ...'

This request for a cocktail confused her; Charlie always mixed the drinks. She dropped ice on the pantry floor, poured a pint or so of gin into the shaker, and tried to correct what appeared to her to be a lethal drink with more vermouth.

'Mr Ludgate here has been telling me how indispensable you are to the life of the parish,' the bishop said, taking his drink.

'I do try,' said Mrs Pastern.

'You have two children.'

'Yes. Sally's at Smith. Carkie's at Colgate. The house seems so empty now. They were confirmed by the old bishop. Bishop Tomlinson.'

'Ah, yes,' the bishop said. 'Oh, yes.'

The presence of the bishop made her nervous. She wished she could give the call a more natural air; she wished

189

at least to make her presence in her own parlor seem real. She was suffering from an intense discomfort that sometimes attacked her during committee meetings, when the parliamentary atmosphere had a disintegrating effect on her personality. She would, sitting in her folding chair, seem to go around the room on her hands and knees, gathering the fragments of herself and cementing them together with some virtue, such as, I am a Good Mother, or, I am a Patient Wife.

'Are you two old friends?' she asked the bishop.

'No!' the bishop exclaimed.

'The bishop was just driving through,' the minister said weakly.

'Could I see your garden?' the bishop asked.

Taking his Martini glass with him, he followed her out the side door onto the terrace. Mrs Pastern was an ardent gardener, but the scene was disappointing. The abundant cycle of bloom was nearly over; there was nothing to see but chrysanthemums. 'I wish you could see it in the spring, especially in the *late* spring,' she said. 'The star magnolia is the first to bloom. Then we have the flowering cherries and plums. Just as they finish, we have the azalea, the laurel, and the hybrid rhododendron. I have bronze tulips under the wisteria. The lilac is white.'

'I see that you have a shelter,' the bishop said.

'Yes.' She had been betrayed by her ducks and gnomes. 'Yes, we have, but it's really nothing to see. This bed is all lily of the valley, all this bed. I feel that roses make a better cutting than an ornamental garden, so I keep the roses behind the house. The border is *fraises des bois*. So sweet, so winy.'

'Have you had the shelter long?'.

'We had it built in the spring,' said Mrs Pastern. 'That hedge is flowering quince. Over there is our little salad garden. Lettuce and herbs. That sort of thing.'

'I would like to see the shelter,' the bishop said.

She was hurt — a hurt that seemed to reverberate all the way back to her childhood, when she had been wounded by the discovery that the friends who came to call on rainy days had not come because they liked her but to eat her cookies and hog her toys. She had never been able to put a good countenance on selfishness, and she scowled as they passed the birdbath and the painted ducks. The gnomes with their mobcaps looked down on the three of them as she unlocked the fire door with a key that she wore around her neck.

'Charming,' the bishop said. 'Charming. Why, I see you even have a library.'

'Yes,' she said. 'The books were chosen for their humor, tranquillity, and hopefulness.'

'It is an unfortunate characteristic of ecclesiastical architecture,' said the bishop, 'that the basement or cellar is confined to a small space under the chancel. This gives us very little room for the salvation of the faithful — a characteristic, I should perhaps add, of our denomination. Some churches have commodious basements. But I shan't take up any more of your time.' He strode back across the lawn toward the house, put his cocktail glass on the terrace wall, and gave her his blessing.

She sat down heavily on her terrace steps and watched the car drive off. He had not come to praise her, she knew that. Was it impious of her to suspect that he was traveling around his domain picking and choosing sanctuaries? Was it possible that he meant to exploit his holiness in this way? The burden of modern life, even if it smelled of plastics – as it seemed to – bore down cruelly on the supports of God, the Family, and the Nation. The burden was top-heavy, and she seemed to hear the foundations give. She had believed all her life in the holiness of the priesthood, and if this belief was genuine, why hadn't she offered the bishop the safety of her shelter at once? But if he believed in the resurrection of the dead and the life of the world to come, why was a shelter anything that he might need?

The telephone rang, and she answered its ringing with a forced lightheartedness. It was a woman named Beatrice, who came to clean Mrs Pastern's house two days a week.

'This is Beatrice, Mrs Pastern,' she said, 'and there is something I think you ought to know. As you know, I'm not a gossip. I'm not like that Adele, who goes around from lady to lady telling that the So-and-Sos aren't sleeping together, and that So-and-So had six empty whiskey bottles in his wastebaskets, and that nobody came to So-and-So's cocktail party. I'm not like that Adele. I'm not a gossip, and you know that, Mrs Pastern. But there is something I think you ought to know. I worked for Mrs Flannagan today, and she showed me a key, and she said it was a key to your bomb shelter, and that your husband gave it to her. I don't know whether it was the truth or not, but I thought you ought to know.'

'Thank you, Beatrice.'

He had dragged her good name through a hundred escapades, debauched her excellence, and thrown away her love, but she had never imagined that he would betray her in their plans for the end of the world. She poured what was left of the bishop's cocktail into a glass. She hated the taste of gin, but her accumulated troubles had grown to seem like the pain of an illness, and gin dimmed this, although it inflamed her indignation. Outside, the sky darkened, the wind changed, it began to rain. What could she do? She couldn't go back to Mother. Mother didn't have a shelter. She couldn't pray for guidance. The bishop's apparent worldliness had reduced the comforts of heaven. She couldn't contemplate her husband's foolish profligacy without drinking more gin. And then she remembered the night – the night of judgment – when they had agreed to let Aunt Ida and Uncle Ralph burn, when she had sacrificed her three-year-old niece and he his five-year-old nephew; when they had conspired like murderers and had decided to deny mercy even to his old mother.

She was quite drunk by the time Charlie came in. 'I couldn't spend two weeks in any hole in the ground with that Mrs Flannagan,' she said.

'What are you talking about?'

'I took the bishop down to show him the shelter and he –'

'What bishop? What was a bishop doing here?'

'Stop interrupting me and listen to what I have to say. Mrs Flannagan has a key to our shelter, and you gave it to her.'

'Who told you this?'

'Mrs Flannagan,' she said, 'has a key to our shelter, and you gave it to her.'

He went back out through the rain to the garage and jammed his fingers in the door. In haste and rage he stalled the car, and, waiting for the carburetor to drain, was faced, in the headlights, with the backstage of his wasteful domestic life which had accumulated in the garage. Here was a fortune in broken garden furniture and power tools. When the car started, he slammed out of his driveway and passed a red light at the first intersection, where, for a moment, his life hung by a thread. He didn't care. Slamming up the hill, he clutched the wheel as if he already had his hands on her plump and silly neck. It was his children's honor and peace of mind that she had damaged. It was his children, his beloved children, that she had harmed.

He stopped the car at the door. The house was lighted, and he could smell wood smoke, but the place was quiet and, peering through the glass pane, he couldn't see any signs of life or hear anything but the rain. He tried the door. It was locked. Then he pounded on the frame with his fist. It was a long time before she appeared, from the living room, and he guessed she must have been asleep. She was wearing the peignoir he had bought her. She straightened her hair. As soon as she opened the door, he pushed his way into the hall and shouted, 'Why did you do it? Why did you do such a damn fool thing?'

'I do not know what you are talking about.'

'Why did you tell my wife you had the key?'

'I did not tell your wife.'

'Then who did you tell?'

'I did not tell anyone.'

She worked her shoulders and looked down at the tip of her slipper. Like most incurable fibbers, she had an extravagant regard for the truth, which she expressed by sending up signals meant to indicate that she was lying. He saw then that he could not get the truth out of her, that he could not shake it out of her with all the strength in his arms, and that her confession, if he had it, would have done him no good.

'Get me something to drink,' he said.

'I think you had better go away and come back later, when you are feeling better,' she said.

'I'm tired,' he said. 'I'm tired. Oh, God, I'm tired. I haven't sat down all day.'

He went into the living room and poured himself a whiskey. He saw his hands, blackened by the trains and the banisters, the doorknobs and the papers, of a long day, and in the mirror he saw that his hair was soaked with rain. He went out of the living room and through the library to the downstairs bathroom. She made a little noise, scarcely a cry. When he opened the bathroom door, he found himself face to face with an absolutely naked stranger.

He shut the door, and then there was that nearly metronomic stillness that precedes a howling confrontation. It was she who broke the silence. 'I do not know who he is, and I have been trying to make him go away ... I know what you are thinking, and I do not care. It is my house, after all, and I did not invite you into it, and I do not have to explain everything that goes on to you.'

'Get away from me,' he said. 'Get away from me or I'll break your neck.'

He drove home through the rain. When he let himself in, he noticed the noise and the smell of cooking from the kitchen. He supposed that these signs and odors must have been one of the first signs of life on the planet, and might be one of the last. The evening paper was in the living room, and, giving it a shake, he shouted, 'Throw a little nuclear hardware at them! Show them who's boss!' And then, falling into a chair, he asked softly, 'Dear Jesus, when will it ever end?'

'I've been waiting for you to say that,' said Mrs Pastern quietly, coming in from the pantry. 'I've been waiting nearly three months now to hear just that. I first began to worry when I saw that you'd sold your cuff links and your studs. I wondered what was the matter then. Then, when you signed the contract for the shelter without a penny to pay for it, I began to see your plan. You *want* the world to end, don't you? Don't you, Charlie, don't you? I've known it all along, but I couldn't admit it to myself, it seemed so ruthless – but then one learns something new every day.' She walked past him into the hallway and started up the stairs. 'There's a hamburger in the frying pan,' she said, 'and some potatoes in the oven. If you want a green vegetable, you can heat up the leftover broccoli. I'm going to telephone the children.'

We travel with such velocity these days that the most we can do is to remember a few place names. The freight of metaphysical speculation will have to catch up with us by slow train, if it catches up with us at all. The rest of the story was recounted by my mother, whose letter caught up with me in Kitzbühel, where I sometimes stay. 'There have been so many changes in the last six weeks,' she wrote, 'that I hardly know where to begin. First, the Pasterns are gone and I mean gone. He's in the county jail serving a two-year sentence for grand larceny. Sally's left college and is working at Macy's, and the boy's still looking for a job, I hear. He's living with his mother somewhere in the Bronx. Someone said they were on home relief. It seems that

Charlie ran through all of that money his mother left him about a year ago and they were just living on credit. The bank took everything and they moved to a motel in Tansford. Then they moved from motel to motel, traveling in a rented car and never paying their bills. The motel and the car-rental people were the first ones to catch up with them. Some nice people named Willoughby bought the house from the bank. And the Flannagans have divorced. Remember her? She used to walk around her garden with a silk parasol. He didn't have to give her a settlement or anything and someone saw her on Central Park West in a thin coat on a cold night. But she did come back. It was very strange. She came back last Thursday. It had just begun to snow. It was a little while after lunch. What an old fool your mother is but as old as I am I never cease to thrill at the miracle of a snowstorm. I had a lot of work to do but I decided to let it go and stand by the window awhile and watch it snow. The sky was very dark. It was a fine, dry snow and covered everything quickly like a spread of light. Then I saw Mrs Flannagan walking up the street. She must have come out on the two-thirty-three and walked up from the station. I don't suppose she can have much money if she can't afford a cab, do you? She was not very warmly dressed and she had on high heels and no rubbers. Well, she walked up the street and she walked right across the Pasterns' lawn, I meant what used to be the Pasterns' lawn, to their bomb shelter and just stood there looking at it. I don't know what in the world she was thinking of but the shelter looks a little like a tomb, you know, and she looked like a mourner standing there with the snow falling on her head and shoulders and it made me sad to think she hardly knew the Pasterns. Then

Mrs Willoughby telephoned me and said there was this strange woman standing in front of her bomb shelter and did I know who it was and I said that I did, that it was Mrs Flannagan who used to live up on the hill, and then she asked what I thought she should do and I said the only thing to do I guessed was to send her away. So then Mrs Willoughby sent her maid down and I saw the maid telling Mrs Flannagan to go away and then in a little while Mrs Flannagan walked back through the snow to the station.'

Reunion

THE LAST TIME I saw my father was in Grand Central Station. I was going from my grandmother's in the Adirondacks to a cottage on the Cape that my mother had rented, and I wrote my father that I would be in New York between trains for an hour and a half, and asked if we could have lunch together. His secretary wrote to say that he would meet me at the information booth at noon, and at twelve o'clock sharp I saw him coming through the crowd. He was a stranger to me – my mother divorced him three years ago and I hadn't been with him since – but as soon as I saw him I felt that he was my father, my flesh and blood, my future and my doom. I knew that when I was grown I would be something like him; I would have to plan my campaigns within his limitations. He was a big, good-looking man, and I was terribly happy to see him again. He struck me on the back and shook my hand. 'Hi, Charlie,' he said. 'Hi, boy. I'd like to take you up to my club, but it's in the Sixties, and if you have to catch an early train I guess we'd better get something to eat around here.' He put his arm around me, and I smelled my father the way my mother sniffs a rose. It was a rich compound of whiskey, after-shave lotion, shoe polish, woolens, and the rankness of a mature male. I hoped that someone would see us together. I wished that we could be photographed. I wanted some record of our having been together.

We went out of the station and up a side street to a restaurant. It was still early, and the place was empty. The bartender was quarreling with a delivery boy, and there was one very old waiter in a red coat down by the kitchen door. We sat down, and my father hailed the waiter in a loud voice. '*Kellner!*' he shouted. '*Garçon! Cameriere! You!*' His boisterousness in the empty restaurant seemed out of place. 'Could we have a little service here!' he shouted. 'Chop-chop.' Then he clapped his hands. This caught the waiter's attention, and he shuffled over to our table.

'Were you clapping your hands at me?' he asked.

'Calm down, calm down, *sommelier*,' my father said. 'If it isn't too much to ask of you – if it wouldn't be too much above and beyond the call of duty, we would like a couple of Beefeater Gibsons.'

'I don't like to be clapped at,' the waiter said.

'I should have brought my whistle,' my father said. 'I have a whistle that is audible only to the ears of old waiters. Now, take out your little pad and your little pencil and see if you can get this straight: two Beefeater Gibsons. Repeat after me: two Beefeater Gibsons.'

'I think you'd better go somewhere else,' the waiter said quietly.

'That,' said my father, 'is one of the most brilliant suggestions I have ever heard. Come on, Charlie, let's get the hell out of here.'

I followed my father out of that restaurant into another. He was not so boisterous this time. Our drinks came, and he cross-questioned me about the baseball season. He then struck the edge of his empty glass with his knife and began shouting again. '*Garçon! Kellner! Cameriere! You!* Could we trouble you to bring us two more of the same.'

'How old is the boy?' the waiter asked.

'That,' my father said, 'is none of your God-damned business.'

'I'm sorry, sir,' the waiter said, 'but I won't serve the boy another drink.'

'Well, I have some news for you,' my father said. 'I have some very interesting news for you. This doesn't happen to be the only restaurant in New York. They've opened another on the corner. Come on, Charlie.'

He paid the bill, and I followed him out of that restaurant into another. Here the waiters wore pink jackets like hunting coats, and there was a lot of horse tack on the walls. We sat down, and my father began to shout again. 'Master of the hounds! Tallyhoo and all that sort of thing. We'd like a little something in the way of a stirrup cup. Namely, two Bibson Geefeaters.'

'Two Bibson Geefeaters?' the waiter asked, smiling.

'You know damned well what I want,' my father said angrily. 'I want two Beefeater Gibsons, and make it snappy. Things have changed in jolly old England. So my friend the duke tells me. Let's see what England can produce in the way of a cocktail.'

'This isn't England,' the waiter said.

'Don't argue with me,' my father said. 'Just do as you're told.'

'I just thought you might like to know where you are,' the waiter said.

'If there is one thing I cannot tolerate,' my father said, 'it is an impudent domestic. Come on, Charlie.'

The fourth place we went to was Italian. '*Buon giorno*,' my father said. '*Per favore, possiamo avere due cocktail americani, forti, forti. Molto gin, poco vermut.*'

'I don't understand Italian,' the waiter said.

'Oh, come off it,' my father said. 'You understand Italian, and you know damned well you do. *Vogliamo due cocktail americani. Subito.*'

The waiter left us and spoke with the captain, who came over to our table and said, 'I'm sorry, sir, but this table is reserved.'

'All right,' my father said. 'Get us another table.'

'All the tables are reserved,' the captain said.

'I get it,' my father said. 'You don't desire our patronage. Is that it? Well, the hell with you. *Vada all' inferno.* Let's go, Charlie.'

'I have to get my train,' I said.

'I'm sorry, sonny,' my father said. 'I'm terribly sorry.' He put his arm around me and pressed me against him. 'I'll walk you back to the station. If there had only been time to go up to my club.'

'That's all right, Daddy,' I said.

'I'll get you a paper,' he said. 'I'll get you a paper to read on the train.'

Then he went up to a newsstand and said, 'Kind sir, will you be good enough to favor me with one of your God-damned, no-good, ten-cent afternoon papers?' The clerk turned away from him and stared at a magazine cover. 'Is it asking too much, kind sir,' my father said, 'is it asking too much for you to sell me one of your disgusting specimens of yellow journalism?'

'I have to go, Daddy,' I said. 'It's late.'

'Now, just wait a second, sonny,' he said. 'Just wait a second. I want to get a rise out of this chap.'

'Goodbye, Daddy,' I said, and I went down the stairs and got my train, and that was the last time I saw my father.

A Vision of the World

THIS IS BEING written in another seaside cottage on another coast. Gin and whiskey have bitten rings in the table where I sit. The light is dim. On the wall there is a colored lithograph of a kitten wearing a flowered hat, a silk dress, and white gloves. The air is musty, but I think it is a pleasant smell – heartening and carnal, like bilge water or the land wind. The tide is high, and the sea below the bluff slams its bulkheads, its doors, and shakes its chains with such power that it makes the lamp on my table jump. I am here alone to rest up from a chain of events that began one Saturday afternoon when I was spading up my garden. A foot or two below the surface I found a small round can that might have contained shoe polish. I pried the can open with a knife. Inside I found a piece of oilcloth, and within this a note on lined paper. It read, 'I, Nils Jugstrum, promise myself that if I am not a member of the Gory Brook Country Club by the time I am twenty-five years old I will hang myself.' I knew that twenty years ago the neighborhood where I live had been farmland, and I guessed that some farmer's boy, gazing off to the green fairways of Gory Brook, had made his vow and buried it in the ground. I was moved, as I always am, by these broken lines of communication in which we express our most acute feelings. The note seemed, like some impulse of romantic love, to let me deeper into the afternoon.

The sky was blue. It seemed like music. I had just cut the grass, and the smell of it was in the air. This reminded me of those overtures and promises of love we know when we are young. At the end of a foot race you throw yourself onto the grass by the cinder track, gasping for breath, and the ardor with which you embrace the schoolhouse lawn is a promise you will follow all the days of your life. Thinking then of peaceable things, I noticed that the black ants had conquered the red ants and were taking the corpses off the field. A robin flew by, pursued by two jays. The cat was in the currant hedge, scouting a sparrow. A pair of orioles passed, pecking each other, and then I saw, a foot or so from where I stood, a copperhead working itself out of the last length of its dark winter skin. What I experienced was not fright or dread; it was shock at my unpreparedness for this branch of death. Here was lethal venom, as much a part of the earth as the running water in the brook, but I seemed to have no space for it in my considerations. I went back to the house to get the shotgun, but I had the misfortune then to meet up with the older of my two dogs, a gun-shy bitch. At the sight of the gun she began to bark and whimper, torn unmercifully by her instincts and anxieties. Her barking brought the second dog, a natural hunter, bounding down the stairs, ready to retrieve a rabbit or a bird, and, followed by two dogs, one barking in joy and the other in horror, I returned to the garden in time to see the viper disappear into a stone wall.

After this I drove into the village and bought some grass seed and then went out to the supermarket on Route 27, to get some brioches my wife had ordered. I think you may need a camera these days to record a supermarket on a Saturday afternoon. Our language is traditional, the accrual of centuries of intercourse. Except for the shapes of the pastry, there was nothing traditional to be seen at the bakery counter where I waited. We were six or seven, delayed by an old man with a long list, a scroll of groceries. Looking over his shoulder I read,

6 eggs

hors d'oeuvres

He saw me reading his document and held it against his chest like a prudent card player. Then suddenly the piped-in music changed from a love song to a cha-cha, and the woman beside me began to move her shoulders shyly and to execute a few steps. 'Would you like to dance, madam?' I asked. She was very plain, but when I held out my arms she stepped into them, and we danced for a minute or two. You could see that she loved to dance, but with a face like that she couldn't have had many chances. She then blushed a deep red, stepped out of my arms, and went over to the glass case, where she studied the Boston cream pies. I felt that we had made a step in the right direction, and when I got my brioches and drove home I was elated. A policeman stopped me at the corner of Alewives Lane, to let a parade go by. First to come was a young girl in boots and shorts that emphasized the fineness of her thighs. She had an enormous nose, wore a busby, and pumped an aluminum baton. She was followed by another girl, with finer and more ample thighs, who marched with her pelvis so far in advance of the rest of her that her spine was strangely curved. She wore bifocals and seemed terribly bored by this forwardness of her pelvis. A band of boys, with here and there a gray-haired ringer, brought up the rear, playing 'The Caissons Go Rolling Along.' They carried no banners, they had no discernible purpose or destination, and it all seemed to me terribly funny. I laughed all the way home.

But my wife was sad.

'What's the matter, darling?' I asked.

'I just have this terrible feeling that I'm a character in a television situation comedy,' she said. 'I mean, I'm nice-looking, I'm well-dressed, I have humorous and attractive children, but I have this terrible feeling that I'm in black-and-white and that I can be turned off by anybody. I just have this terrible feeling that I can be turned *off.*' My wife is often sad because her sadness is not a sad sadness, sorry because her sorrow is not a crushing sorrow. She grieves because her grief is not an acute grief, and when I tell her that this sorrow over the inadequacies of her sorrow may be a new hue in the spectrum of human pain, she is not con-soled. Oh, I sometimes think of leaving her. I could con-ceivably make a life without her and the children, I could get along without the companionship of my friends, but I could not bring myself to leave my lawns and gardens, I could not part from the porch screens that I have repaired and painted, I cannot divorce myself from the serpentine brick walk I have laid between the side door and the rose garden; and so, while my chains are forged of turf and house paint, they will still bind me until I die. But I was grateful to my wife then for what she had said, for stating that the externals of her life had the quality of a dream. The unin-hibited energies of the imagination had created the supermarket, the viper, and the note in the shoe-polish can. Compared to these, my wildest reveries had the literalness of double-entry bookkeeping. It pleased me to think that our external life has the quality of a dream and that in our dreams we find the virtues of conservatism. I then went into the house, where I found the cleaning woman smoking a stolen Egyptian cigarette and piecing together the torn letters in the wastebasket.

We went to Gory Brook that night for dinner. I checked the list of members, looking for Nils Jugstrum, but he wasn't there, and I wondered if he had hanged himself. And for what? It was the usual. Gracie Masters, the only daughter of a millionaire funeral director, was dancing with Pinky Townsend. Pinky was out on fifty thousand dollars' bail for stockmarket manipulation. When bail was set, he took the fifty thousand out of his wallet. I danced a set with Millie Surcliffe. The music was 'Rain,' 'Moonlight on the Ganges,' 'When the Red Red Robin Comes Bob Bob Bobbin' Along,' 'Five Foot Two, Eyes of Blue,' 'Carolina in the Morning,' and 'The Sheik of Araby.' We seemed to be dancing on the grave of social coherence. But while the scene was plainly revolutionary, where was the new day, the world to come? The next set was 'Lena from Palesteena,' 'I'm Forever Blowing Bubbles,' 'Louisville Lou,' 'Smiles,' and 'The Red Red Robin' again. That last one really gets us jumping, but when the band blew the spit out of their instruments I saw them shaking their heads in deep moral disapproval of our antics. Millie went back to her table, and I stood by the door, wondering why my heart should heave when I see people leave a dance floor at the end of a set – heave as it heaves when I see a crowd pack up and leave a beach as the shadow of the cliff falls over the water and the sand, heave as if I saw in these gentle departures the energies and the thoughtlessness of life itself.

Time, I thought, strips us rudely of the privileges of the bystander, and in the end that couple chatting loudly in bad French in the lobby of the Grande Bretagne (Athens) turns out to be us. Someone else has got our post behind the potted palms, our quiet corner in the bar, and, exposed, perforce we cast around for other avenues of observation. What I wanted to identify then was not a chain of facts but an essence – something like the indecipherable collision of contingencies that can produce exaltation or despair. What I wanted to do was to grant my dreams, in so incoherent a world, their legitimacy. None of this made me moody, and I danced, drank, and told stories at the bar until about one, when we went home. I turned on the television set to a commercial that, like so much else I had seen that day, seemed terribly funny. A young woman with a boarding-school accent was asking, 'Do you offend with wet-furcoat odor? A fifty-thousand-dollar sable cape caught in a thundershower can smell worse than an old hound dog who's been chasing a fox through a swamp. *Nothing* smells worse than wet mink. Even a light mist can make lamb, opossum, civet, baum marten, and other less costly and serviceable furs as malodorous as a badly ventilated lion house in a zoo. Safeguard yourself from embarrassment and anxiety by light applications of Elixircol before you wear your furs ...' She belonged to the dream world, and I told her so before I turned her off. I fell asleep in the moonlight and dreamed of an island.

I was with some other men, and seemed to have reached the place on a sailing boat. I was sunburned, I remember, and, touching my jaw, I felt a three- or four-day stubble. The island was in the Pacific. There was a smell of rancid cooking oil in the air – a sign of the China coast. It was in the middle of the afternoon when we landed, and we seemed to have nothing much to do. We wandered through the streets. The place either had been occupied by the Army or had served as a military way station, because many of the signs in the windows were written in an approximation of English. 'Crews Cutz,' I read on a sign in an Oriental barbershop. Many of the stores had displays of imitation American whiskey. Whiskey was spelled 'Whikky'. Because we had nothing better to do, we went into a local museum. There were bows, primitive fishhooks, masks, and drums. From the museum we went to a restaurant and ordered a meal. I had a struggle with the local language, but what surprised me was that it seemed to be an informed struggle. I seemed to have studied the language before coming ashore. I distinctly remembered putting together a sentence when the waiter came up to the table. '*Porpozec ciebie nie prosze dorzanin albo zyolpocz ciwego,*' I said. The waiter smiled and complimented me, and, when I woke from the dream, the fact of the language made the island in the sun, its population, and its museum real, vivid, and enduring. I thought with longing of the quiet and friendly natives and the easy pace of their lives.

Sunday passed swiftly and pleasantly in a round of cocktail parties, but that night I had another dream. I dreamed that I was standing at the bedroom window of the cottage in Nantucket that we sometimes rent. I was looking south along the fine curve of the beach. I have seen finer, whiter, and more splendid beaches, but when I look at the yellow of the sand and the arc of the curve, I always have the feeling that if I look at the cove long enough it will reveal something to me. The sky was cloudy. The water was gray. It was Sunday – although I couldn't have said how I knew this. It was late, and from the inn I could hear that most pleasant sound of dishes being handled, while families would be eating their Sunday-night suppers in the old matchboard dining room. Then I saw a single figure coming down the beach. It seemed to be a priest or a bishop. He carried a crozier, and wore the miter, cope, soutane, chasuble, and alb for high votive Mass. His vestments were heavily worked with gold, and now and then they were lifted by the sea wind. His face was clean-shaven. I could not make out his features in the fading light. He saw me at my window, raised his hand, and called: 'Porpozec ciebie nie prosze dorzanin albo zyolpocz ciwego.' Then he hurried along the sand, striking his crozier down like a walking stick, his stride impeded by the voluminousness of his vestments. He passed the window where I stood and disappeared where the curve of the bluff overtakes the curve of the shore.

I worked on Monday, and on Tuesday morning woke at about four from a dream in which I had been playing touch football. I was on the winning team. The score was six to eighteen. It was a scrub Sunday-afternoon game on somebody's lawn. Our wives and daughters watched from the edge of the grass, where there were chairs and tables and things to drink. The winning play was a long end run, and when the touchdown had been scored a big blonde named Helene Farmer got up and organized the women into a cheering section. 'Rah, rah, rah,' they said. 'Porpozec ciebie nie prosze dorzanin albo zyolpocz ciwego. Rah, rah, rah.'

211

I found none of this disconcerting. It was what I had wanted, in a way. Isn't the unconquerable force in man the love of discovery? The repetition of this sentence had the excitement of discovery for me. The fact that I had been on the winning team made me feel happy, and I went cheerfully down to breakfast, but our kitchen, alas, is a part of dreamland. With its pink, washable walls, chilling lights, built-in television (where prayers were being said), and artificial potted plants, it made me nostalgic for my dream, and when my wife passed me the stylus and Magic Tablet on which we write our breakfast orders, I wrote, '*Porpozec ciebie nie prosze dorzanin albo zyolpocz ciwego.*' She laughed and asked me what I meant. When I repeated the sentence – it seemed, indeed, to be the only thing I wanted to say – she began to cry, and I saw in the bitterness of her tears that I had better take a rest. Dr Howland came over to give me a sedative, and I took a plane to Florida that afternoon.

Now it is late. I drink a glass of milk and take a sleeping pill. I dream that I see a pretty woman kneeling in a field of wheat. Her lightbrown hair is full and so are the skirts of her dress. Her clothing seems old-fashioned – it seems before my time – and I wonder how I can know and feel so tenderly toward a stranger who is dressed in clothing that my grandmother might have worn. And yet she seems real – more real than the Tamiami Trail four miles to the east, with its Smorgorama and Giganticburger stands, more real than the back streets of Sarasota. I do not ask her who she is. I know what she will say. But then she smiles and starts to speak before I can turn away. '*Porpozec ciebie ...*' she begins. Then either I awake in despair or am waked by the sound of rain on the palms. I think of some farmer who, hearing the noise of rain, will stretch his lame bones and smile, feeling that the rain is falling into his lettuce and his cabbages, his hay and his oats, his parsnips and his corn. I think of some plumber who, waked by the rain, will smile at a vision of the world in which all the drains are miraculously cleansed and free. Right-angle drains, crooked drains, root-choked and rusty drains all gurgle and discharge their waters into the sea. I think that the rain will wake some old lady, who will wonder if she has left her copy of *Dombey and Son* in the garden. Her shawl? Did she cover the chairs? And I know that the sound of the rain will wake some lovers, and that its sound will seem to be a part of that force that has thrust them into one another's arms. Then I sit up in bed and exclaim aloud to myself, 'Valor! Love! Virtue! Compassion! Splendor! Kindness! Wisdom! Beauty!' The words seem to have the colors of the earth, and as I recite them I feel my hopefulness mount until I am contented and at peace with the night.

Montraldo

THE FIRST TIME I robbed Tiffany's, it was raining. I bought an imitation-diamond ring at a costume-jewelry place in the Forties. Then I walked up to Tiffany's in the rain and asked to look at rings. The clerk had a haughty manner. I looked at six or eight diamond rings. They began at eight hundred and went up to ten thousand. There was one priced at three thousand that looked to me like the paste in my pocket. I was examining this when an elderly woman – an old customer, I guessed – appeared on the other side of the counter. The clerk rushed over to greet her, and I switched rings. Then I called, 'Thank you very much. I'll think it over.' 'Very well,' the clerk said haughtily, and I went out of the store. It was as simple as pie. I walked down to the diamond market in the Forties and sold the ring for eighteen hundred. No questions were asked. Then I went to Thomas Cook and found that the *Conte di Salvini* was sailing for Genoa at five. This was in August, and there was plenty of space on the eastbound crossing. I took a cabin in first class and was standing at the bar when she sailed. The bar was not officially open, of course, but the bar Jack gave me a Martini in a tumbler to hold me until we got into international waters. The *Salvini* had an exceptionally percussive whistle, and you may have heard it if you were anywhere near midtown, although who ever is at five o'clock on an August afternoon?

That night I met Mrs Winwar and her elderly husband at the horse races. He promptly got seasick, and we plunged into the marvelous skulduggery of illicit love. The passed notes, the phony telephone calls, the affected indifference, and what happened when we were behind the closed door of my cabin made my theft of a ring seem guileless. Mr Winwar recovered in Gibraltar, but this only seemed like a challenge, and we carried on under his nose. We said good-bye in Genoa, where I bought a secondhand Fiat and started down the coast.

I got to Montraldo late one afternoon. I stopped there because I was tired of driving. There was a semicircular bay, set within high stone cliffs, and one of those beaches that are lined with cafés and bathing houses. There were two hotels, a Grand and a National, and I didn't care for either one of them, and a waiter in a café told me I could rent a room in the villa on the cliff. It could be reached, he said, either by a steep and curving road or by a flight of stone steps – one hundred and twenty-seven, I discovered later – that led from the back garden down into the village. I took my car up the curving road. The cliff was covered with rosemary, and the rosemary was covered with the village laundry, drying in the sun. There were signs on the door in five languages, saying that rooms were for rent. I rang, and a thickset, bellicose servant opened the door. I learned that her name was Assunta. I never saw any relaxation of her bellicosity. In church, when she plunged up the aisle to take Holy Communion, she looked as if she were going to knock the priest down and mess up the acolyte. She said I could have a room if I paid a week's rent in advance, and I had to pay her before I was allowed to cross the threshold.

The place was a ruin, but the whitewashed room she showed me into was in a little tower, and through a broken window the room had a broad view of the sea. The one luxury was a gas ring. There was no toilet, and there was no running water; the water I washed in had to be hauled out of a well in a leaky marmalade can. I was obviously the only guest. That first afternoon, while Assunta was praising the healthfulness of the sea air, I heard a querulous and elegant voice calling to us from the courtyard. I went down the stairs ahead of the servant, and introduced myself to an old woman standing by the well. She was short, frail, and animated, and spoke such a flowery Roman that I wondered if this wasn't a sort of cultural or social dust thrown into one's eyes to conceal the fact that her dress was ragged and dirty. 'I see you have a gold wristwatch,' she said. 'I, too, have a gold wristwatch. We will have this in common.'

The servant turned to her and said, 'Go to the devil!'

'But it is a fact. The gentleman and I do both have gold wristwatches,' the old lady said, it will make us sympathetic.'

'Bore,' the servant said. 'Rot in hell.'

'Thank you, thank you, treasure of my house, light of my life,' the old lady said, and made her way toward an open door.

The servant put her hands on her hips and screamed, 'Witch! Frog! Pig!'

'Thank you, thank you, thank you infinitely,' the old lady said, and went in at the door.

★

That night, at the café, I asked about the signorina and her servant, and the waiter was fully informed. The signorina, he said, came from a noble Roman family, from which she had been expelled because of a romantic and unsuitable love affair. She had lived as a hermit in Montraldo for fifty years. Assunta had been brought here from Rome to be her *donna di servizio*, but all she did for the old lady these days was to go into the village and buy her some bread and wine. She had robbed the old woman of all her possessions – she had even taken the bed from her room – and she now kept her a prisoner in the villa. Both the Grand Hotel and the National were luxurious and commodious. Why did I stay in such a place?

I stayed because of the view, because I had paid my rent in advance, and because I was curious about the eccentric old spinster and her cranky servant. They began quarreling early the next morning. Assunta opened up with obscenity and abuse. The signorina countered with elaborate sarcasm. It was a depressing performance. I wondered if the old lady was really a prisoner, and later in the morning, when I saw her alone in the courtyard, I asked her if she would like to drive with me to Tambura, the next village up the coast. She said, in her flowery Roman, that she would be delighted to join me. She wanted to have her watch, her gold watch, repaired. The watch was of great value and beauty and there was only one man she dared entrust it to. He was in Tambura. While we were talking, Assunta joined us.

'Why do you want to go to Tambura?' she asked the old lady.

'I want to have my gold watch repaired,' the old lady said.

'You don't have a gold watch,' Assunta said.

'That is true,' the old lady said. 'I no longer have a gold watch, but I used to have a gold watch. I used to have a gold watch, and I used to have a gold pencil.'

'You can't go to Tambura to have your watch repaired if you don't have a watch,' Assunta said.

'That is true, light of my life, treasure of my house,' the old lady said, and she went in at her door.

I spent most of my time on the beach and in the cafés. The fortunes of the resort seemed to be middling. The waiters complained about business, but then they always do. The smell of the sea was riggish but unfresh, and I used to think with homesickness of the wild and magnificent beaches of my own country. Gay Head is, I know, sinking into the sea, but the sinkage at Montraldo seemed to be spiritual – as if the waves were eroding the vitality of that place. The sea was incandescent; the light was clear but not brilliant. The flavor of Montraldo, as I remember it, was immutable, intimate, depleted – everything I detest; for shouldn't the soul of man be as limpid and cutting as a diamond? The waves spoke in French or Italian – now and then a word of dialect – but they seemed to speak without force.

One afternoon a remarkably beautiful woman came down the beach, followed by a boy of about eight, I should say, and an Italian woman dressed in black – a maid. They carried sandwich bags from the Grand Hotel, and my guess was that the boy lived mostly in hotels. He was pitiful. The maid took some toys from an assortment she carried in a string bag. They seemed to be all wrong for his age. There was a sand bucket, a shovel, some molds, a whiffle ball, and an old-fashioned pair of water wings. I suspected that the mother, stretched out on a blanket with an American novel, was a divorcee, and that she would presently have a drink with me in the café. With this in mind, I got to my feet and offered to play whiffle ball with the boy. He was delighted to have some company, but he could neither throw nor catch a ball, and, making a guess at his tastes, I asked, with one eye on the mother, if he would like me to build him a sand castle. He would. I built a water moat, then an escarpment with curved stairs, a dry moat, a crenelated wall with cannon positions, and a cluster of round towers with parapets. I worked as if the impregnability of the place was a reality, and when it was completed I set flags, made of candy wrappers, flying from every tower. I thought naïvely that it was beautiful, and so did the boy, but when I called his mother's attention to my feat she said, '*Andiamo.*' The maid gathered up the toys, and off they went, leaving me, a grown man in a strange country, with a sand castle.

At Montraldo, the high point of the day came at four, when there was a band concert. This was the largesse of the municipality. The bandstand was wooden, Turkish in inspiration, and weathered by sea winds. The musicians sometimes wore uniforms, sometimes bathing suits, and their number varied from day to day, but they always played Dixieland. I don't think they were interested in the history of jazz. I just think they'd found some old arrangements in a trunk and were stuck with them. The music was comical, accelerated – they seemed to be playing for some ancient ballroom team. 'Clarinet Marmalade,' 'China Boy,' 'Tiger Rag,' 'Careless Love' – how stirring it was to hear this old, old jazz explode in the salty air. The concert ended at five, when most of the musicians packed up their instruments and went out to sea with the sardine fleet and the bathers returned to the cafés and the village. Men, women, and children on a beach, band music, sea grass, and sandwich hampers remind me much more forcibly than classical landscapes of our legendary ties to paradise. So I would go up with the others to the café, where, one day, I befriended Lord and Lady Rockwell, who asked me for cocktails. You may wonder why I put these titles down so breathlessly, and the reason is that my father was a waiter.

He wasn't an ordinary waiter; he used to work at a dinner-dance spot in one of the big hotels. One night he lost his temper at a drunken brute, pushed his face into a plate of cannelloni, and left the premises. The union suspended him for three months, but he was, in a way, a hero, and when he went back to work they put him on the banquet shift, where he passed mushrooms to Kings and Presidents. He saw a lot of the world, but I sometimes wonder if the world ever saw much more of him than the sleeve of his red coat and his suave and handsome face, a little above the candlelight. It must have been like living in a world divided by a sheet of one-way glass. Sometimes I am reminded of him by those pages and guards in Shakespeare who come in from the left and stand at a door, establishing by their costumes the fact that this is Venice or Arden. You scarcely see their faces, they never speak a line; nor did my father, and when the after-dinner speeches began he would vanish like the pages on stage. I tell people that he was in the administrative end of the hotel business, but actually he was a waiter, a banquet waiter.

The Rockwells' party was large, and I left at about ten. A hot wind was blowing off the sea. I was later told that this was the sirocco. It was a desert wind, and so oppressive that I got up several times during the night to drink some mineral water. A boat offshore was sounding its foghorn. In the morning, it was both foggy and suffocating. While I was making some coffee, Assunta and the signorina began their morning quarrel. Assunta started off with the usual 'Pig! Dog! Witch! Dirt of the streets!' Leaning from an open window, the whiskery old woman sent down her flowery replies: 'Dear one. Beloved. Blessed one. Thank you, thank you.' I stood in the door with my coffee, wishing they would schedule their disputes for some other time of day. The quarrel was suspended while the signorina came down the stairs to get her bread and wine. Then it started up again: 'Witch! Frog! Frog of frogs! Witch of witches!' etc. The old lady countered with 'Treasure! Light! Treasure of my house! Light of my life!' etc. Then there was a scuffle – a tug-of-war over the loaf of bread. I saw Assunta strike the old woman cruelly with the edge of her hand. She fell on the steps and began to moan 'Aiee! Aieee!' Even these cries of pain seemed florid. I ran across the courtyard to where she lay in a disjointed heap. Assunta began to scream at me, 'I am not culpable, I am not culpable!' The old lady was in great pain. 'Please, signore,' she asked, 'please find the priest for me!' I picked her up. She weighed no more than a child, and her clothing smelled of soil. I carried her up the stairs into a high-ceilinged room festooned with cobwebs and put her onto a couch. Assunta was on my heels, screaming, 'I am not culpable!' Then I started down the one hundred and twenty-seven steps to the village.

The fog streamed through the air, and the African wind felt like a furnace draft. No one answered the door at the priest's house, but I found him in the church, sweeping the floor with a broom made of twigs. I was excited and impatient, and the more excited I became, the more slow-moving was the priest. First, he had to put his broom in a closet. The closet door was warped and wouldn't shut, and he spent an unconscionable amount of time trying to close it. I finally went outside and waited on the porch. It took him half an hour to get collected, and then, instead of starting for the villa, we went down into the village to find an acolyte. Presently a young boy joined us, pulling on a soiled lace soutane, and we started up the stairs. The priest negotiated ten steps and then sat down to rest. I had time to smoke a cigarette. Then ten more steps and another rest, and when we were halfway up the stairs, I began to wonder if he would ever make it. His face had turned from red to purple, and the noises from his respiratory tract were harsh and desperate. We finally arrived at the door of the villa. The acolyte lit his censer. Then we made our way into that ruined place. The windows were open. There was sea fog in the air. The old woman was in great pain, but the notes of her voice remained genteel, as I expect they truly were. 'She is my daughter,' she said. 'Assunta. She is my daughter, my child.'

Then Assunta screamed, 'Liar! Liar!'

'No, no, no,' the old lady said, 'you are my child, my only child. That is why I have cared for you all my life.'

Assunta began to cry, and stamped down the stairs. From the window, I saw her crossing the courtyard. When the priest began to administer the last rites, I went out.

I kept a sort of vigil in the café. The church bells tolled at three, and a little later news came down from the villa that

the signorina was dead. No one in the café seemed to suspect that they were anything but an eccentric old spinster
and a cranky servant. At four o'clock the band concert
opened up with 'Tiger Rag.' I moved that night from the
villa to the Hotel National, and left Montraldo in the
morning.

Percy

REMINISCENCE, ALONG WITH the cheese boards and ugly pottery sometimes given to brides, seems to have a manifest destiny with the sea. Reminiscences are written on such a table as this, corrected, published, read, and then they begin their inevitable journey toward the bookshelves in those houses and cottages one rents for the summer. In the last house we rented, we had beside our bed the *Memories of a Grand Duchess*, the *Recollections of a Yankee Whaler*, and a paperback copy of *Goodbye to All That*, but it is the same all over the world. The only book in my hotel room in Taormina was *Recordi d'un Soldato Garibaldino*, and in my room in Yalta I found «Повесть о Жизни.» Unpopularity is surely some part of this drifting toward salt water, but since the sea is our most universal symbol for memory, might there not be some mysterious affinity between these published recollections and the thunder of waves? So I put down what follows with the happy conviction that these pages will find their way into some bookshelf with a good view of a stormy coast. I can even see the room – see the straw rug, the window glass clouded with salt, and feel the house shake to the ringing of a heavy sea.

Great-uncle Ebenezer was stoned on the streets of New-buryport for his abolitionist opinions. His demure wife,

Georgiana (an artiste on the pianoforte), used once or twice a month to braid feathers into her hair, squat on the floor, light a pipe, and, having been given by psychic forces the personality of an Indian squaw, receive messages from the dead. My father's cousin, Anna Boynton, who had taught Greek at Radcliffe, starved herself to death during the Armenian famine. She and her sister Nanny had the copper skin, high cheekbones, and black hair of the Natick Indians. My father liked to recall the night he drank all the champagne on the New York – Boston train. He started drinking splits with some friend before dinner, and when they finished the splits they emptied the quarts and the magnums and were working on a jeroboam when the train reached Boston. He felt that this guzzling was heroic. My Uncle Hamlet – a black-mouthed old wreck who had starred on the Newburyport Volunteer Fire Department ball team – called me to the side of his deathbed and shouted, 'I've had the best fifty years of this country's history. *You* can have the rest.' He seemed to hand it to me on a platter – droughts, depressions, convulsions of nature, pestilence, and war. He was wrong, of course, but the idea pleased him. This all took place in the environs of Athenian Boston, but the family seemed much closer to the hyperbole and rhetoric that stem from Wales, Dublin, and the various principalities of alcohol than to the sermons of Phillips Brooks.

One of the most vivid members of my mother's side of the family was an aunt who called herself Percy, and who smoked cigars. There was no sexual ambiguity involved. She was lovely, fair, and intensely feminine. We were never very close. My father may have disliked her, although I don't recall this. My maternal grandparents had emigrated from England in the 1890s with their six children. My Grandfather Holinshed was described as a bounder — a word that has always evoked for me the image of a man leaping over a hedge just ahead of a charge of buckshot. I don't know what mistakes he had made in England, but his transportation to the New World was financed by his father-in-law, Sir Percy Devere, and he was paid a small remittance so long as he did not return to England. He detested the United States and died a few years after his arrival here. On the day of his funeral, Grandmother announced to her children that there would be a family conference in the evening. They should be prepared to discuss their plans. When the conference was called, Grandmother asked the children in turn what they planned to make of their lives. Uncle Tom wanted to be a soldier. Uncle Harry wanted to be a sailor. Uncle Bill wanted to be a merchant. Aunt Emily wanted to marry. Mother wanted to be a nurse and heal the sick. Aunt Florence — who later called herself Percy — exclaimed, 'I wish to be a great painter, like the Masters of the Italian Renaissance!' Grandmother then said, 'Since at least one of you has a clear idea of her destiny, the rest of you will go to work and Florence will go to art school.' That is what they did, and so far as I know none of them ever resented this decision.

How smooth it all seems and how different it must have been. The table where they gathered would have been lighted by whale oil or kerosene. They lived in a farmhouse in Dorchester. They would have had lentils or porridge or at best stew for dinner. They were very poor. If it was in the winter, they would be cold, and after the conference the wind would extinguish Grandmother's candle — stately

226

Grandmother – as she went down the back path to the malodorous outhouse. They couldn't have bathed more than
once a week, and I suppose they bathed out of pails. The
succinctness of Percy's exclamation seemed to have obscured
the facts of a destitute widow with six children. Someone
must have washed all those dishes, and washed them in
greasy water, drawn from a pump and heated over a fire.

The threat of gentility in such recollections is Damo-
clean, but these were people without pretense or affecta-
tion, and when Grandmother spoke French at the dinner
table, as she often did, she merely meant to put her education to some practical use. It was, of course, a much simpler
world. For example, Grandmother read in the paper one
day that a drunken butcher, the father of four, had chopped
up his wife with a meat cleaver, and she went directly to
Boston by horsecar or hansom – whatever transportation
was available. There was a crowd around the tenement
where the murder had taken place, and two policemen
guarded the door. Grandmother got past the policemen and
found the butcher's four terrified children in a bloody
apartment. She got their clothes together, took the children
home with her, and kept them for a month or longer, when
other homes were found. Cousin Anna's decision to starve
and Percy's wish to become a painter were made with the
same directness. It was what Percy thought she could do
best – what would make most sense of her life.

She began to call herself Percy in art school, because she
felt that there was some prejudice against women in the
arts. In her last year in art school she did a six-by-fourteen-
foot painting of Orpheus taming the beasts. This won her a
gold medal and a trip to Europe, where she studied at the

Beaux-Arts for a few months. When she returned, she was given three portrait commissions, but she was much too skeptical to succeed at this. Her portraits were pictorial indictments, and all three of them were unacceptable. She was not an aggressive woman, but she was immoderate and critical.

After her return from France she met a young doctor named Abbott Tracy at some yacht club on the North Shore. I don't mean the Corinthian. I mean some briny huddle of driftwood nailed together by weekend sailors. Moths in the billiard felt. Salvaged furniture. Two earth closets labeled 'Ladies' and 'Gentlemen,' and moorings for a dozen of those wide-waisted catboats that my father used to say sailed like real estate. Percy and Abbott Tracy met in some such place, and she fell in love. He had already begun a formidable and clinical sexual career, and seemed unacquainted in any way with sentiment, although I recall that he liked to watch children saying their prayers. Percy listened for his footsteps, she languished in his absence, his cigar cough sounded to her like music, and she filled a portfolio with pencil sketches of his face, his eyes, his hands, and, after their marriage, the rest of him.

They bought an old house in West Roxbury. The ceilings were low, the rooms were dark, the windows were small, and the fireplaces smoked. Percy liked all of this, and shared with my mother a taste for drafty ruins that seemed odd in such high-minded women. She turned a spare bedroom into a studio and did another large canvas – Prometheus bringing fire to man. This was exhibited in Boston, but no one bought it. She then painted a nymph and centaur. This used to be in the attic, and the centaur looked exactly like

Uncle Abbott. Uncle Abbott's practice was not very profit-
able, and I guess he was lazy. I remember seeing him eating
his breakfast in pajamas at one in the afternoon. They must
have been poor, and I suppose Percy did the housework,
bought the groceries, and hung out the wash. Late one
night when I had gone to bed, I overheard my father shouting, 'I cannot support that cigar-smoking sister of yours any
longer.' Percy spent some time copying paintings at Fenway
Court. This brought in a little money, but evidently not
enough. One of her friends from art school urged her to try
painting magazine covers. This went deeply against all of
her aspirations and instincts, but it must have seemed to her
that she had no choice, and she began to turn out deliberately sentimental pictures for magazines. She got to be quite
famous at this.

She was never pretentious, but she couldn't forget that
she had not explored to the best of her ability those gifts
that she may have had, and her enthusiasm for painting was
genuine. When she was able to employ a cook, she gave the
cook painting lessons. I remember her saying, toward the
end of her life, 'Before I die, I must go back to the Boston
Museum and see the Sargent watercolors.' When I was sixteen or seventeen, I took a walking tour in Germany with
my brother and bought Percy some van Gogh reproduc-
tions in Munich. She was very excited by these. Painting,
she felt, had some organic vitality – it was the exploration
of continents of consciousness, and here was a new world.
The deliberate puerility of most of her work had damaged
her draftsmanship, and at one point she began to hire a
model on Saturday mornings and sketch from life. Going
there on some simple errand – the return of a book or a

newspaper clipping – I stepped into her studio and found, sitting on the floor, a naked young woman. 'Nellie Casey,' said Percy, 'this is my nephew, Ralph Warren.' She went on sketching. The model smiled sweetly – it was nearly a social smile and seemed to partially temper her monumental nakedness. Her breasts were very beautiful, and the nipples, relaxed and faintly colored, were bigger than silver dollars. The atmosphere was not erotic or playful, and I soon left. I dreamed for years of Nellie Casey. Percy's covers brought in enough money for her to buy a house on the Cape, a house in Maine, a large automobile, and a small painting by Whistler that used to hang in the living room beside a copy Percy had made of Titian's *Europa*.

Her first son, Lovell, was born in the third year of her marriage. When he was four or five years old, it was decided that he was a musical genius, and he did have unusual manual dexterity. He was great at unsnarling kite lines and fishing tackle. He was taken out of school, educated by tutors, and spent most of his time practicing the piano. I detested him for a number of reasons. He was extremely dirty-minded, and used oil on his hair. My brother and I wouldn't have been more disconcerted if he had crowned himself with flowers. He not only used oil on his hair but when he came to visit us he left the hair-oil bottle in our medicine cabinet. He had his first recital in Steinway Hall when he was eight or nine, and he always played a Beethoven sonata when the family got together.

Percy must have perceived, early in her marriage, that her husband's lechery was compulsive and incurable, but she was determined, like any other lover, to authenticate her suspicion. How could a man that she adored be faithless?

She hired a detective agency, which tracked him down to an apartment house near the railroad station called the Orpheus. Percy went there and found him in bed with an unemployed telephone operator. He was smoking a cigar and drinking whiskey. 'Now, Percy,' he is supposed to have said, 'why did you have to go and do this?' She then came to our house and stayed with us for a week or so. She was pregnant, and when her son Beaufort was born his brain or his nervous system was seriously damaged. Abbott always claimed that there was nothing wrong with his son, but when Beaufort was five or six years old he was sent off to some school or institution in Connecticut. He used to come home for the holidays, and had learned to sit through an adult meal, but that was about all. He was an arsonist, and he once exposed himself at an upstairs window while Lovell was playing the 'Waldstein.' In spite of all this, Percy was never bitter or melancholy, and continued to worship Uncle Abbott.

The family used to gather, as I recall, almost every Sunday. I don't know why they should have spent so much time in one another's company. Perhaps they had few friends or perhaps they held their family ties above friendship. Standing in the rain outside the door of Percy's old house, we seemed bound together not by blood and not by love but by a sense that the world and its works were hostile. The house was dark. It had a liverish smell.

The guests often included Grandmother and old Nanny Boynton, whose sister had starved herself to death. Nanny taught music in the Boston public schools until her retirement, when she moved to a farm on the South Shore. Here she raised bees and mushrooms, and read musical scores

— Puccini, Mozart, Debussy, Brahms, etc. — that were mailed to her by a friend in the public library. I remember her very pleasantly. She looked, as I've said, like a Natick Indian. Her nose was beaked, and when she went to the beehives she covered herself with cheesecloth and sang *Vissi d'arte.* I once overheard someone say that she was drunk a good deal of the time, but I don't believe it. She stayed with Percy when the winter weather was bad, and she always traveled with a set of the Britannica, which was set up in the dining room behind her chair to settle disputes.

The meals at Percy's were very heavy. When the wind blew, the fireplaces smoked. Leaves and rain fell outside the windows. By the time we retired to the dark living room, we were all uncomfortable. Lovell would then be asked to play. The first notes of the Beethoven sonata would transform that dark, close, malodorous room into a landscape of extraordinary beauty. A cottage stood in some green fields near a river. A woman with flaxen hair stepped out of the door and dried her hands on an apron. She called her lover. She called and called, but something was wrong. A storm was approaching. The river would flood. The bridge would be washed away. The bass was massive, gloomy, and prophetic. Beware, beware! Traffic casualties were unprecedented. Storms lashed the west coast of Florida. Pittsburgh was paralyzed by a blackout. Famine gripped Philadelphia, and there was no hope for anyone. Then the lyric treble sang a long song about love and beauty. When this was done, down came the bass again, fortified by more bad news reports. The storm was traveling north through Georgia and Virginia. Traffic casualties were mounting. There was cholera in Nebraska. The Mississippi was over its banks. A live volcano had erupted in the Appalachians. Alas, alas! The treble resumed its part of the argument, persuasive, hopeful, purer than any human voice I had ever heard. Then the two voices began their counterpoint, and on it went to the end.

One afternoon, when the music was finished, Lovell, Uncle Abbott, and I got into the car and drove into the Dorchester slums. It was in the early winter, already dark and rainy, and the rains of Boston fell with great authority. He parked the car in front of a frame tenement and said that he was going to see a patient.

'You think he's going to see a patient?' Lovell asked.

'Yes,' I said.

'He's going to see his girl friend,' Lovell said. Then he began to cry.

I didn't like him. I had no sympathy to give him. I only wished that I had more seemly relations. He dried his tears, and we sat there without speaking until Uncle Abbott returned, whistling, contented, and smelling of perfume. He took us to a drugstore for some ice cream, and then we went back to the house, where Percy was opening the living-room windows to let in some air. She seemed tired but still high-spirited, although I suppose that she and everyone else in the room knew what Abbott had been up to. It was time for us to go home.

Lovell entered the Eastman Conservatory when he was fifteen, and performed the Beethoven G–Major Concerto with the Boston orchestra the year he graduated. Having been drilled never to mention money, it seems strange that I should recall the financial details of his debut. His tails cost one hundred dollars, his coach charged five hundred, and the orchestra paid him three hundred for two performances. The family was scattered throughout the hall, so we were unable to concentrate our excitement, but we were all terribly excited. After the concert we went to the greenroom and drank champagne. Koussevitzky did not appear, but Burgin, the concertmaster, was there. The reviews in the *Herald* and the *Transcript* were fairly complimentary, but they both pointed out that Lovell's playing lacked sentiment. That winter, Lovell and Percy went on a tour that took them as far west as Chicago, and something went wrong. They may, as travelers, have been bad company for one another; he may have had poor notices or small audiences; and while nothing was ever said, I recall that the tour was not triumphant. When they returned, Percy sold a piece of property that adjoined the house and went to Europe for the summer. Lovell could surely have supported himself as a musician, but instead he took a job as a manual laborer for some electrical-instrument company. He came to see us before Percy returned, and told me what had been happening that summer.

'Daddy didn't spend much time around the house after Mother went away,' he said, 'and I was alone most evenings. I used to get my own supper, and I spent a lot of time at the movies. I used to try and pick up girls, but I'm skinny and I don't have much self-confidence. Well, one Sunday I drove down to this beach in the old Buick. Daddy let me have the old Buick. I saw this very fat couple with a young daughter. They looked lonely. Mrs Hirshman is very fat, and she makes herself up like a clown, and she has a little dog. There is a kind of fat woman who always has a little dog. So then I said something about how I loved dogs, and they seemed happy to talk with me, and then I ran into the waves and showed off my crawl and came back and sat with them. They were Germans, and they had a funny accent, and I think their funny English and their fatness made them lonely. Well, their daughter was named Donna-Mae, and she was all wrapped up in a bathrobe, and she had on a hat, and they told me she had such fair skin she had to keep out of the sun. Then they told me she had beautiful hair, and she took off her hat, and I saw her hair for the first time. It *was* beautiful. It was the color of honey and very long, and her skin was pearly. You could see that the sun would burn it. So we talked, and I got some hot dogs and tonic, and took Donna-Mae for a walk up the beach, and I was very happy. Then, when the day was over, I offered to drive them home – they'd come to the beach in a bus – and they said they'd like a ride if I'd promise to have supper with them. They lived in a sort of a slum, and he was a house painter. Their house was behind another house. Mrs Hirshman said while she cooked supper why didn't I wash Donna-Mae off with the hose? I remember this very clearly, because it's when I fell in love. She put on her bathing suit again, and I put on my bathing suit, and I sprayed her very gently with the hose. She squealed a little, naturally, because the water was cold, and it was getting dark, and in the house next door someone was playing the Chopin C-Sharp-Minor, Opus 28. The piano was out of tune, and the person didn't know how to play, but the music and the hose and Donna-Mae's pearly skin and golden hair and the smells of supper from the kitchen and the twilight all seemed to be a kind of paradise. So I had supper with them and went home, and the next night I took Donna-Mae to the movies. Then I had supper with them again, and when I told Mrs Hirshman that my mother was away and that I almost never saw my father, she said that they had a spare room and why didn't I stay there? So the next night I packed some clothes and moved into their spare room, and I've been there ever since.'

It is unlikely that Percy would have written my mother after her return from Europe, and, had she written, the letter would have been destroyed, since that family had a crusading detestation of souvenirs. Letters, photographs, diplomas – anything that authenticated the past was always thrown into the fire. I think this was not, as they claimed, a dislike of clutter but a fear of death. To glance backward was to die, and they did not mean to leave a trace. There was no such letter, but had there been one it would, in the light of what I was told, have gone like this:

Dear Polly:

Lovell met me at the boat on Thursday. I bought him a Beethoven autograph in Rome, but before I had a chance to give it to him he announced that he was engaged to be married. He can't afford to marry, of course, and when I asked him how he planned to support a family he said that he had a job with some electrical-instrument company. When I asked about his music he said he would keep it up in the evenings. I do not want to run his life and I want him to be happy but I could not forget the amount of money that has been poured into his musical education. I had looked forward to coming home and I was very upset to receive this news as soon as I got off the boat. Then he told me that he no longer lived with his father and me. He lives with his future parents-in-law.

I was kept busy getting settled and I had to go into Boston several times to find work so I wasn't able to entertain his fiancée until I had been back a week or two. I asked her for tea. Lovell asked me not to smoke cigars and I agreed to this. I could see his point. He is very uneasy about what he calls my 'bohemianism' and I wanted to make a good impression. They came at four. Her name is Donna-Mae Hirshman. Her parents are German immigrants. She is twenty-one years old and works as a clerk in some insurance office. Her voice is high. She giggles. The one thing that can be said in her favor is that she has a striking head of yellow hair. I suppose Lovell may be attracted by her fairness but this hardly seems reason enough to marry. She giggled when we were introduced. She sat on the red sofa and as soon as she saw *Europa* she giggled again. Lovell could not take his eyes off her. I poured her tea and asked if she wanted lemon or cream. She said she didn't know. Then I asked politely what she usually took in her tea and she said she'd never drunk tea before. Then I asked what she usually drank and she said she drank mostly tonic and sometimes beer. I gave her tea with milk and sugar, and tried to think of something to say. Lovell broke the ice by asking me if I didn't think her hair was beautiful. I said that it was very beautiful. Well, it's a lot of work, she said. I have to wash it twice a week in whites of egg. Oh, there's been plenty of times when I've wanted to cut it off. People don't understand. People think that if God crowns you with a beautiful head of hair you ought to treasure it but it's just as much work as a sinkful of dishes. You have to wash it and dry it and comb it and brush it and put it up at night. I know it's hard to understand but honest to God there's days when I would just like to chop it off but Mummy made me promise on the Bible that I wouldn't. I'll take it down for you if you'd like.

I'm telling you the truth, Polly. I am not exaggerating. She went to the mirror, took a lot of pins out of her hair, and let it down. There was a great deal of it. I suppose she could sit on it although I didn't ask. I said that it was very beautiful several times. Then she said that she had known I would appreciate it because Lovell had told her I was artistic and interested in beautiful things. Well she displayed her hair for some time and then began the arduous business of getting it back into place again. It was hard work. Then she went on to say that some people thought her hair was dyed and that this made her angry because she felt that women who dyed their hair were immoral. I asked her if she would like another cup of tea and she said no. Then I asked her if she had ever heard Lovell play the piano and she said no, they didn't have a piano. Then she looked at Lovell and said that it was time to go. Lovell drove her home and then came back to ask, I suppose, for some words of approval. Of course my heart was broken in two. Here was a great musical career ruined by a head of hair. I told him I never wanted to see her again. He said he was going to marry her and I said I didn't care what he did.

Lovell married Donna-Mae. Uncle Abbott went to the wedding, but Percy kept her word and never saw her daughter-in-law again. Lovell came to the house four times a year to pay a ceremonial call on his mother. He would not go near the piano. He had not only given up his music, he hated music. His simple-minded taste for obsceneness seemed to have transformed itself into simple-minded piety. He had transferred from the Episcopal church to the Hirshmans' Lutheran congregation, which he attended twice on Sundays. They were raising money to build a new church when I last spoke with him. He spoke intimately of the Divinity. 'He has helped us in our struggles, again and again. When everything seemed hopeless, He has given us encouragement and strength. I wish I could get you to understand how wonderful He is, what a blessing it is to love Him …' Lovell died before he was thirty, and since everything must have been burned, I don't suppose there was a trace left of his musical career.

But the darkness in the old house seemed, each time we went there, to deepen. Abbott continued his philandering, but when he went fishing in the spring or hunting in the fall Percy was desperately unhappy without him. Less than a year after Lovell's death, Percy was afflicted with some cardiovascular disease. I remember one attack during Sunday dinner. The color drained out of her face, and her breathing became harsh and quick. She excused herself and was mannered enough to say that she had forgotten something. She went into the living room and shut the door, but her accelerated breathing and her groans of pain could be heard. When she returned, there were large splotches of red up the side of her face. 'If you don't see a doctor, you will die,' Uncle Abbott said.

'You are my husband and you are my doctor,' she said.

'I have told you repeatedly that I will not have you as a patient.'

'You are my doctor.'

'If you don't come to your senses, you will die.'

He was right, of course, and she knew it. Now, as she saw the leaves fall, the snow fall, as she said goodbye to friends in railroad stations and vestibules, it was always with a sense that she would not do this again. She died at three in the morning, in the dining room, where she had gone to get a glass of gin, and the family gathered for the last time at her funeral.

There is one more incident. I was taking a plane at Logan Airport. As I was crossing the waiting room, a man who was sweeping the floor stopped me.

'Know you,' he said thickly. 'I know who you are.'

'I don't remember,' I said.

'I'm Cousin Beaufort,' he said. 'I'm your cousin Beaufort.'

I reached for my wallet and took out a ten-dollar bill.

'I don't want any money,' he said. 'I'm your cousin. I'm your cousin Beaufort. I have a job. I don't want any money.'

'How are you, Beaufort?' I asked.

'Lovell and Percy are dead,' he said. 'They buried them in the earth.'

'I'm late, Beaufort,' I said, 'I'll miss my plane. It was nice to see you. Goodbye.' And so off to the sea.

The Swimmer

It was one of those midsummer Sundays when everyone sits around saying, 'I *drank* too much last night.' You might have heard it whispered by the parishioners leaving church, heard it from the lips of the priest himself, struggling with his cassock in the *vestiarium*, heard it from the golf links and the tennis courts, heard it from the wildlife preserve where the leader of the Audubon group was suffering from a terrible hangover. 'I *drank* too much,' said Donald Westerhazy. 'We all *drank* too much,' said Lucinda Merrill. 'It must have been the wine,' said Helen Westerhazy. 'I *drank* too much of that claret.'

This was at the edge of the Westerhazys' pool. The pool, fed by an artesian well with a high iron content, was a pale shade of green. It was a fine day. In the west there was a massive stand of cumulus cloud so like a city seen from a distance – from the bow of an approaching ship – that it might have had a name. Lisbon. Hackensack. The sun was hot. Neddy Merrill sat by the green water, one hand in it, one around a glass of gin. He was a slender man – he seemed to have the especial slenderness of youth – and while he was far from young he had slid down his banister that morning and given the bronze backside of Aphrodite on the hall table a smack, as he jogged toward the smell of

241

coffee in his dining room. He might have been compared to a summer's day, particularly the last hours of one, and while he lacked a tennis racket or a sail bag the impression was definitely one of youth, sport, and clement weather. He had been swimming and now he was breathing deeply, stertorously as if he could gulp into his lungs the components of that moment, the heat of the sun, the intenseness of his pleasure. It all seemed to flow into his chest. His own house stood in Bullet Park, eight miles to the south, where his four beautiful daughters would have had their lunch and might be playing tennis. Then it occurred to him that by taking a dogleg to the southwest he could reach his home by water.

His life was not confining and the delight he took in this observation could not be explained by its suggestion of escape. He seemed to see, with a cartographer's eye, that string of swimming pools, that quasi-subterranean stream that curved across the county. He had made a discovery, a contribution to modern geography; he would name the stream Lucinda after his wife. He was not a practical joker nor was he a fool but he was determinedly original and had a vague and modest idea of himself as a legendary figure. The day was beautiful and it seemed to him that a long swim might enlarge and celebrate its beauty.

He took off a sweater that was hung over his shoulders and dove in. He had an inexplicable contempt for men who did not hurl themselves into pools. He swam a choppy crawl, breathing either with every stroke or every fourth stroke and counting somewhere well in the back of his mind the one-two one-two of a flutter kick. It was not a serviceable stroke for long distances but the domestication of swimming had saddled the sport with some customs and in his part of the world a crawl was customary. To be embraced and sustained by the light green water was less a pleasure, it seemed, than the resumption of a natural condition, and he would have liked to swim without trunks, but this was not possible, considering his project. He hoisted himself up on the far curb – he never used the ladder – and started across the lawn. When Lucinda asked where he was going he said he was going to swim home.

The only maps and charts he had to go by were remembered or imaginary but these were clear enough. First there were the Grahams, the Hammers, the Lears, the Howlands, and the Crosscups. He would cross Ditmar Street to the Bunkers and come, after a short portage, to the Levys, the Welchers, and the public pool in Lancaster. Then there were the Hallorans, the Sachses, the Biswangers, Shirley Adams, the Gilmartins, and the Clydes. The day was lovely, and that he lived in a world so generously supplied with water seemed like a clemency, a beneficence. His heart was high and he ran across the grass. Making his way home by an uncommon route gave him the feeling that he was a pilgrim, an explorer, a man with a destiny, and he knew that he would find friends all along the way; friends would line the banks of the Lucinda River.

He went through a hedge that separated the Westerhazys' land from the Grahams', walked under some flowering apple trees, passed the shed that housed their pump and filter, and came out at the Grahams' pool. 'Why, Neddy,' Mrs Graham said, 'what a marvelous surprise. I've been trying to get you on the phone all morning. Here, let me get you a drink.' He saw then, like any explorer, that the

243

hospitable customs and traditions of the natives would have to be handled with diplomacy if he was ever going to reach his destination. He did not want to mystify or seem rude to the Grahams nor did he have the time to linger there. He swam the length of their pool and joined them in the sun and was rescued, a few minutes later, by the arrival of two carloads of friends from Connecticut. During the uproarious reunions he was able to slip away. He went down by the front of the Grahams' house, stepped over a thorny hedge, and crossed a vacant lot to the Hammers'. Mrs Hammer, looking up from her roses, saw him swim by although she wasn't quite sure who it was. The Lears heard him splashing past the open windows of their living room. The Howlands and the Crosscups were away. After leaving the Howlands' he crossed Ditmar Street and started for the Bunkers', where he could hear, even at that distance, the noise of a party.

The water refracted the sound of voices and laughter and seemed to suspend it in midair. The Bunkers' pool was on a rise and he climbed some stairs to a terrace where twenty-five or thirty men and women were drinking. The only person in the water was Rusty Towers, who floated there on a rubber raft. Oh, how bonny and lush were the banks of the Lucinda River! Prosperous men and women gathered by the sapphire-colored waters while caterer's men in white coats passed them cold gin. Overhead a red de Haviland trainer was circling around and around and around in the sky with something like the glee of a child in a swing. Ned felt a passing affection for the scene, a tenderness for the gathering, as if it was something he might touch. In the distance he heard thunder. As soon as Enid Bunker saw him she began to scream: 'Oh, look who's here! What a marvel-ous surprise! When Lucinda said that you couldn't come I though I'd *die*.' She made her way to him through the crowd, and when they had finished kissing she led him to the bar, a progress that was slowed by the fact that he stopped to kiss eight or ten other women and shake the hands of as many men. A smiling bartender he had seen at a hundred parties gave him a gin and tonic and he stood by the bar for a moment, anxious not to get stuck in any con-versation that would delay his voyage. When he seemed about to be surrounded he dove in and swam close to the side to avoid colliding with Rusty's raft. At the far end of the pool he bypassed the Tomlinsons with a broad smile and jogged up the garden path. The gravel cut his feet but this was the only unpleasantness. The party was confined to the pool, and as he went toward the house he heard the bril-liant, watery sound of voices fade, heard the noise of a radio from the Bunkers' kitchen, where someone was listening to a ball game. Sunday afternoon. He made his way through the parked cars and down the grassy border of their drive-way to Alewives Lane. He did not want to be seen on the road in his bathing trunks but there was no traffic and he made the short distance to the Levys' driveway, marked with a PRIVATE PROPERTY sign and a green tube for the *New York Times*. All the doors and windows of the big house were open but there were no signs of life; not even a dog barked. He went around the side of the house to the pool and saw that the Levys had only recently left. Glasses and bottles and dishes of nuts were on a table at the deep end, where there was a bathhouse or gazebo, hung with Japanese lanterns. After swimming the pool he got himself a glass and poured a drink. It was his fourth or fifth drink and he had swum nearly half the length of the Lucinda River. He felt tired, clean, and pleased at that moment to be alone; pleased with everything.

It would storm. The stand of cumulus cloud – that city – had risen and darkened, and while he sat there he heard the percussiveness of thunder again. The de Haviland trainer was still circling overhead and it seemed to Ned that he could almost hear the pilot laugh with pleasure in the afternoon; but when there was another peal of thunder he took off for home. A train whistle blew and he wondered what time it had gotten to be. Four? Five? He thought of the provincial station at that hour, where a waiter, his tuxedo concealed by a raincoat, a dwarf with some flowers wrapped in newspaper, and a woman who had been crying would be waiting for the local. It was suddenly growing dark; it was that moment when the pin-headed birds seem to organize their song into some acute and knowledgeable recognition of the storm's approach. Then there was a fine noise of rushing water from the crown of an oak at his back, as if a spigot there had been turned. Then the noise of fountains came from the crowns of all the tall trees. Why did he love storms, what was the meaning of his excitement when the door sprang open and the rain wind fled rudely up the stairs, why had the simple task of shutting the windows of an old house seemed fitting and urgent, why did the first watery notes of a storm wind have for him the unmistakable sound of good news, cheer, glad tidings? Then there was an explosion, a smell of cordite, and rain lashed the Japanese lanterns that Mrs Levy had bought in Kyoto the year before last, or was it the year before that?

He stayed in the Levys' gazebo until the storm had passed. The rain had cooled the air and he shivered. The force of the wind had stripped a maple of its red and yellow leaves and scattered them over the grass and the water. Since it was midsummer the tree must be blighted, and yet he felt a peculiar sadness at this sign of autumn. He braced his shoulders, emptied his glass, and started for the Welchers' pool. This meant crossing the Lindleys' riding ring and he was surprised to find it overgrown with grass and all the jumps dismantled. He wondered if the Lindleys had sold their horses or gone away for the summer and put them out to board. He seemed to remember having heard something about the Lindleys and their horses but the memory was unclear. On he went, barefoot through the wet grass, to the Welchers', where he found their pool was dry.

This breach in his chain of water disappointed him absurdly, and he felt like some explorer who seeks a torrential headwater and finds a dead stream. He was disappointed and mystified. It was common enough to go away for the summer but no one ever drained his pool. The Welchers had definitely gone away. The pool furniture was folded, stacked, and covered with a tarpaulin. The bathhouse was locked. All the windows of the house were shut, and when he went around to the driveway in front he saw a FOR SALE sign nailed to a tree. When had he last heard from the Welchers – when, that is, had he and Lucinda last regretted an invitation to dine with them? It seemed only a week or so ago. Was his memory failing or had he so disciplined it in the repression of unpleasant facts that he had damaged his

sense of the truth? Then in the distance he heard the sound
of a tennis game. This cheered him, cleared away all his
apprehensions and let him regard the overcast sky and the
cold air with indifference. This was the day that Neddy
Merrill swam across the county. That was the day! He
started off then for his most difficult portage.

Had you gone for a Sunday afternoon ride that day you
might have seen him, close to naked, standing on the shoulders of Route 424, waiting for a chance to cross. You might
have wondered if he was the victim of foul play, had his car
broken down, or was he merely a fool. Standing barefoot in
the deposits of the highway – beer cans, rags, and blowout
patches – exposed to all kinds of ridicule, he seemed pitiful.
He had known when he started that this was a part of his
journey – it had been on his maps – but confronted with
the lines of traffic, worming through the summery light, he
found himself unprepared. He was laughed at, jeered at, a
beer can was thrown at him, and he had no dignity or
humor to bring to the situation. He could have gone back,
back to the Westerhazys', where Lucinda would still be sitting in the sun. He had signed nothing, vowed nothing,
pledged nothing, not even to himself. Why, believing as he
did, that all human obduracy was susceptible to common
sense, was he unable to turn back? Why was he determined
to complete his journey even if it meant putting his life in
danger? At what point had this prank, this joke, this piece of
horseplay become serious? He could not go back, he could
not even recall with any clearness the green water at the
Westerhazys', the sense of inhaling the day's components,
the friendly and relaxed voices saying that they had *drunk*

too much. In the space of an hour, more or less, he had covered a distance that made his return impossible.

An old man, tooling down the highway at fifteen miles an hour, let him get to the middle of the road, where there was a grass divider. Here he was exposed to the ridicule of the northbound traffic, but after ten or fifteen minutes he was able to cross. From here he had only a short walk to the Recreation Center at the edge of the village of Lancaster, where there were some handball courts and a public pool.

The effect of the water on voices, the illusion of brilliance and suspense, was the same here as it had been at the Bunkers' but the sounds here were louder, harsher, and more shrill, and as soon as he entered the crowded enclosure he was confronted with regimentation, 'ALL SWIMMERS MUST TAKE A SHOWER BEFORE USING THE POOL. ALL SWIMMERS MUST USE THE FOOTBATH. ALL SWIMMERS MUST WEAR THEIR IDENTIFICATION DISKS.' He took a shower, washed his feet in a cloudy and bitter solution, and made his way to the edge of the water. It stank of chlorine and looked to him like a sink. A pair of lifeguards in a pair of towers blew police whistles at what seemed to be regular intervals and abused the swimmers through a public address system. Neddy remembered the sapphire water at the Bunkers' with longing and thought that he might contaminate himself – damage his own prosperousness and charm – by swimming in this murk, but he reminded himself that he was an explorer, a pilgrim, and that this was merely a stagnant bend in the Lucinda River. He dove, scowling with distaste, into the chlorine and had to swim with his head above water to avoid collisions, but even so he was bumped into, splashed, and jostled. When he got to the shallow end both lifeguards were shouting at him: 'Hey, you, you with-out the identification disk, get outa the water.' He did, but they had no way of pursuing him and he went through the reek of suntan oil and chlorine out through the hurricane fence and passed the handball courts. By crossing the road he entered the wooded part of the Halloran estate. The woods were not cleared and the footing was treacherous and difficult until he reached the lawn and the clipped beech hedge that encircled their pool.

The Hallorans were friends, an elderly couple of enor-mous wealth who seemed to bask in the suspicion that they might be Communists. They were zealous reformers but they were not Communists, and yet when they were accused, as they sometimes were, of subversion, it seemed to gratify and excite them. Their beech hedge was yellow and he guessed this had been blighted like the Levys' maple. He called hullo, hullo, to warn the Hallorans of his approach, to palliate his invasion of their privacy. The Hallorans, for rea-sons that had never been explained to him, did not wear bathing suits. No explanations were in order, really. Their nakedness was a detail in their uncompromising zeal for reform and he stepped politely out of his trunks before he went through the opening in the hedge.

Mrs Halloran, a stout woman with white hair and a serene face, was reading the *Times*. Mr Halloran was taking beech leaves out of the water with a scoop. They seemed not surprised or displeased to see him. Their pool was per-haps the oldest in the country, a fieldstone rectangle, fed by a brook. It had no filter or pump and its waters were the opaque gold of the stream.

'I'm swimming across the county,' Ned said.

'Why, I didn't know one could,' exclaimed Mrs Halloran.

'Well, I've made it from the Westerhazys',' Ned said. 'That must be about four miles.'

He left his trunks at the deep end, walked to the shallow end, and swam this stretch. As he was pulling himself out of the water he heard Mrs Halloran say, 'We've been *terribly* sorry to hear about all your misfortunes, Neddy.'

'My misfortunes?' Ned asked, I don't know what you mean.'

'Why, we heard that you'd sold the house and that your poor children ...'

'I don't recall having sold the house,' Ned said, 'and the girls are at home.'

'Yes,' Mrs Halloran sighed. 'Yes ...' Her voice filled the air with an unseasonable melancholy and Ned spoke briskly. 'Thank you for the swim.'

'Well, have a nice trip,' said Mrs Halloran.

Beyond the hedge he pulled on his trunks and fastened them. They were loose and he wondered if, during the space of an afternoon, he could have lost some weight. He was cold and he was tired and the naked Hallorans and their dark water had depressed him. The swim was too much for his strength but how could he have guessed this, sliding down the banister that morning and sitting in the Westerhazys' sun? His arms were lame. His legs felt rubbery and ached at the joints. The worst of it was the cold in his bones and the feeling that he might never be warm again. Leaves were falling down around him and he smelled wood smoke on the wind. Who would be burning wood at this time of year?

He needed a drink. Whiskey would warm him, pick him up, carry him through the last of his journey, refresh his

feeling that it was original and valorous to swim across the
county. Channel swimmers took brandy. He needed a stimu-
lant. He crossed the lawn in front of the Hallorans' house
and went down a little path to where they had built a house
for their only daughter, Helen, and her husband, Eric Sachs.
The Sachses' pool was small and he found Helen and her
husband there.

'Oh, *Neddy,*' Helen said. 'Did you lunch at Mother's?'

'Not *really,*' Ned said. 'I *did* stop to see your parents.' This
seemed to be explanation enough. 'I'm terribly sorry to
break in on you like this but I've taken a chill and I wonder
if you'd give me a drink.'

'Why, I'd *love* to,' Helen said, 'but there hasn't been anything in this house to drink since Eric's operation. That was
three years ago.'

Was he losing his memory, had his gift for concealing pain-
ful facts let him forget that he had sold his house, that his
children were in trouble, and that his friend had been ill? His
eyes slipped from Eric's face to his abdomen, where he saw
three pale, sutured scars, two of them at least a foot long. Gone
was his navel, and what, Neddy thought, would the roving
hand, bed-checking one's gifts at 3 A.M., make of a belly with
no navel, no link to birth, this breach in the succession?

'I'm sure you can get a drink at the Biswangers',' Helen
said. 'They're having an enormous do. You can hear it from
here. Listen!'

She raised her head and from across the road, the lawns,
the gardens, the woods, the fields, he heard again the brilliant noise of voices over water. 'Well, I'll get wet,' he said,
still feeling that he had no freedom of choice about his
means of travel. He dove into the Sachses' cold water and,

gasping, close to drowning, made his way from one end of the pool to the other. 'Lucinda and I want *terribly* to see you,' he said over his shoulder, his face set toward the Biswangers'. 'We're sorry it's been so long and we'll call you *very* soon.'

He crossed some fields to the Biswangers' and the sounds of revelry there. They would be honored to give him a drink, they would be happy to give him a drink. The Biswangers invited him and Lucinda for dinner four times a year, six weeks in advance. They were always rebuffed and yet they continued to send out their invitations, unwilling to comprehend the rigid and undemocratic realities of their society. They were the sort of people who discussed the price of things at cocktails, exchanged market tips during dinner, and after dinner told dirty stories to mixed company. They did not belong to Neddy's set – they were not even on Lucinda's Christmas-card list. He went toward their pool with feelings of indifference, charity, and some unease, since it seemed to be getting dark and these were the longest days of the year. The party when he joined it was noisy and large. Grace Biswanger was the kind of hostess who asked the optometrist, the veterinarian, the real-estate dealer, and the dentist. No one was swimming and the twilight, reflected on the water of the pool, had a wintry gleam. There was a bar and he started for this. When Grace Biswanger saw him she came toward him, not affectionately as he had every right to expect, but bellicosely.

'Why, this party has everything,' she said loudly, 'including a gate crasher.'

She could not deal him a social blow – there was no question about this and he did not flinch. 'As a gate crasher,' he asked politely, 'do I rate a drink?'

'Suit yourself,' she said. 'You don't seem to pay much attention to invitations.'

She turned her back on him and joined some guests, and he went to the bar and ordered a whiskey. The bartender served him but he served him rudely. His was a world in which the caterer's men kept the social score, and to be rebuffed by a part-time barkeep meant that he had suffered some loss of social esteem. Or perhaps the man was new and uninformed. Then he heard Grace at his back say: 'They went for broke overnight – nothing but income – and he showed up drunk one Sunday and asked us to loan him five thousand dollars ...' She was always talking about money. It was worse than eating your peas off a knife. He dove into the pool, swam its length and went away.

The next pool on his list, the last but two, belonged to his old mistress, Shirley Adams. If he had suffered any injuries at the Biswangers' they would be cured here. Love – sexual roughhouse in fact – was the supreme elixir, the pain killer, the brightly colored pill that would put the spring back into his step, the joy of life in his heart. They had had an affair last week, last month, last year. He couldn't remember. It was he who had broken it off, his was the upper hand, and he stepped through the gate of the wall that surrounded her pool with nothing so considered as self-confidence. It seemed in a way to be his pool, as the lover, particularly the illicit lover, enjoys the possessions of his mistress with an authority unknown to holy matrimony. She was there, her hair the color of brass, but her figure, at the edge of the lighted, cerulean water, excited in him no profound memories. It had been, he thought, a lighthearted affair, although she had wept when he broke it off. She seemed confused to see him and he wondered if she was still wounded. Would she, God forbid, weep again?

'What do you want?' she asked.

'I'm swimming across the county.'

'Good Christ. Will you ever grow up?'

'What's the matter?'

'If you've come here for money,' she said, 'I won't give you another cent.'

'You could give me a drink.'

'I could but I won't. I'm not alone.'

'Well, I'm on my way.'

He dove in and swam the pool, but when he tried to haul himself up onto the curb he found that the strength in his arms and shoulders had gone, and he paddled to the ladder and climbed out. Looking over his shoulder he saw, in the lighted bathhouse, a young man. Going out onto the dark lawn he smelled chrysanthemums or marigolds – some stubborn autumnal fragrance – on the night air, strong as gas. Looking overhead he saw that the stars had come out, but why should he seem to see Andromeda, Cepheus, and Cassiopeia? What had become of the constellations of mid-summer? He began to cry.

It was probably the first time in his adult life that he had ever cried, certainly the first time in his life that he had ever felt so miserable, cold, tired, and bewildered. He could not understand the rudeness of the caterer's barkeep or the rudeness of a mistress who had come to him on her knees and showered his trousers with tears. He had swam too long, he had been immersed too long, and his nose and his throat were sore from the water. What he needed then was a drink, some company, and some clean, dry clothes, and while he could have cut directly across the road to his home he went on to the Gilmartins' pool. Here, for the first time in his life, he did not dive but went down the steps into the icy water and swam a hobbled sidestroke that he might have learned as a youth. He staggered with fatigue on his way to the Clydes' and paddled the length of their pool, stopping again and again with his hand on the curb to rest. He climbed up the ladder and wondered if he had the strength to get home. He had done what he wanted, he had swum the county, but he was so stupefied with exhaustion that his triumph seemed vague. Stooped, holding on to the gate-posts for support, he turned up the driveway of his own house.

The place was dark. Was it so late that they had all gone to bed? Had Lucinda stayed at the Westerhazys' for supper? Had the girls joined her there or gone someplace else? Hadn't they agreed, as they usually did on Sunday, to regret all their invitations and stay at home? He tried the garage doors to see what cars were in but the doors were locked and rust came off the handles onto his hands. Going toward the house, he saw that the force of the thunder-storm had knocked one of the rain gutters loose. It hung down over the front door like an umbrella rib, but it could be fixed in the morning. The house was locked, and he thought that the stupid cook or the stupid maid must have locked the place up until he remembered that it had been some time since they had employed a maid or a cook. He shouted, pounded on the door, tried to force it with his shoulder, and then, looking in at the windows, saw that the place was empty.

The World of Apples

ASA BASCOMB, THE old laureate, wandered around his work house or study – he had never been able to settle on a name for a house where one wrote poetry – swatting hornets with a copy of *La Stampa* and wondering why he had never been given the Nobel Prize. He had received nearly every other sign of renown. In a trunk in the corner there were medals, citations, wreaths, sheaves, ribbons, and badges. The stove that heated his study had been given to him by the Oslo P.E.N. Club, his desk was a gift from the Kiev Writer's Union, and the study itself had been built by an inter-national association of his admirers. The presidents of both Italy and the United States had wired their congratulations on the day he was presented with the key to the place. Why no Nobel Prize? Swat, swat. The study was a barny, raftered building with a large northern window that looked off to the Abruzzi. He would sooner have had a much smaller place with smaller windows but he had not been consulted. There seemed to be some clash between the altitude of the mountains and the disciplines of verse. At the time of which I'm writing he was eighty-two years old and lived in a villa below the hill town of Monte Carbone, south of Rome.

He had strong, thick white hair that hung in a lock over his forehead. Two or more cowlicks at the crown were usually disorderly and erect. He wet them down with soap for formal receptions, but they were never supine for more than an hour or two and were usually up in the air again by the time champagne was poured. It was very much a part of the impression he left. As one remembers a man for a long nose, a smile, birthmark, or scar, one remembered Bascomb for his unruly cowlicks. He was known vaguely as the Cézanne of poets. There was some linear preciseness to his work that might be thought to resemble Cézanne but the vision that underlies Cézanne's paintings was not his. This mistaken comparison might have arisen because the title of his most popular work was *The World of Apples* – poetry in which his admirers found the pungency, diversity, color, and nostalgia of the apples of the northern New England he had not seen for forty years.

Why had he – provincial and famous for his simplicity – chosen to leave Vermont for Italy? Had it been the choice of his beloved Amelia, dead these ten years? She had made many of their decisions. Was he, the son of a farmer, so naïve that he thought living abroad might bring some color to his stern beginnings? Or had it been simply a practical matter, an evasion of the publicity that would, in his own country, have been an annoyance? Admirers found him in Monte Carbone, they came almost daily, but they came in modest numbers. He was photographed once or twice a year for *Match* or *Epoca* – usually on his birthday – but he was in general able to lead a quieter life than would have been possible in the United States. Walking down Fifth Avenue on his last visit home he had been stopped by strangers and asked to autograph scraps of paper. On the streets of Rome no one knew or cared who he was and this was as he wanted it.

Monte Carbone was a Saracen town, built on the summit of a loaf-shaped butte of sullen granite. At the top of the town were three pure and voluminous springs whose water fell in pools or conduits down the sides of the mountain. His villa was below the town and he had in his garden many fountains, fed by the springs on the summit. The noise of falling water was loud and unmusical – a clapping or clattering sound. The water was stinging cold, even in midsummer, and he kept his gin, wine, and vermouth in a pool on the terrace. He worked in his study in the mornings, took a siesta after lunch, and then climbed the stairs to the village.

The tufa and pepperoni and the bitter colors of the lichen that takes root in the walls and roofs are no part of the consciousness of an American, even if he has lived for years, as Bascomb had, surrounded by this bitterness. The climb up the stairs winded him. He stopped again and again to catch his breath. Everyone spoke to him. *Salve, maestro, salve!* When he saw the bricked-up transept of the twelfth-century church he always mumbled the date to himself as if he were explaining the beauties of the place to some companion. The beauties of the place were various and gloomy. He would always be a stranger there, but his strangeness seemed to him to be some metaphor involving time as if, climbing the strange stairs past the strange walls, he climbed through hours, months, years, and decades. In the piazza he had a glass of wine and got his mail. On any day he received more mail than the entire population of the village. There were letters from admirers, propositions to lecture, read, or simply show his face, and he seemed to be on the invitation list of every honorary society in the

Western world excepting, of course, that society formed by
the past winners of the Nobel Prize. His mail was kept in a
sack, and if it was too heavy for him to carry, Antonio, the
postina's son, would walk back with him to the villa. He
worked over his mail until five or six. Two or three times a
week some pilgrims would find their way to the villa and if
he liked their looks he would give them a drink while he
autographed their copy of *The World of Apples*. They almost
never brought his other books, although he had published
a dozen. Two or three evenings a week he played backgammon with Carbone, the local padrone. They both thought
that the other cheated and neither of them would leave the
board during a game, even if their bladders were killing
them. He slept soundly.

Of the four poets with whom Bascomb was customarily
grouped one had shot himself, one had drowned himself,
one had hanged himself, and the fourth had died of delir-
ium tremens. Bascomb had known them all, loved most of
them, and had nursed two of them when they were ill, but
the broad implication that he had, by choosing to write
poetry, chosen to destroy himself was something he rebelled
against vigorously. He knew the temptations of suicide as
he knew the temptations of every other form of sinfulness
and he carefully kept out of the villa all firearms, suitable
lengths of rope, poisons, and sleeping pills. He had seen in
Z – the closest of the four – some inalienable link between
his prodigious imagination and his prodigious gifts for
self-destruction, but Bascomb in his stubborn, countrified
way was determined to break or ignore this link – to over-
throw Marsyas and Orpheus. Poetry was a lasting glory and
he was determined that the final act of a poet's life should

not – as had been the case with Z – be played out in a dirty room with twenty-three empty gin bottles. Since he could not deny the connection between brilliance and tragedy he seemed determined to bludgeon it.

Bascomb believed, as Cocteau once said, that the writing of poetry was the exploitation of a substratum of memory that was imperfectly understood. His work seemed to be an act of recollection. He did not, as he worked, charge his memory with any practical tasks but it was definitely his memory that was called into play – his memory of sensation, landscapes, faces, and the immense vocabulary of his own language. He could spend a month or longer on a short poem but discipline and industry were not the words to describe his work. He did not seem to choose his words at all but to recall them from the billions of sounds that he had heard since he first understood speech. Depending on his memory, then, as he did, to give his life usefulness he sometimes wondered if his memory were not failing. Talking with friends and admirers he took great pains not to repeat himself. Waking at two or three in the morning to hear the unmusical clatter of his fountains he would grill himself for an hour on names and dates. Who was Lord Cardigan's adversary at Balaklava? It took a minute for the name of Lord Lucan to struggle up through the murk but it finally appeared. He conjugated the remote past of the verb *esse*, counted to fifty in Russian, recited poems by Donne, Eliot, Thomas, and Wordsworth, described the events of the Risorgimento beginning with the riots in Milan in 1812 up through the coronation of Vittorio Emanuele, listed the ages of prehistory, the number of kilometers in a mile, the planets of the solar system, and the

261

speed of light. There was a definite retard in the responsive-
ness of his memory but he remained adequate, he thought.
The only impairment was anxiety. He had seen time destroy
so much that he wondered if an old man's memory could
have more strength and longevity than an oak; but the pin
oak he had planted on the terrace thirty years ago was dying
and he could still remember in detail the cut and color of
the dress his beloved Amelia had been wearing when they
first met. He taxed his memory to find its way through cities. He imagined walking from the railroad station in Indi-
anapolis to the memorial fountain, from the Hotel Europe
in Leningrad to the Winter Palace, from the Eden-Roma
up through Trastevere to San Pietro in Montori. Frail,
doubting his faculties, it was the solitariness of this inquisi-
tion that made it a struggle.

His memory seemed to wake him one night or morning, asking him to produce the first name of Lord Byron.
He could not. He decided to disassociate himself momen-
tarily from his memory and surprise it in possession of
Lord Byron's name but when he returned, warily, to this
receptacle it was still empty. Sidney? Percy? James? He got
out of bed – it was cold – put on some shoes and an over-
coat and climbed up the stairs through the garden to his
study. He seized a copy of *Manfred* but the author was listed
simply as Lord Byron. The same was true of *Childe Harold*.
He finally discovered, in the encyclopedia, that his lordship
was named George. He granted himself a partial excuse for
this lapse of memory and returned to his warm bed. Like
most old men he had begun a furtive glossary of food that
seemed to put lead in his pencil. Fresh trout. Black olives.
Young lamb roasted with thyme. Wild mushrooms, bear,

venison, and rabbit. On the other side of the ledger were all frozen foods, cultivated greens, overcooked pasta, and canned soups.

In the spring, a Scandinavian admirer wrote, asking if he might have the honor of taking Bascomb for a day's trip among the hill towns. Bascomb, who had no car of his own at the time, was delighted to accept. The Scandinavian was a pleasant young man and they set off happily for Monte Felici. In the fourteenth and fifteenth centuries the springs that supplied the town with water had gone dry and the population had moved halfway down the mountain. All that remained of the abandoned town on the summit were two churches or cathedrals of uncommon splendor. Bascomb loved these. They stood in fields of flowering weeds, their wall paintings still brilliant, their façades decorated with griffins, swans, and lions with the faces and parts of men and women, skewered dragons, winged serpents, and other marvels of metamorphoses. These vast and fanciful houses of God reminded Bascomb of the boundlessness of the human imagination and he felt lighthearted and enthusiastic. From Monte Felici they went on to San Giorgio, where there were some painted tombs and a little Roman theatre. They stopped in a grove below the town to have a picnic. Bascomb went into the woods to relieve himself and stumbled on a couple who were making love. They had not bothered to undress and the only flesh visible was the stranger's hairy backside. *Tanti, scusi*, mumbled Bascomb and he retreated to another part of the forest but when he rejoined the Scandinavian he was uneasy. The struggling couple seemed to have dimmed his memories of the cathedrals. When he returned to his villa some nuns from a Roman convent were waiting for him to autograph their copies of *The World of Apples*. He did this and asked his housekeeper, Maria, to give them some wine. They paid him the usual compliments – he had created a universe that seemed to welcome man; he had divined the voice of moral beauty in a rain wind – but all that he could think of was the stranger's back. It seemed to have more zeal and meaning than his celebrated search for truth. It seemed to dominate all that he had seen that day – the castles, clouds, cathedrals, mountains, and fields of flowers. When the nuns left he looked up to the mountains to raise his spirits but the mountains looked then like the breasts of women. His mind had become unclean. He seemed to step aside from its recalcitrance and watch the course it took. In the distance he heard a train whistle and what would his wayward mind make of this? The excitements of travel, the *prix fixe* in the dining car, the sort of wine they served on trains? It all seemed innocent enough until he caught his mind sneaking away from the dining car to the venereal stalls of the Wagon-Lit and thence into gross obscenity. He thought he knew what he needed and he spoke to Maria after dinner. She was always happy to accommodate him, although he always insisted that she take a bath. This, with the dishes, involved some delays but when she left him he definitely felt better but he definitely was not cured.

In the night his dreams were obscene and he woke several times trying to shake off his venereal pall or torpor. Things were no better in the light of morning. Obscenity – gross obscenity – seemed to be the only factor in life that possessed color and cheer. After breakfast he climbed up to his study and sat at his desk. The welcoming universe, the rain wind that sounded through the world of apples had vanished. Filth was his destiny, his best self, and he began with relish a long ballad called The Fart That Saved Athens. He finished the ballad that morning and burned it in the stove that had been given to him by the Oslo P.E.N. The ballad was, or had been until he burned it, an exhaustive and revolting exercise in scatology, and going down the stairs to his terrace he felt genuinely remorseful. He spent the afternoon writing a disgusting confession called The Favorite of Tiberio. Two admirers – a young married couple – came at five to praise him. They had met on a train, each of them carrying a copy of his *Apples*. They had fallen in love along the lines of the pure and ardent love he described. Thinking of his day's work, Bascomb hung his head.

On the next day he wrote The Confessions of a Public School Headmaster. He burned the manuscript at noon. As he came sadly down the stairs onto his terrace he found there fourteen students from the University of Rome who, as soon as he appeared, began to chant 'The Orchards of Heaven' – the opening sonnet in *The World of Apples*. He shivered. His eyes filled with tears. He asked Maria to bring them some wine while he autographed their copies. They then lined up to shake his impure hand and returned to a bus in the field that had brought them out from Rome. He glanced at the mountains that had no cheering power – looked up at the meaningless blue sky. Where was the strength of decency? Had it any reality at all? Was the gross bestiality that obsessed him a sovereign truth? The most harrowing aspect of obscenity, he was to discover before the end of the week, was its boorishness. While he tackled his indecent projects with ardor he finished them with boredom and shame. The pornographer's course seems inflexible and he found himself repeating that tedious body of work that is circulated by the immature and the obsessed. He wrote The Confessions of a Lady's Maid, The Baseball Player's Honeymoon, and A Night in the Park. At the end of ten days he was at the bottom of the pornographer's barrel; he was writing dirty limericks. He wrote sixty of these and burned them. The next morning he took a bus to Rome.

He checked in at the Minerva, where he always stayed, and telephoned a long list of friends, but he knew that to arrive unannounced in a large city is to be friendless, and no one was home. He wandered around the streets and, stepping into a public toilet, found himself face to face with a male whore, displaying his wares. He stared at the man with the naïveté or the retard of someone very old. The man's face was idiotic – doped, drugged, and ugly – and yet, standing in his unsavory orisons, he seemed to old Bascomb angelic, armed with a flaming sword that might conquer banality and smash the glass of custom. He hurried away. It was getting dark and that hellish eruption of traffic noise that rings off the walls of Rome at dusk was rising to its climax. He wandered into an art gallery on the Via Sistina where the painter or photographer – he was both – seemed to be suffering from the same infection as Bascomb, only in a more acute form. Back in the streets he wondered if there was a universality to this venereal dusk that had settled over his spirit. Had the world, as well as he, lost its way? He passed a concert hall where a program of songs was advertised and thinking that music might cleanse the thoughts of his heart he bought a ticket and went in. The concert was poorly attended. When the accompanist appeared, only a third of the seats were taken. Then the soprano came on, a splendid ash blonde in a crimson dress, and while she sang *Die Liebhaber der Brücken* old Bascomb began the disgusting and unfortunate habit of imagining that he was disrobing her. Hooks and eyes? he wondered. A zipper? While she sang *Die Feldspar* and went on to *Le Temps des lilas et le temps des roses ne reviendra plus* he settled for a zipper and imagined unfastening her dress at the back and lifting it gently off her shoulders. He got her slip over her head while she sang *L'Amore Nascondere* and undid the hooks and eyes of her brassiere during *Les Rêves de Pierrot*. His reverie was suspended when she stepped into the wings to gargle but as soon as she returned to the piano he got to work on her garter belt and all that it contained. When she took her bow at the intermission he applauded uproariously but not for her knowledge of music or the gifts of her voice. Then shame, limpid and pitiless as any passion, seemed to encompass him and he left the concert hall for the Minerva but his seizure was not over. He sat at his desk in the hotel and wrote a sonnet to the legendary Pope Joan. Technically it was an improvement over the limericks he had been writing but there was no moral improvement. In the morning he took the bus back to Monte Carbone and received some grateful admirers on his terrace. The next day he climbed to his study, wrote a few limericks, and then took some Petronius and Juvenal from the shelves to see what had been accomplished before him in this field of endeavor.

Here were candid and innocent accounts of sexual mer-
riment. There was nowhere that sense of wickedness he
experienced when he burned his work in the stove each
afternoon. Was it simply that his world was that much older,
its social responsibilities that much more grueling, and that
lewdness was the only answer to an increase of anxiety?
What was it that he had lost? It seemed then to be a sense
of pride, an aureole of lightness and valor, a kind of crown.
He seemed to hold the crown up to scrutiny and what did
he find? Was it merely some ancient fear of Daddy's razor
strap and Mummy's scowl, some childish subservience to
the bullying world? He well knew his instincts to be rowdy,
abundant, and indiscreet and had he allowed the world and
all its tongues to impose upon him some structure of transparent values for the convenience of a conservative economy, an established church, and a bellicose army and navy?
He seemed to hold the crown, hold it up into the light, it
seemed made of light and what it seemed to mean was the
genuine and tonic taste of exaltation and grief. The limericks he had just completed were innocent, factual, and
merry. They were also obscene, but when had the facts of
life become obscene and what were the realities of this virtue he so painfully stripped from himself each morning?
They seemed to be the realities of anxiety and love: Amelia
standing in the diagonal beam of light, the stormy night his
son was born, the day his daughter married. One could
disparage them as homely but they were the best he knew
of life – anxiety and love – and worlds away from the limerick on his desk that began: There was a young consul
named Caesar / Who had an enormous fissure.' He burned
his limerick in the stove and went down the stairs.

The next day was the worst. He simply wrote F - - k again and again covering six or seven sheets of paper. He put this into the stove at noon. At lunch Maria burned her finger, swore lengthily, and then said: 'I should visit the sacred angel of Monte Giordano.' 'What is the sacred angel?' he asked. 'The angel can cleanse the thoughts of a man's heart,' said Maria. 'He is in the old church at Monte Giordano. He is made of olivewood from the Mount of Olives, and was carved by one of the saints himself. If you make a pilgrimage he will cleanse your thoughts.' All Bascomb knew of pilgrimages was that you walked and for some reason carried a seashell. When Maria went up to take a siesta he looked among Amelia's relics and found a seashell. The angel would expect a present, he guessed, and from the box in his study he chose the gold medal the Soviet government had given him on Lermontov's Jubilee. He did not wake Maria or leave her a note. This seemed to be a conspicuous piece of senility. He had never before been, as the old often are, mischievously elusive, and he should have told Maria where he was going but he didn't. He started down through the vineyards to the main road at the bottom of the valley.

As he approached the river a little Fiat drew off the main road and parked among some trees. A man, his wife, and three carefully dressed daughters got out of the car and Bascomb stopped to watch them when he saw that the man carried a shotgun. What was he going to do? Commit murder? Suicide? Was Bascomb about to see some human sacrifice? He sat down, concealed by the deep grass, and watched. The mother and the three girls were very excited. The father seemed to be enjoying complete sovereignty.

They spoke a dialect and Bascomb understood almost nothing they said. The man took the shotgun from its case and put a single shell in the chamber. Then he arranged his wife and three daughters in a line and put their hands over their ears. They were squealing. When this was all arranged he stood with his back to them, aimed his gun at the sky, and fired. The three children applauded and exclaimed over the loudness of the noise and the bravery of their dear father. The father returned the gun to its case, they all got back into the Fiat and drove, Bascomb supposed, back to their apartment in Rome.

Bascomb stretched out in the grass and fell asleep. He dreamed that he was back in his own country. What he saw was an old Ford truck with four flat tires, standing in a field of buttercups. A child wearing a paper crown and a bath towel for a mantle hurried around the corner of a white house. An old man took a bone from a paper bag and handed it to a stray dog. Autumn leaves smoldered in a bathtub with lion's feet. Thunder woke him, distant, shaped, he thought, like a gourd. He got down to the main road, where he was joined by a dog. The dog was trembling and he wondered if it was sick, rabid, dangerous, and then he saw that the dog was afraid of thunder. Each peal put the beast into a paroxysm of trembling and Bascomb stroked his head. He had never known an animal to be afraid of nature. Then the wind picked up the branches of the trees and he lifted his old nose to smell the rain, minutes before it fell. It was the smell of damp country churches, the spare rooms of old houses, earth closets, bathing suits put out to dry – so keen an odor of joy that he sniffed noisily. He did not, in spite of these transports, lose sight of his practical need for shelter. Beside the road was a little hut for bus travelers and he and the frightened dog stepped into this. The walls were covered with that sort of uncleanliness from which he hoped to flee and he stepped out again. Up the road was a farmhouse – one of those schizophrenic improvisations one sees so often in Italy. It seemed to have been bombed, spatch-cocked, and put together, not at random but as a deliberate assault on logic. On one side there was a wooden lean-to where an old man sat. Bascomb asked him for the kindness of his shelter and the old man invited him in.

The old man seemed to be about Bascomb's age but he seemed to Bascomb enviably untroubled. His smile was gentle and his face was clear. He had obviously never been harried by the wish to write a dirty limerick. He would never be forced to make a pilgrimage with a seashell in his pocket. He held a book in his lap – a stamp album – and the lean-to was filled with potted plants. He did not ask his soul to clap hands and sing, and yet he seemed to have reached an organic peace of mind that Bascomb coveted. Should Bascomb have collected stamps and potted plants? Anyhow it was too late. Then the rain came, thunder shook the earth, the dog whined and trembled, and Bascomb caressed him. The storm passed in a few minutes and Bascomb thanked his host and started up the road.

He had a nice stride for someone so old and he walked, like all the rest of us, in some memory of prowess – love or football, Amelia, or a good dropkick – but after a mile or two he realized that he would not reach Monte Giordano until long after dark and when a car stopped and offered him a ride to the village he accepted it, hoping that this would not put a crimp in his cure. It was still light when he reached Monte Giordano. The village was about the same size as his own, with the same tufa walls and bitter lichen. The old church stood in the center of the square but the door was locked. He asked for the priest and found him in a vineyard, burning prunings. He explained that he wanted to make an offering to the sainted angel and showed the priest his golden medal. The priest wanted to know if it was true gold and Bascomb then regretted his choice. Why hadn't he chosen the medal given him by the French government or the medal from Oxford? The Russians had not hallmarked the gold and he had no way of proving its worth. Then the priest noticed that the citation was written in the Russian alphabet. Not only was it false gold; it was Communist gold and not a fitting present for the sacred angel. At that moment the clouds parted and a single ray of light came into the vineyard, lighting the medal. It was a sign. The priest drew a cross in the air and they started back to the church.

It was an old, small, poor country church. The angel was in a chapel on the left, which the priest lighted. The image, buried in jewelry, stood in an iron cage with a padlocked door. The priest opened this and Bascomb placed his Lermontov medal at the angel's feet. Then he got to his knees and said loudly: 'God bless Walt Whitman. God Bless Hart Crane. God bless Dylan Thomas. God bless William Faulkner, Scott Fitzgerald, and especially Ernest Hemingway.' The priest locked up the sacred relic and they left the church together. There was a café on the square where he got some supper and rented a bed. This was a strange engine of brass with brass angels at the four corners, but they

272

seemed to possess some brassy blessedness since he dreamed of peace and woke in the middle of the night finding in himself that radiance he had known when he was younger. Something seemed to shine in his mind and limbs and lights and vitals and he fell asleep again and slept until morning.

On the next day, walking down from Monte Giordano to the main road, he heard the trumpeting of a waterfall. He went into the woods to find this. It was a natural fall, a shelf of rock and a curtain of green water, and it reminded him of a fall at the edge of the farm in Vermont where he had been raised. He had gone there one Sunday afternoon when he was a boy and sat on a hill above the pool. While he was there he saw an old man, with hair as thick and white as his was now, come through the woods. He had watched the old man unlace his shoes and undress himself with the haste of a lover. First he had wet his hands and arms and shoulders and then he had stepped into the torrent, bellowing with joy. He had then dried himself with his underpants, dressed, and gone back into the woods and it was not until he disappeared that Bascomb had realized that the old man was his father.

Now he did what his father had done – unlaced his shoes, tore at the buttons of his shirt, and knowing that a mossy stone or the force of the water could be the end of him he stepped naked into the torrent, bellowing like his father. He could stand the cold for only a minute but when he stepped away from the water he seemed at last to be himself. He went on down to the main road, where he was picked up by some mounted police, since Maria had

273

sounded the alarm and the whole province was looking for the maestro. His return to Monte Carbone was triumphant and in the morning he began a long poem on the inalienable dignity of light and air that, while it would not get him the Nobel Prize, would grace the last months of his life.